INVITATION TO MURDER

ALEXANDRA

THE WESTPORT ROMANTIC MYSTERIES

BETH PRENTICE

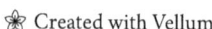

For everyone who believed in me—thank you!

Like trees our lives grow in many directions,
Yet our roots keep us connected!
Westport Television Network reunion
Catch up with old friends and reminisce as you hunt for a murderer!
Saturday 23rd August
1 Television Avenue
Westport
The fun will begin at 5 pm and finish when the sun rises, so bring your
sleuthing skills!

RSVP: Rachel on 0433 615446

PROLOGUE

"*Y*ou have dialed emergency triple zero. Your call is being connected."

I waited a beat whilst I was connected to an operator.

"Do you need police, fire, or ambulance?"

"Ummm, police."

"Please hold. I will connect you to the nearest center."

The phone went quiet whilst I was being transferred (very quickly I may add).

"Police emergency. What is the location of the emergency?"

"Ummm..." *Oh God.* They sounded so efficient. "It's unit 403, 59 Amity Avenue, Westport, Australia." I probably hadn't needed to tell them I was in Australia. I was sure they already knew that. But I *was* grateful my voice sounded a lot more controlled than I felt.

"Please tell me your emergency." The male voice sounded reassuring in my ear.

"I think I've been broken into," I explained, my voice only wobbling slightly. I wasn't going to cry. I wasn't. Okay, that was a lie. I was totally going to cry. I was known in my family as being a crybaby. I'd cry at a McDonald's advertisement. Why did I even think I wouldn't cry when my home had been broken into while I was sleeping on the couch?

"Are you in danger? Is the perpetrator still present?" asked the very-in-control voice.

"Ummm, no. Well, I don't think so." I looked wildly around the room, my eyes stopping on the open balcony doors. I normally never fell asleep without closing and locking the security screen, but today I'd drifted off like a baby.

"What's your name?"

"Alexandra, but my friends call me Alex." Why did I say that? This guy wasn't my friend, but he sounded friendly, and right now, I needed friendly.

"Okay, Alex. Can you explain the situation please?" The voice sounded like its owner might be good-looking. How can you tell by the sound of a voice? Well, you just could, okay?

I quickly filled him in on what had happened.

"And you're sure there is no one on the premises still?"

"Yes. I'm positive. Only me." I hoped. I mean, I hadn't checked *all* the cupboards. My eyes drifted to the cabinets attached high on the wall. Surely nobody could hide in those.

"Alex, break-ins should be reported to your local police station direct. I'll give you their number for future use. However, on this occasion, I will contact them for you. Please stay on the line while I do that now."

"Oh, okay." I waited a beat for the voice to return.

"The local police have been informed and will be there as soon as possible. If you feel you are in danger, call triple zero again, but please remember this line is for life-threatening emergencies only. We need the lines to stay clear for those who need us urgently." I heard his smile over the phone. "You're lucky today is a quiet day."

"Sorry," I muttered, my cheeks flaming at my mistake. "And thanks."

"You're welcome. And don't hesitate to call back if the situation changes."

I heard the connection click off. Placing my phone on the counter, I felt alone and scared.

I sank my bottom to the tiled floor and put my head between my knees. It had really been a strange day. First, I'd received an invitation to my old workplace reunion containing nine dead butterflies. Yes, *nine*. A tenth one had still been alive in the box, but when I'd set him free off my balcony, gravity had seemed stronger than his wings. I'd really hoped that wasn't a bad omen for the rest of the day, but I should have known better.

Then, during lunch, a news bulletin had flashed across the television screen announcing my dentist, Stacey, was missing. *Missing.* Now Stacey wasn't *just* my dentist—she was a friend. Sure, we were a lot closer when we were at primary school together, but I definitely still had her in the friend category. And now she was missing.

To finish off my day, I'd waken from an afternoon siesta to find my apartment had been broken into. *Broken into!* These things didn't happen to me! I was a normal twenty-eight-year-old living in Westport. And Westport was a quiet town. Our crime rate wasn't that high. I knew that because I read the town newsletter that got delivered every second month, and last month's edition informed me the crime rate was dropping. Westport had only had three house break-ins, two acts of vandalism, and one out-of-control senior citizen chasing a hooligan. So what were the chances of me being broken into?

Thankfully, the police arrived pretty quickly. And I'd admit to Sergeant Ed Helms being extraordinary eye candy. In fact, if word got out that our police force was that good-looking, there'd be a spike in crime by women hoping to get arrested.

Sergeant Helms sat on the couch, his large, muscular frame taking up way more space than I ever did, as his partner Constable Davidson sat next to him. Constable Davidson looked like he had just arrived from the academy. His blond hair and blue eyes gave him the innocent, adorable boy look.

Sergeant Helms opened his notebook and looked at me patiently. I quickly filled them in on what had happened.

"Okay," he said, "you mentioned you made a list of what's missing."

"Yes. It's a strange list though."

"In what way?" asked Constable Davidson.

"Well, nothing of any real value has gone. It's all personal stuff that's virtually worthless to anyone but me." I passed the list to Sergeant Helms. He read aloud.

"Gray sweater from Just Jeans, old jeans with the hole in the knee, fluffy winter socks, ugly necklace Grandma gave me, old WTN T-shirt, photo album from WTN days, my favorite MAC eye shadow, tampons, and the book from my bedside table." He stopped reading and looked at me. "Tampons? You didn't just run out of them, did you?"

"No, I only just bought a new box." The tips of my ears started to burn. Geez, this conversation quickly turned personal. "They were on the bathroom counter." I shrugged. "Maybe the burglar was female and had a bit of a situation." Honestly, I had no idea why they would have taken my tampons, but they were definitely gone.

"What does your WTN T-shirt look like?"

"It's navy blue with a white Westport Television Network logo on the front. It was a kind of uniform that I got when I worked there a few years ago. My job was in the traffic department with my BFF, Georgie, and our manager, Rachel. We made and timed the schedules for everything that went to air. I've actually just received an invite to their reunion to celebrate the station being fifty years old. I don't really want to go, but who knows? I'm still friends with some of them on Facebook." When I'm nervous, I really over share.

"Okay. Can we take a look around?"

"Sure. Go for it," I replied, sinking my back into the couch cushions.

I watched from my spot as the two officers looked around my bedroom and bathroom, making notes as they went. It didn't take long. My one-bedroom apartment wasn't that big. Constable Davidson took a few fingerprint dustings (which was really interesting, and if it had been in anyone else's home, I would have been a bit excited about it). They were just moving back to the lounge when I heard their radios crackle. Constable Davidson adjusted the volume on his and listened to the dispatcher. Personally, I had no idea what she was talking about as it was all in numbered codes, but I did recognize the address when it was called. Apartment 303, 59 Amity Avenue, Westport. The apartment directly under mine.

Surely, this day couldn't get any worse?

CHAPTER 1

 wo weeks later

I PULLED my car to a stop at the red light and looked at up the storm clouds, a feeling of dread settling in my stomach. I wasn't sure why. Maybe it was because I didn't know what I was driving into. Maybe I was worried about what people would think of me now. More likely, it was the fact I was about to come face to face with my ex and his gorgeous new wife. I let out the breath I'd been holding.

I was on my way to the reunion. I'm not really a fan of reunions. I always figured that if I liked somebody enough, I would stay in touch with them. If I didn't stay in touch, I probably didn't like them enough, so why would I want to catch up with them years later? Well, I was here under duress from my BFF, Georgie.

My job at WTN had been to book the commercials. Georgie's was to make sure we actually had the material the advertiser wanted to air, and our manager Rachel's job was to make sure the whole thing timed-out with the programming. I'd confess to it having been my favorite job. And I've had a few.

Unfortunately, the great gods, otherwise known as network executives, decided our station would be far more profitable if we merged with another network. So a sad day was had by all when fifty redundancy packages were handed out, and we were sent on our merry way.

However, what the executives hadn't foreseen was a much larger network buying out the entire group and keeping the newsroom operating, which was why Westport still technically had a television station in operation and why we were all invited to a get together to reminisce about old times and celebrate the fiftieth anniversary.

The last time I set foot inside the building I was a tiny, naïve twenty-three-year-old with all sorts of hopes and dreams for the future. My hopes and dreams were still exactly that, but I was no longer tiny. Still naïve? Probably.

I glanced over at my best friend, Georgie, as I waited for the traffic light to turn green.

"It's going to pour down, isn't it?" I said, more as a statement than a question. Of course it was. According to our local weatherman, Tony, a massive storm cell was heading for Westport. Of all the days the skies would open up, it had to be today. I'd put extra care into my appearance, making sure my almond-shaped green eyes were framed to perfection and that my long, straight, white-blonde hair fell in silky smooth locks. Actually, the silky smooth locks bit was all due to my amazing hairdresser, Danny. Usually my hair resembled albino rat tails. Looking at those clouds, Danny's hard work wouldn't last long.

I took another moment to reassess my outfit. I had chosen to wear my favorite white top and new jeans that sat just low enough to be sexy but not low enough to be slutty. My sheer top cleverly disguised my fashionably large bottom, and even though it was sheer, it wasn't transparent. Unless of course it was wet, then everyone would get the perfect view of my new bra.

I sighed as I watched the traffic light turn green, put my car in gear, and moved up the hill toward the clouds.

"It'll be all right, Alex," said Georgie. "They've set up a marquee in case it rains, but I think we'll be inside for most of it." She smiled. "And anyway, a bit of rain never hurt anyone."

She would think that. Georgie and I had been best friends since we worked together at WTN. She was about the same height as I (five foot five in heels), a year older than I, and *way* more intelligent.

She had big gray eyes, ridiculously long eyelashes, and when she was standing next to me, she looked gorgeous. Actually, standing next to anybody she looked gorgeous. She pulled down the sun visor and used the mirror to adjust her short brown hair.

"I'm so excited for this," she said, the delight clear on her face. "There're going to be so many people that I haven't seen in ages but I've kept in contact with on Facebook. It's going to be fun seeing them again." Georgie was the socialite. She loved everybody.

I looked back at the clouds and let out another breath, wishing I felt the same enthusiasm. But then again, Georgie didn't have an ex that she was about to come face to face with.

The television station was perched high on the edge of the mountain range, overlooking Westport, the river, and the ocean. On a lovely sunny afternoon, it was spectacular. On a wet and stormy afternoon, it was cold, damp, and depressing.

My car gave a sigh of relief as it reached the top of the hill, and I turned into the circular driveway. The square, two-story, block-like building still stood with the same cement façade and peeling gray paint it had five years ago.

I slowed my car as I worked my way around to the back and pulled into the parking lot shaded by the large jacaranda tree. The tree stood tall, overlooking the original old house, the helipad, and a makeshift marquee that stood on the grounds. Five years ago, the old house had been used by the station for storing props etc., but whatever it was used for now, it looked creepier than ever.

I shivered as I looked around at the other cars and saw another yellow Mazda 3 just like the one I was driving. The car reminded me of a particularly embarrassing incident I'd had recently in the parking lot of my apartment block.

What happened was, another resident owned the same car as well, but I didn't know that, did I? So of course, I got caught trying to get into the wrong car. Why couldn't it have happened when nobody else was around to witness my humiliation? I sighed at the memory and pulled my car into a parking spot opposite it. I stepped out, waited for Georgie to do the same, and then beeped the doors locked behind me. I felt the wind whip up and pulled on my jacket in an attempt to keep out the chill that crept up my spine.

I have four sisters, and the only thing that set me apart from them is my gypsy-like intuition. If it feels wrong, it generally is wrong. However, I'm known for *ignoring* that intuition, which, according to my mother, is really something I needed to work on. She was probably right. On more than one occasion it had saved me from getting hurt.

In hindsight, this was one of those moments where I should have listened to my intuition. If I had, I would have put my car in reverse, gone home, snuggled up in bed, and read a good book. But no, that would have made life boring, wouldn't it?

"Look out for the pothole in the concrete," I said to Georgie who was busy sending a message on her phone. She continued what she was doing but sidestepped it nicely. Georgie was good like that. She could multitask.

"There are no signs telling us how to get in," I commented as I walked a little bit faster away from the old house. It appeared a lot creepier than the last time I saw it.

"Let's try this door," suggested Georgie, motioning toward the side entrance with one hand and pushing her phone into her bag with the other.

A feeling of déjà vu ran over me as she pulled open the glass door, and we stepped inside, walked past the ladies' toilets, and headed down the whitewashed hall toward the studio where all the noise was coming from.

Stepping behind Georgie, I followed her into the large room. The studio was almost the same. The only difference now was the station logo hanging behind the news desk, lights beaming down on it as if we were ready to go on air. Instead of reading *Westport Television Network*, it now read *WTN, A Division of the Hope Network*.

The crowd was gathering quite nicely as I allowed Georgie to lead the way. I hated being the leader walking into a room filled with people. I felt self-conscious as they all looked our way. Thankfully, it didn't take long to find a familiar face and one who recognized us. Actually, I should say someone who recognized Georgie. It turned out I wasn't very memorable.

"Hi, Georgie," said Sally, smiling.

I remembered Sally from sales. She worked here long before I did. Even though we were a similar age, she used to be on the chubbier side, very well dressed, and had the prettiest face I'd ever seen. The pretty face was still there, but the puppy fat, as my mum would call it, had definitely disappeared. Her short skirt and fitted jumper showed her new curves beautifully.

"Oh my God, Sally," gushed Georgie, leaning in for a hug. "Look at you. You look amazing!"

"Oh, thank you," she replied, blushing, pulling out of Georgie's embrace and stepping back, looking at me expectantly. After a second, she still couldn't pick who I was.

"Hi, Sally." I smiled, giving her a small wave. I would have liked a hug as well, but judging by the look on her face, I thought it might have been awkward. "Alex. From Traffic," I added.

"Oh yes, of course. Hi, Alex. I'm so sorry. You look different now." I didn't. I looked the same. I dressed the same. I wasn't one for change really, but that was okay. I wouldn't take it personally. I just hoped this wouldn't be a pattern tonight.

I stood back and listened as she told us how she still worked here as a copywriter for the commercials the station still made. She also brought us up to date on how proudly her mum had told everybody about Sally's stint on the state's baseball team.

I remembered Sally's mum. She was always quite ill, and Sally had the responsibility of looking after her. It was good to hear she was still with the living, doing well, and a proud supporter of her daughter.

Turning away, I saw Wes walking toward us. This reunion was his idea, but with the help of our former department manager, Rachel, tonight was actually happening.

Wes used to work in the production area and was a really sweet guy. Age was being reasonably kind to him. The only difference was that he now had a little less hair and was slightly rounder in the tummy area. He was a bit older than Georgie and I. I guessed somewhere in his forties.

"Hi, Georgie. Hi, Alex. Welcome. It's so good to see you both again." He smiled, reaching forward for an awkward kiss on the cheek. I'm not much of a cheek kisser, I will admit. I always found it a bit awkward, really.

"Hi, Wes. You look good," I commented, lying about his yellow floral shirt and secretly wishing I could reach up and wipe my cheek. He was a sloppy kisser. I watched him blush.

"Thanks, Alex. That's really nice of you to say, and I'll add that you look fantastic. But then again, you always did." *I did?* I'd seen the photos, and let me tell you, that wasn't how I remembered it.

Georgie laughed. "Oh, Wes, you're funny." She giggled.

Humph.

"How've you been, Alex? Did you ever get that business up and running?" he asked.

This was *one* of the things I'd been dreading about coming here tonight—having to explain the last five years and the numerous jobs I'd had. Not that it was all bad—at least I was working—but when I'd been handed my redundancy, I told everybody it was fine by me as I was about to open my own business as a beauty therapist.

I had indeed gone to beauty school and opened my own business—with Mum's money, no less—but that business had failed miserably. That was a story I was not looking forward to repeating tonight. Especially if I saw my ex-boyfriend, Jake.

"Umm…"

Thankfully, I was saved from answering. Walking up behind Wes was Rachel, her loud, booming voice drowning out anything I was about to say.

Rachel was five-foot-eight, had a big ego, and a temper to match. Her skinny jeans and skintight red shirt showed off all her assets perfectly.

She ignored Georgie and me completely and pulled Wes aside, whispering something in his ear. I heard him mumble a reply, which obviously hadn't pleased her as she flicked her dark hair over her shoulder and spun on her heel away from us. Wes blushed and turned his attention back to Georgie.

"Sorry about that. Now, what were you saying?"

Georgie continued telling him her life story, but after a few minutes, I got bored and wandered off for a look around the studio. The walls had been transformed into a gallery of old photos taken at various times over the last fifty years of the station's history. I remembered some of the faces in the photos, but even those I didn't remember shone happily, reminding me of the fun we had working here.

Once I'd done a lap of the room, I stepped over to Georgie, who'd moved on from Wes and was now chatting with an elderly gentleman I didn't recognize.

"Well hello, lovely lady." He smiled at me.

"Hello," I replied.

"This is Arthur." Georgie made the introduction. "He works here helping Mum and Dad." Georgie's mum and dad were still employed here, acting as jacks-of-all-trades.

"Oh wow!" I said excitedly.

"You look familiar," he said. Finally, someone recognized me. "Did I work with you in the seventies?" he asked.

I felt the blush start at my neck and spread rapidly north.

"No, sorry, you didn't. I wasn't born until 1986," I mumbled. Quickly changing the subject, I whispered to Georgie, "Hey, who is that woman over there standing next to Sally?" The woman in question had done exactly what she had been asked to do and had put on a name badge. Maybe this was something I should've done.

"Her name tag says Katie. I don't remember her though. Why?"

"She keeps staring at me as if she knows me, but I don't remember her either." I had been discreetly looking at her for the past ten minutes, wondering if I knew her. I really hoped I wouldn't do to her what everyone seemed to do to me. It was a bit embarrassing to keep having to repeat who I was.

"She looks about our age." Georgie was right. Katie looked to be in her late twenties. Her blonde hair was pulled back in a ponytail. Her white shirt was tight under her navy-blue jacket. Her jeans sat low on her hips, and her makeup was immaculate. "Maybe she's a current employee."

"But she's looking at me like she knows me."

"Sorry, I don't know who she is." Georgie shrugged.

Me neither. So why was my intuition buzzing?

CHAPTER 2

I wanted to question Georgie more about her, but the lights dimmed, and Rachel walked into the spotlight, stopping behind the microphone stand. She tapped it to see if it was working, and I cringed at the squealing sound coming through the speakers. She laughed and flipped her long, mousy-blonde hair over her shoulder with her free hand, lifting the microphone from its base as she did so.

"Hello, everyone!" she sang into the microphone. "Are we all having a great time?"

She obviously was. She swayed as she put her hand up to shield her eyes and survey the crowd. I figured she needed to slow down on her alcohol intake. Either that or she needed urgent medical attention, as that sway could not be normal.

I looked around the room to see who was listening to her. It appeared I was the only one, probably because she scared the crap out of me. I was far too afraid *not* to listen when she spoke.

"Hellooo," she called, her voice much louder than the first time.

Still, nobody stopped what they were doing.

"Hey!" she yelled, her eyebrows knitting together as her

magnified voice boomed around the studio walls and rang in my ears.

Okay... *That* got everyone's attention. Fifty or so sets of eyes turned her way, and the noise level in the room dropped until all I could hear was the rustle of clothing.

"Great," trilled Rachel, but I could see the annoyance in her shoulders. Rachel had a bad temper. You really didn't want to get on the wrong side of her. *Maybe I should run and get her another drink. Oops, too late.* Wes had already done it. She accepted the glass and leaned back into him.

I raised my eyebrows as I looked at Georgie. "They look cozy," I whispered, turning my attention to Wes's wife, who stood by the food table. I suddenly remembered why I loved working here so much.

"Huh?" she murmured, looking up from her phone.

"Wes and Rachel." I nodded toward the stage.

"Oh, yeah. Some history there."

There was?

I opened my mouth to ask Georgie about it when Rachel's voice boomed around the room once again.

"I hope everyone has remembered our theme tonight." She giggled, raising her glass and taking a sip of her drink. "I'm sure you're all keen to get started," she continued. "Now, what will happen shortly is there will be a murder! Who will the victim be?"

Looking around the room, I could have had a guess, but maybe actually killing Rachel was taking things to the extreme. She was a bit of a cow, but murdering her was a little over the top.

"You'll have to wait and see," she continued, giggling again, her drink sloshing around in her glass. "First, we need to get into groups as you'll all be competing to see who can solve the mystery first. And, of course, we need team leaders!" I felt my stomach flip at the memory that I'd been chosen as a team leader.

Wes stepped offstage and returned, carrying a pile of envelopes. I felt the excitement pick up around the room as people started to whisper to one another.

"The team leaders already know who they are, and I certainly hope you all remembered to bring the boxes I sent with your invite," continued Rachel.

I'd left the box at home, but I did have the contents with me. I patted my handbag, shivering as I remembered that awful moment when I'd opened the box containing my invite and nine dead butterflies had stared back at me, one poor lone survivor fluttering its wings in a desperate attempt to escape the box. I have no idea why Rachel thought mailing a box of butterflies would be a good idea or why she thought the Westport Post Office would have delivered them fast enough for the butterflies to have survived the trip. I'd returned the butterflies to the earth, but I did bring the other items that were in the box.

It had contained a letter, a map, a photo, a notepad, a cipher key, and the most hideous headband I had ever seen, stating I was a team leader.

"Team leaders," called Rachel, almost swallowing the microphone as she spoke. "Please open your box, and put your headgear on. This is how your team will recognize you tonight!"

Was she serious? There was no way in hell I was wearing that headband!

"Where's yours, Alex?" she asked, a smug smile playing on her lips.

I huffed, opened my handbag, and retrieved the offending object. It was fluorescent pink with lots of sparkly beads and a big purple butterfly bouncing on a spring. Painted across the band were the words *Team Leader*. I closed my eyes and wondered why I hadn't thought to leave it at home.

"Okay, leaders, please step up to the stage. We're about to announce your teams."

The noise level in the room picked up as ten of us moved

forward. I pushed my way through the crowd and found myself with a group containing a few current employees mixed with some older ones, but it was the last lady to step forward who bothered me—Katie, the woman who smiled like she knew me. I smiled back and figured I'd avoid eye contact after that, as I still had absolutely no idea who she was. Unfortunately, she decided to stand shoulder-to-shoulder with me, her butterfly-less green headband sitting proudly atop her head.

"Come on, leaders, suit up!" said Rachel, giggling.

I watched as the men put on caps and the women put on their headbands. That was so unfair. How come the men got caps? And how come I was the only one with a big purple butterfly hanging off my headband?

"Come on, Alex. Put your headband on!"

The spotlight moved to illuminate me. I cringed and thought Rachel was paying me back for the *one* time I'd stood up to her all those years ago. I considered lying, hiding it behind my back and saying I'd forgotten it, but everyone was staring at me, so I sighed and pulled it onto my head as my blush raced north. The big purple butterfly bounced happily, annoying me every two seconds when it bounced so low it caught my vision. *Arghh.* Rachel looked at me and grinned.

"Okay. Wes will hand you an envelope. It contains the list of your team members," she explained as Wes walked past and handed each of us an envelope. I turned mine over, put my finger under the seal, and ripped it open.

"Now, people," Rachel continued, the joy in her voice apparent, "when you hear your name called, please come and stand beside your team leader."

Wes stepped up to the first guy in the line—Brent. Brent was known as the workplace lothario. Looking at the way he stood, confidence oozing from every pore, he obviously still thought he was.

We listened as he read his all-female list. My eyebrows moved somewhere near my hairline as I realized he'd had affairs with at least two of his group. I wondered if his current girlfriend, Deanne, knew that.

Katie was next to call her list. I listened to the names, including Georgie's, and thought how they were all from my era. Funny how I didn't remember Katie, though?

I looked at Georgie and raised my eyebrows, wondering why she wasn't in my group.

Then it was my turn. Wes moved to stand alongside me and placed the microphone to my lips.

Removing the A4-sized piece of paper from its envelope, I unfolded it and read the list. In my group I had Matt Wilson, my *ex*-boyfriend Jake Radburn, and Sam McDermott.

Matt, a reporter for WTN news, stepped up immediately. I'd seen his gorgeous face on the six o'clock news every night. In fact, he was the only reason I switched it on. He was about my age, had short sandy-blond hair that curled sexily at his collar, vibrant blue eyes, was close to six feet tall, and fit his clothes exceptionally well. And I'll admit, I did give a little nervous giggle the second I shook his hand.

Next up was Jake. I counted my heartbeats as I waited for him to step forward. When I met Jake, he was the best-looking guy at the station. He had the most beautiful dark eyes, shiny black hair, and the smile of a god. Unfortunately, he knew it, but all those years ago, I was too young and naïve to know that.

As the crowd parted and allowed him through, our eyes met. I could tell he was no happier about this than I was. And age was treating him well. *Damn.*

As Jake stepped up and stood beside Matt, I looked back at the paper and called the last name on the list. "Sam."

As he hurriedly stepped forward, a handheld news camera in his hand, his grin was almost infectious. I felt my heart rate increase for a whole different reason. I remembered Sam, but in my memory, he didn't look like that. He'd blossomed, as my mum would say. He stood over six feet tall, had sun-bleached blond hair, an extremely sexy mouth, and was all muscle from head to gorgeous toe. I felt my palms go sweaty merely standing in his presence. *Oh boy.* Tonight would be a challenge.

"Hi, Sam," I heard Georgie say from behind me.

I was actually quite impressed at how steady her voice sounded. I didn't think mine would be anywhere near that steady. I turned to look at her.

"Hi, Georgie," he said, leaning in for a cheek kiss. Georgie looked back at me and smiled.

"Sam, you remember Alex, don't you? Alex, Sam is Matt's cameraman. Remember I was telling you about him a few weeks ago?"

Yes, I did remember her telling me about him, and she did tell me how sexy he was, but she failed to mention that this was the same Sam whom we had worked with years ago. The one who, at the time, was scrawny and constantly asking me out. Well, at least that's what I thought he was trying to do. He never actually came out and asked me directly.

It was always things like, "Hi, Alex, what are you doing tonight?"

And I'd reply, "Going out with friends." At which point he would just retreat back behind the senior cameraman he was working with. When I started dating Jake, Sam never spoke to me again.

I stared up at Sam and the five o'clock shadow framing his soft, full lips. His smile showed the dimple in his right cheek. My eyes moved to meet his, and I shivered as they twinkled back at me, as blue as the sky.

Suddenly, I was rethinking my opinion on cheek kisses. Maybe now would be a good time to overcome my dislike of them. And there could always be the added bonus of leaning the wrong way and meeting those lips. Actually, scratch that. I think if those lips came anywhere near mine, my heart would actually stop beating. I silently cursed myself for never accepting his offer all those years ago.

"Hi, Alex." He smiled slowly, showing his perfectly straight teeth. He then leaned in for the cheek kiss, and I felt my heart rate kick up and become erratic. I held my breath as I felt the warmth of his breath touch my cheek, and a feather-light kiss whispered over my skin.

"H...hi," I replied, breathlessly.

I was saved from having to say any more as someone walked behind Matt, causing him to bump into me and spill his beer all down the front of my shirt. He blushed and immediately tried to wipe it off.

"Matt!" cried Georgie.

Personally, it wasn't that I was not enjoying the attention my cleavage was receiving from him, but I'd heard he had a girl-friend, so it probably wasn't the most appropriate thing for him to be doing.

"What?" he said, stopping mid-wipe and looking at Georgie.

"You virtually have your hand down her top," she explained, waving her hand toward me.

Matt looked at his hand and then up into my eyes. His blushing kicked up to full heat.

"I...I...I'm really sorry," he stammered, finally removing his hand.

I smiled back at him but didn't want to admit that was the most attention my chest had had in a very long time.

Thankfully, the next group was announced, pulling everyone's attention away from my cleavage.

"Tonight's going to be fun!" said Sam, his lips close to my ear as he put the camera on his shoulder and moved it around our group.

I hated cameras. In fact, as much as I'd loved my job here, cameras were the downside, seemingly everywhere you bloody turned.

"Hello, Alex," whispered Jake. I changed my scowl to my very best smile and turned to face him.

"Hello, Jake," I replied. "How are you?"

"Good, thank you," he replied, an awkward smile firmly in place.

"Whose group is Faith in? I was hoping she'd be in ours," said Georgie, referring to Jake's new wife and reaching up to give him the appropriate cheek kiss. I gave him a look that said, *don't even bother looking for a kiss from me*, and he gave me a look back that said, *as if I would*.

"I don't know," he answered tightly. "I thought she'd be with me. Maybe I should go talk to Rachel," he said, turning away and pushing through the crowd now gathering around the stage as the groups filled up.

"Great. Thanks for that, Georgie," I said. "It wasn't awkward enough just with Jake. You had to ask for the wife to be part of the group too." I was going to add, *and when did you become that close a friend with her, that you wanted her in your group?* But I didn't. Jake and I were a long time ago. I had no reason for not wanting Georgie to be her friend.

"Sorry. I wasn't thinking."

"I wouldn't worry," said Matt, looking up from the notebook he'd been scribbling in. "Faith'll be cool with it." Yeah, maybe *she* would, but this wasn't about her, was it?

"Rachel has certainly gathered some interesting groups," commented Georgie, looking around the room. "There's a lot of history here, and I for one would have kept them apart. She could easily have reorganized them so people were with those they actually liked."

"Yeah, but Rachel was always a troublemaker," I said, a feeling of unease causing my skin to crawl. "She likes drama."

"I think she'll get what she wants then." Georgie sighed.

I stood chewing my thumb as Georgie turned to a member of her group and asked about her family.

My thoughts drifted to Jake. We met when I first started working at the station, and it didn't take him long to ask me out. He was my first real love and definitely the first one I'd been past first base with. We were together for three years and only split just after I'd been made redundant. He gave me no explanation as to why, only saying he wasn't able to commit to me the way I wanted. Whatever that meant.

I sighed and looked at the people around me, my thoughts moving to Georgie's assumption that Rachel was looking for trouble. She was right. I could already feel the tension in the groups. The more I looked around, the more I realized these groups had been carefully handpicked, and the more the feeling of unease prickled my skin.

It was only when Jake walked back toward me that I pulled my attention back to my own group. Jake was accompanied by Rachel and another woman I assumed to be his wife. I gulped as I took her in. This woman was stunning. Her ridiculously shiny blonde hair shimmered under the lights, her green-blue eyes sparkled, and her sexy curves made me feel very beige.

"Sorry, guys," smiled Rachel. "You're going to get an extra team member. I forgot to put poor Faith's name on your list, Alex. I hope you don't mind having her in your group?" she asked me sweetly.

I saw the challenge in her eyes. "Not at all," I replied cheerily.

If Rachel wanted drama, she wasn't getting it from me. Faith smiled a super-white smile and fluttered her eyelashes innocently. I looked at Jake and wondered if she knew our history. As she looped her arm through his, claiming her stake, I figured the answer was yes, she did know.

"Excellent. I'll leave you to it then." With that, Rachel flicked her hair over her shoulder and turned on her heel, ready to face the next unhappy coworker, sideswiping Georgie as she went.

I looked at Faith awkwardly. She wore three-inch spiked heels that made her stand a few inches shorter than Jake. Her skinny jeans molded her body perfectly. Her black top floated about her dreamily showing just enough cleavage, and her green silk scarf accented the color of her eyes.

Damn Jake. Why couldn't he have married an ugly woman? If not ugly, then just not one quite so gorgeous. I sighed as she smiled triumphantly back at me. There was something familiar about her. I have a really good memory for faces, just not a very good memory for *how* I knew the face. This time was no different, apparently.

"Well, this is fun!" said Sam, returning with the camera firmly pointed at me.

I looked away from Faith to Sam as he spoke. Even though his face was covered by the camera, I could see his firm stomach as his T-shirt lifted above the waistband of his jeans when he held the camera on his shoulder. I may also have noticed the soft patch of hair on his stomach move its way into the top of those jeans as they sat low on his hips and showed the perfect V-shaped muscle and glistening, smooth golden skin. The saliva in my mouth dried up as it hung open, and all thoughts of Jake and Faith fled from my mind.

It was only as he lowered the camera that I realized he'd probably caught me perving on him on video. *Shit.*

I cleared my throat and brought my mind back out of the gutter.

"Umm... I can think of better ways of having fun," I said.

"Me too!" He smiled. I felt the blush race up my neck and stop at my ears. Thankfully, I was saved from responding as the speakers came to life once more, and Rachel's voice boomed out across the room.

"Now that we all are in our groups, it's time for the rules!" she sang. "Team leaders, you should have your tools with you," she said.

I looked at Jake. "Yep, got one tool right here," I commented. He scowled back at me.

"Okay, now the first rule is the team must stay together! If you're not all together at the end, you cannot win the game!"

"What do we win?" I heard someone yell.

Rachel smiled a very sly smile. "You'll have to wait and see, but I guarantee you, it's worth the wait!"

It had better be. I looked at Jake as Faith held possessively tight to his arm. "How long have they been married?" I asked Georgie quietly.

"Ummm...about a year, but they've known each other for a long time." Georgie squirmed uncomfortably. She knew more than she was letting on.

"Rule number two!" called Rachel, interrupting us before I could question Georgie further. "You'll also get bonus points if you photograph your opposition being sabotaged!"

Great. This sounded like a fun game, didn't it?

"Spying on your opposition may also help you solve your clues quicker as they may have figured out something that you missed!"

I heard the excitement go around the room as people were already pulling out their smartphones and taking happy snaps.

"Why did I have to be leader?" I asked. I sucked at puzzles, and nobody wanted to be with me when I was trying to read a map.

"Because you've got the headband," laughed Sam.

Crap. I'd forgotten about that thing. I snatched it off my head and smoothed my hair down as I looked at Faith and noticed her snigger. Maybe her personality wasn't quite as gorgeous as her exterior.

"Now, everyone grab yourself a drink and hope it's not one of you who's murdered!" Rachel raised her glass to the room and chugged back what was left in it.

CHAPTER 3

*I*t wasn't much longer before we heard the fake scream alerting us to the fact that a body had been found.

Indeed, on closer inspection, it was Rachel who we found on the floor, fake blood pouring from the cut across her throat. Hmm, if this were a real murder, I didn't know who my most likely candidate for bad guy would have been.

One by one, our teams were allowed to get closer to her to inspect the body and the crime scene. It appeared Rachel's fake death involved a lot of fake blood. Fake or not, it made my stomach churn, and the possibility of passing out became a real one. So, I did what any good leader would do. I delegated.

Thankfully, Matt and Jake didn't share the same phobia I did and happily stepped up to check her body. Sam stood back and filmed the entire thing in case we needed to double-check anything later on.

I did notice a few of the other groups admiring this technique as they pulled out their smartphones and switched them to video. Faith stood next to me, probably feeling the same way I did about the blood.

As we stepped away to allow Brent's team their turn, Matt

opened his notepad and scribbled a few things down. I looked over his shoulder to see what he had written. God, he smelled good.

"Wes's wife, Kelly, found the body, so she's top of the list for me," he said, showing me his notebook. I shook my head to clear my senses and read his list.

"Wow. You've got quite a few names on there already."

"Well, on this list," he said, flipping the page backward in the notebook, "I've listed the names of everyone I could recall being in the room with us in the time between Rachel leaving the room and when her body was found. And this list," he said, returning to the original page, "is the list of everyone else."

Wow, was I lucky Matt was in my group. He was super-cute *and* intelligent.

"But what motive would Kelly have for murdering her?"

"Wes and Rachel seemed pretty cozy up on the stage when the envelopes were being handed out. I was at the bar at the time, and Kelly definitely didn't seem impressed."

"I don't think that was for the show," commented Sam. "Rumors are Wes and Rachel had an affair."

"What?" I asked, shocked. "No way. Surely he wouldn't do that?" Wes was a really nice guy, and even though age seemed to have been reasonably kind to him, he did have a noticeably receding hairline and a fairly round tummy. He just didn't seem like Rachel's type.

"It was a long time ago now, and apparently Wes patched things up with Kelly."

"I thought Rachel had the affair with Marty," said Matt.

"She did. Wes was before Marty."

"Geez, Rachel was a busy girl," I said.

"You don't know the half of it," finished Sam. "She had an affair with just about everyone. Male and female!"

"Really?" I asked, shocked at the revelation. "How do you both know all of this?"

Sam smiled a really wicked smile, and I felt my heart miss a beat. "Matt is a really excellent reporter. He investigates everything."

"Georgie told us," said Matt, correcting Sam.

"Don't give all our secrets away," chastised Sam, playfully. "We want Alex to think we're super-smart and awesome. And by the way, I never slept with Rachel," he added.

Good to know.

"Me either," said Matt. "Until they organized this reunion, I'd never even met her."

Jake remained silent. Did he have a history with Rachel I didn't know about? Faith glared at him, obviously wondering the same thing. Minutes later, I heard her mumble some sharp words in his ear, but he still remained silent. I figured he'd pay for that at some point in time.

Brent's team pushed past us, moved through the door and out of the studio, following their first clue.

"I think we should start in Bernie's office," said Matt.

Bernie was—and still is—the station manager. "Really? Why?" I asked, surprised.

"I believe she was killed by having her throat cut with a broken bottle, specifically a *Scotch* bottle. Tonight's makeshift bar didn't serve spirits. It only served beer and wine, but I know Bernie keeps the best Scotch in his office. I reckon we should start there and see if we can find any clues."

Bernie having Scotch in his office didn't surprise me, but the fact that Matt had figured that out just by looking at Rachel did.

"How do you know that's how she fake-died?"

"Well, the wounds she sustained looked like the murder weapon was blunt and uneven. I'm no expert on forensics or anything, but I've seen a few crimes scenes, and to me, it definitely looked like it was done by a broken bottle. And she smelled of Scotch, so my guess is the bottle would have held Scotch."

"I don't think the smell came from the murder weapon," said Sam, grinning.

"You figured all that out just by looking at her?" I asked, completely impressed.

"Nah, I had a tip-off about the murder weapon," said Matt, touching his nose to indicate this was all very Secret Squirrel stuff only reporters could know about, and gave me a wink.

"Who gave you the tip-off?" I asked anyway.

"Can't say."

Oh well, no harm in asking, right? "So Bernie's office, hey? Sam, lead the way!"

THE LAYOUT of the station building was pretty simple even though it was extremely large. On the ground floor was the studio we'd been in, various offices, including Bernie's, an old storage room that once upon a time held all the dubs, a board-room, the newsroom, a reception area, and the toilets. Oh, there was also a small storage room hidden under a flight of stairs. Three staircases headed up. We ignored all of it as we moved down the hall, past the reception desk, and toward Bernie's office.

I'd only ever had the opportunity to be in this office once before, and even though I no longer worked here, I still felt intimidated walking into it. The room was large and imposing, and his furniture was oversized and made of dark timber. Some might have said he had a Napoleon complex, and some might have been right, but I would never have said that to his face.

To be honest, I was surprised that Rachel had gotten away with this room being included in tonight's events. Then again, with the information Sam had shared about her bedroom activities, maybe she'd pulled in some favors. Or maybe we were completely wrong in our sleuthing and shouldn't be in here at all, but hey, I didn't work here anymore.

I stood at the door as Matt moved into the office followed by Sam and Jake. Faith had joined Georgie and headed in the opposite direction from us, saying she needed a quick stop at the ladies' toilets. Personally, I thought she was sulking after the lovers' tiff I'd overheard in the studio between her and Jake, but I was definitely not getting involved. Between you and me, though, I thought the point she made to Jake about remaining quiet on the whole Rachel business was actually spot on. I, too, would have wanted an answer as to whether or not he'd ever slept with her.

Matt opened the mahogany door on the cabinetry running the length of the back wall, and I heard the appropriate gasps of admiration from the boys when they saw the interior of it. Not only did it hold a fully stocked refrigerator, it also contained bottles of bourbon, rum, and gin. And that was only naming the bottles I recognized.

Sam let out a long, low whistle. "And I always thought his secretary was his favorite part of the job."

"That's a lot of alcohol," I said. "But how do we know if it's what we are looking for?" As I spoke, a flash lit the window behind me. The storm was moving in.

"Whoa!" jumped Sam, moving closer.

He looked down at me and grinned, and I figured he wasn't *really* scared of a storm. As he grabbed my arm, my stomach flipped, but I told myself it was maybe because I was a *little* bit scared of storms and had nothing to do with Sam's smile. Or the fact that my skin tingled under his touch.

"The storm's ages away," said Jake. "Count the seconds between the lightning and thunder, and you'll know how far away it is."

Right on cue, the thunder rumbled, and the walls of the office trembled. I didn't have to count the seconds to know it was still a long way off. Sam moved to sit in Bernie's desk chair, wiggled the mouse backward and forward, and the computer came to life.

"What are you doing?" I asked, my heart missing another beat.

"Browsing," replied Sam, his cheeky grin firmly in place.

Matt turned to look at him. "You know the password to Bernie's computer?" he asked, impressed.

"Yeah, I was in here with him one day when he entered it. It didn't take a genius to figure out it was his wife's name."

Sam gestured to an ugly crystal photo frame containing a happy snap of Bernie's family, his wife smiling, holding center stage. I'd never met his family, but I had to admit they were a good-looking bunch. They obviously got their looks from their mother.

"Sam, you can't just snoop around someone's computer like that," I said, feeling really uneasy.

"Well, technically the computer belongs to the station, so Bernie shouldn't have anything personal on it."

"No, but it might have some classified information on there you're not supposed to know about."

"This isn't the FBI," said Sam, his dimple flashing as he spoke. "Anyway, Rachel said we were supposed to spy on our opposition."

"Bernie's not our opposition. He's not even here tonight," I added.

"Yes, he is," added Jake. "I saw him earlier. He was talking to Rachel."

"Really? The website set up for the reunion said he wasn't coming."

"Well, he was definitely here."

Hmmm, that was odd. "I even remember Wes telling me he wasn't coming," I insisted. "I specifically asked because I was intending to avoid him if he were here. If his breath smells as bad as it used to, then I didn't want to get stuck talking to him."

"It's okay, Alex. Relax. He's not even going to know I've been looking around," said Sam, clicking the mouse a few times and studying the screen. "I only want to see if he Googles porn throughout the day."

I scoffed. "Nobody does that!"

"Sure they do. Look, right here," said Sam, swiveling the screen to show me. "Right there—*Some Like It Hot*. Porn." Sam was flipping through the history on Bernie's computer.

"That's a movie," I added.

"Oh," replied Sam, disappointed.

"What's that site?" asked Jake, leaning over Sam's shoulder, obviously as interested in Bernie's internet surfing as Sam was.

"Let's click on it and find out." Within seconds, the screen was filled with a betting site.

Matt whistled. "He's doing that on company time?" he asked.

"Seems that way."

"Well, I guess it's really none of our business," I said, wanting to get out of there before Bernie appeared. Sweat broke out on my upper lip as fear rolled in my stomach. I figured I wasn't cut out for snooping.

"See if you can open his betting account," said Matt.

"Matt! You can't do that!"

"I'm not going to do anything with it. I just want to check out a couple of things."

It appeared it didn't matter what I said, the boys did what they wanted to anyway. Within seconds, they were all looking at each other seriously, and Matt was scribbling in his notebook. Jake was pointing to something on the screen, and Sam was clicking on whatever he was pointing to. I sat down on the opposite side of the desk from them, not wanting any part of it.

Bernie's desk was open to me, and I could see Sam's long legs stretched out close to mine. I was distracting myself from what they were doing by admiring his athletic muscles pulling against the fabric of his jeans, when I noticed some-thing on the floor, stuck between the desk and the paper shredder. I knelt down and crawled under the desk to retrieve it. It was a piece of paper that seemed to have missed the shredder.

Sam popped his head under the desk. "Look, Alex, I'm flattered, but maybe another time would be more appropriate."

His grin spread from ear to ear. Matt roared with laughter. I didn't know what Jake did as my head was under the desk only inches away from Sam's legs.

It took me a moment to realize what Sam was talking about, but when I caught up, my face was so hot from embarrassment I thought I might just self-combust. I quickly got myself back to the chair.

"No! That... That's not what I was doing," I stuttered.

Sam's laugh erupted, deep and masculine. Jake scowled at him, and for the first time tonight, I appreciated him.

"I was just picking this up," I finished quietly.

"Sorry, Alex. I know what you were doing. I just couldn't resist teasing you." Sam's smile faded. Maybe he realized how embarrassed I was. "What is that?"

I turned the paper over in my hand. "I'm guessing it was supposed to be shredded. It's part of an itinerary for an airline." My ears were still burning, but I'd managed to regain some composure.

Matt moved to look over my shoulder. "Mind if I take a look?" he asked.

I handed him the paper and stood up, wanting some of the cooler air in the hall. As I did, I heard the sound of footsteps moving toward us.

Oh God! "Someone's coming," I hissed, my heart rate increasing from its normal seventy-something beats per minute to approximately a million beats per minute in less than a second. Okay, maybe I was exaggerating a bit. It was more like half a million beats per minute.

Sam quietly closed down the computer as Jake and Matt

moved away from him. I turned to move from the room and came face to face with Wes. I let out a small scream.

"I can't find anything that could be a clue here," said Matt loudly. "There's definitely no Scotch. Maybe we should check the old house before this storm gets any closer," he added, looking at his watch. "I know there's a stash of bottles out there."

Matt pushed the paper into his jacket pocket as Sam stood and quietly pushed the chair back into place.

"What are you all doing in here?" asked Wes, looking surprised to see us there.

"Just looking for clues to tonight's mystery," added Sam, jovially.

"Well you shouldn't be looking in here," said Wes, his tone suggesting his annoyance. "This room's off-limits. I seriously thought you would have known that."

I felt the reprimand like a slap across the face. I didn't like disappointing people, and right now, I felt I had disappointed Wes.

"Sorry, Wes," I said, quietly. "We were just leaving."

"Good."

He watched as we all moved past him out of the room, and then he moved into it himself, quietly closing the door.

Matt watched him over his shoulder as we made our way down the hall. "What's *he* doing in there, would be my question," he whispered.

I didn't care. I just wanted to get out of there.

Lightning flashed brightly in the floor-to-ceiling glass walls as we made our way down the hall. As we passed the reception desk, Katie's group stood scratching their heads, looking confused.

"Where's Faith?" asked Jake, looking at Georgie for an answer.

"I left her in the toilet."

"Why?"

"What?"

"Why did you leave her? Aren't you women supposed to hold hands or something to go to the toilet?"

"Jake, that is so sexist!" she snapped.

"No, it's not. I've just never met a woman who would go to the toilet alone," he explained.

"Well, she was in the cubicle talking to someone on her phone when I finished my business, so I told her where I was going and left. She's probably still trying to get a good phone signal and hasn't even done what she needed to do yet."

"Who was she talking too?" asked Jake, a frown marring his perfect forehead.

"Well, it was really none of my business, but I thought she said 'Hi, Mum,' so my guess would be her mother."

"She doesn't have a mother. She died when Faith was a baby."

Georgie sighed. "Sorry, then I have no idea who she was talking to."

Jake's frown deepened. "Maybe I'll send her a message and tell her where to meet us," he said, looking at me.

Like I cared what he did.

Sam put his arm around Jake's shoulders and pulled him in close for a manly shoulder hug. "Jake, my friend," he said. "Take my advice. If a woman is annoyed at you, a text message isn't going to help. You need to kneel in front of her and beg for forgiveness."

"And flowers. Lots of flowers," added Matt.

Geez, where were these men when Jake dumped *me*.

Jake sighed and nodded his agreement. "Yeah, you're right. Even though I didn't do anything wrong."

"Of course you didn't!" said Sam, now slapping him on the back. "But that argument won't help when you're sleeping alone."

As we headed down the hall, leaving Katie's group behind, Sam turned to Matt. "What was on the piece of paper Alex found?"

Matt retrieved it from where he'd pushed it into his pocket.

"Well, I didn't get a great look before, but it seems to be a flight itinerary for Bernie. He leaves late tonight." Matt frowned.

"Why the frown?" I asked.

"It just seems a bit odd, that's all."

"Really? Why? Anyone can take a holiday."

"It's a one-way ticket to France. If it were a holiday, he would have booked a return flight."

To be honest, what Bernie did was none of my business. Nor was it a priority. All I needed to be concerned about right now was leading my team to victory and hopefully avoiding a visit to the old house. Which was exactly where Matt was planning on taking us.

───

Do you ever wish you could rewind a moment in your life? I do. Actually, I wished I could rewind more than a moment. In fact, I reckon I'd have chosen about ten minutes. If I could do that, I would have gone back and made the boys come with me. Make our team stick together. That way I would not have been walking down a very creepy hall alone, in a building that seemed eerily quiet as night had descended during a storm that had moved in quickly.

But no, when I'd received the iMessage from an unknown sender advising me to—*Meet under the stairs...immediately! I have a clue for you! Come alone!!!!*—I'd decided that was exactly what I would do. And in my defense, I did need to use the ladies' and definitely didn't want the boys' help to do that. Plus, I figured this was much more efficient. They could continue to search for clues to solve the murder mystery while I answered the call of nature and kept to the terms set out by my secret snitch.

If I was heading for the correct set of stairs, I knew the area in question was filled with boxes, dust, and dirt. *Seriously?* Why couldn't we have met in the lunchroom? It was far nicer, *and* it had coffee. I sighed again, pulled my phone from my bag, and reread the message.

I left the boys to take their detour to the studio. They said they wanted to revisit the crime scene, but personally, I thought they wanted to revisit the bar. Once again, I thought how I should have made them come with me. Or stayed with them. The bar definitely seemed like the better option right now.

Jake had reverted to his original idea of groveling to Faith via text. Wasn't sure how successful that would be. Unless he could use iMessage like my unknown snitch had. Cell signal up here sucked. I never really understood why. Someone once told me it had something to do with the positioning of cell towers, but we were on the highest point in Westport, so you would have thought signal strength would have been amazing. Outside I guessed it was better, but inside these cement walls, signal strength was almost zero. Australia wasn't known for having the best service coverage, and I was with one of the smaller networks. Maybe if I'd gone with the major provider I could have gotten a better service, but who could afford them?

I glanced at the little signal bar on my phone and noticed it jumping from one bar to none as I walked along the hall. I sighed and pushed my phone into my jeans pocket.

As I continued toward my meeting place, I thought about this evening and the fake murder we'd been presented with. I was sure Matt was wishing he'd been picked for a different team.

I shivered at the memory of the fake blood pooling around Rachel as she'd lain on the floor, pretending to be dead. I hated blood—even when it was fake. If it had been left to me, her body probably wouldn't have been checked. I would have just followed one of the other groups around until we came up with an idea, but apparently that wasn't the way real detectives did it. Whoever thought I was anything like a real detective, though, was an idiot.

Thankfully, the toilets were on the way to the staircase, so it wouldn't delay my meeting too much.

Reaching my destination, I put my hand to the outer door and pushed it open. It led to a tiny area with two other doors leading off of it—one going to the ladies' toilets and one to the men's. I had my hand on the inner door to the ladies' before the outer one closed behind me. However, it caught my shoulder bag as it closed, which pulled me up short. I cursed as I was unexpectedly pulled backward. Damn it.

The door had closed on my bag, so I tugged at the shoulder strap to release it. As it ripped free, the contents spilled all over the floor.

Have I mentioned how much stuff I keep in my bag? You just never know when you're going to need something, right? And it's all very organized. Well it was. I looked at the floor and let out another curse.

"Shit!" I said more loudly than I actually should have.

I hoped no one was about to walk into the toilets, swinging the door open and hitting me in the head as I bent to retrieve everything.

It took me a bit longer than necessary as I tried to put everything back where it came from. I put my pen in the pen holder, my lip gloss in the side pocket for easy access, my car keys hung back on the little hook thing that mum gave me for Christmas last year—great invention. Have never lost my keys since.

I eventually gave up and pushed the rest of the contents in, thinking how I could sit and organize it again when we stopped for a meal break. Right now, I had a deadline to meet someone who was going to give me a clue. And we needed all the clues we could get.

I stood and pulled my bag back over my shoulder and pushed the inner door open. My intuition screamed at me. I really should have listened to my intuition because if I had, I would have picked up my bag, gone home, and snuggled up in bed with a good book. I would have preferred snuggling with a good man, but until an hour ago, I didn't even know Sam was sexy now. I mentally chastised myself for having inappropriate thoughts.

Entering the small room, memories poured out at me as I remembered how this had been our gathering spot for workplace gossip.

I looked around. Absolutely nothing had changed. There were still only two cubicles. Both had sickly green, laminate walls and ancient plumbing. The mirror above the sink was still cracked, and the lighting was still bad.

I checked the locks on the doors to make sure they weren't occupied. One of the cubicle doors swung open when I touched it, but the other remained closed. The lock said it was vacant, and I couldn't see any feet under the door. Jake's assessment of Faith finding a quiet corner to sulk had obviously been correct. Okay, sulk hadn't been his exact word, but it was what I figured he meant.

The lights flickered as the storm moved closer, causing the power to surge. I shivered and quickly moved to the cubicle that had swung open. The closed one felt just a little bit creepy.

I dropped my jeans to my ankles and squatted over the seat. There was no way any part of my tush was touching a public toilet.

As I was looking upward, willing my bladder to empty faster as my legs were starting to shake from the squat, I noticed one of the polystyrene ceiling tiles was askew, creating a space to see into the void beyond it. I hated things like that, as I always felt like someone was in there watching me.

I shivered and finished the task at hand. Pulling my jeans up, I hurriedly moved out of the toilet. As I did so, I bumped the laminated wall between the cubicles, and the door to the adjoining toilet creaked open.

Goose bumps broke out at the sound, but I ignored them and stepped up to the sink, hoping to get the hell out of there as quickly as possible. I turned the tap on to wash my hands and quickly checked my reflection in the mirror as I went. That was when I noticed someone was in the other toilet. I let out a small squeak and turned quickly.

My heart stopped, and my squeak turned into a blood-curdling scream.

My ex-boyfriend's brand new wife, Faith, was sitting on the toilet, her feet propped up against the toilet roll. Her head hung to one shoulder. Her eyes stared back at me blankly, and blood had gushed from a very large gash in her temple.

My stomach rolled as the smell of blood filled my nostrils, my vision blackened, and I passed out.

CHAPTER 4

I opened my eyes. I lay on the cold, hard, vinyl-covered floor. I moved to sit, my mind jumbled as to what had happened. I looked around me, my thoughts slowly coming together, and saw Faith, her position unnatural and the blood now soaking her scarf. I felt my stomach lurch as I remembered why I was lying there.

Pushing myself to a sitting position, I managed to get to the adjoining toilet before I threw up. Panic took over, and adrenaline kicked in, causing my body to shake, my face to get clammy, and ringing to start in my ears. I had to get control and calm down. I wasn't helping anyone in the state I was in.

I tried to take a deep breath and moved back to Faith. I was pretty sure she was dead, but I still thought I should check. I looked at the wound, and tears stung my eyes. She'd hit her head hard. And judging by her position on the toilet, I thought that hit hadn't been from a fall.

I moved closer to her, willing my stomach to stop heaving. I really didn't want to touch her, but I had to. Didn't I?

I watched for breathing, but tears caused my vision to blur. I looked back at the wound. Her blood had run down her neck where I had to check for her pulse. As the bile rose into my throat, I thought my knowledge of first aid was nil, so I couldn't perform CPR even if I needed to. No, all I could do for her was get help.

I stumbled out of the toilets and back into the hallway, running toward the studio. I needed to get help, to tell someone what had happened.

My lungs burned as I breathed deeply, the studio feeling much farther away than it actually was.

Reaching the door, I flung it open and ran inside, calling for help as I went.

Only no one was there. I scanned the room, hoping for a sign someone was around. I ran behind the news desk—no one. I ran behind the set. No one there either. I didn't know how long I'd been unconscious, but I did know that it couldn't have been that long because surely my teammates would have come looking for me.

I reached the spiral staircase behind the set and climbed up to the production booth positioned above, hoping that was where they were now. It was empty. I sank to the floor, shock setting in.

As I hugged my knees to my chest, I tried to slow my breathing and think clearly. I felt my phone dig into my hip, and I remembered that was where I had pushed it after rereading the message. *Yes.* I could call for help!

I stretched my leg and pulled it out, reading the message again. I'd actually forgotten I was supposed to be meeting someone. The stairs were only a few meters from the toilets, so why didn't I think to run there for help?

I hit my forehead with the palm of my hand as I pressed Georgie's number, silently praying she would answer and that she would bring help. After all, I was having a hard time stopping the shaking that seemed to have taken over my body. Thinking was obviously something I wasn't doing clearly.

I listened to the silence over the phone, waiting for it to

connect, but soon realized that my signal strength was on zero. Bloody cement walls! I stood and lifted my phone in the air, waving it about as I paced the room, willing the little signal line to go up.

Come on. You can do it. You can do it.

No such luck. I spotted a phone on the desk, lifted the receiver, and, with shaking fingers, punched in Georgie's number.

I waited for the dial-tone beep as it attempted to connect with Georgie, but all I got was her message bank. Wherever she was in the station, she had no cell signal either. I didn't know any of the numbers for my teammates, and I didn't know Rachel's number. I'd had no reason to know. Now I wished I'd taken more notice of the invitation I'd received for tonight. It had Rachel's number written on the bottom of it. I could picture the invite very clearly in my mind, but no matter how hard I tried, I couldn't see the phone number.

Should I call triple zero? Surely this was an emergency? Last time I called them, they considered my problem not an emergency because I wasn't in any imminent danger. Well, Faith looked dead, so no ambulance could help her now. But a dead body suggested an emergency, didn't it?

I wasn't made for this kind of thing. I was a girl who lived in a happy world. I didn't handle stress very well. *And where the hell was everyone?* I felt the panic take hold, wanting someone to take control of this for me. *If only I could rewind time!*

Tears spilled over my lashes again as I pressed the numbers on the keypad.

Thankfully, the door swung open behind me, and in walked Sam, his smiling, happy face warming my soul. I dropped the phone back into the cradle as Matt and Jake followed him in. Seeing Jake, my heart ached. How did I tell him what I just saw? Sure, he was the *ex*-boyfriend who had dumped me so unceremoniously, but he was still a person with feelings. And as much as I detested him for how he'd treated me, I didn't want to hurt him the way I was about to. I wouldn't want to do that to my worst enemy.

Seeing me, Sam dropped his news camera onto the desk and took hold of my shoulders. His blue eyes radiated concern.

"Alex, what's wrong?" he asked, his voice filled with urgency.

I fell forward into him as his strong arms surrounded me, and his warmth seeped into my skin. I took a moment to enjoy the feeling of safety, grateful for him for the first time in my life.

"It's…it's Faith. She…she's in the t…toilet…d…dead," I managed to say, almost hyperventilating. I saw Jake's face pale, and he turned and ran from the room.

"No! Jake!" I called to him, but he ignored me and continued on. "Someone stop him!" I screamed. "He can't go alone." I grabbed Sam's arms, panicked that Jake would find Faith the way I'd left her. "We need to stop him." Sam looked deep into my eyes and nodded.

"Okay. Come on," he said, taking my hand. "If we go down through the studio, we should be able to head him off."

I wiped my face with the back of my free hand as Sam pulled me along. Matt followed closely on our heels. I wanted to say he was about to get the story of his life, but Matt seemed like a really nice guy, and I knew that was an unfair assessment of him.

Sam held tight to my hand as we ran down the spiral staircase, through the studio, and into the hall that led back to the ladies' toilets. Thankfully, we beat Jake.

He was just running toward us as we stepped out of the studio. Matt grabbed his arm and slowed him down, whilst Sam ran ahead. We all stopped outside the toilet door, Jake trying desperately to get away from Matt.

I doubled at the waist and tried to suck in air, the hyperventilating threatening to take over. I didn't want to go in and see her again. Once had been enough. I sank to my bottom with my back against the wall and waited.

I held my breath as Sam entered the room. Jake broke away from Matt and pushed past him as I strangled the cry in my throat. I heard the curse escape Matt's lips as he followed Jake.

Seconds later, Jake reappeared, his face dark with anger. I guess I could understand that emotion. I'd be angry if someone had done that to my loved one. He turned to me and glared.

"What do you think you're playing at?" he demanded.

"What?" I whispered. Why was he angry at me? "I didn't do it, Jake. Surely you'd know that I couldn't do...that?"

Sam stepped out of the door as Jake grabbed my arm and pulled me to my feet.

"Jake, leave her. There has to be some misunderstanding."

Misunderstanding?

Sam turned to me. "Alex, what did you see in there?"

I swallowed the saliva that was threatening to drown me. "Faith!"

"In the toilet?"

"Yes! The cubicle closest to the far wall."

"Is this some kind of *sick* joke?" spat Jake, his black eyes boring into mine.

"What? No... I didn't do it, Jake. You have to know that!"

"Didn't do what, exactly?" asked Sam.

"Kill Faith," I whispered, looking directly at him.

"But Faith's not in there," he said.

What?

I pushed past Jake and moved back into the toilet, preparing myself for what I was about to see again. Jake and Sam followed me. Moving to the end cubicle, I pushed the door open, ready to see Faith and show them what I'd seen. Not that I really believed they could have missed her, but something was wrong here. Instead of seeing Faith, I saw Matt crouched down, checking the area for evidence.

What the...?

"But...but... She was there. Right there!" I stammered. I took a step closer to Matt, looking for any signs that she'd been there. It's not like she could have got up and left. Could she?

"She was there!" I said again, turning to look at Sam. "She had her feet propped against the wall, and she'd been hit—here," I explained, pointing to the right side of my own head to show them exactly where she'd been hit. "There was a lot of blood on her scarf and…and…" I closed my eyes, visions of Faith filling my mind. "Her eyes were open," I finished, swallowing the bile that had risen in my own throat.

"Did you check her pulse?" demanded Jake. "You said she was dead. What did you do, Alex?"

I looked past Sam to Jake. He had his hands in his hair, pulling hard as his denim shirt rode up, showing the leather belt that I'd given him when we'd been dating. I wanted to answer, but my mind just couldn't keep up.

"Alex! What did you do?" he shouted, panic taking hold of him.

"I passed out," I said lamely.

"And?"

"And when I woke up, she was still there!"

"Surely if she'd been hit in here, there would be blood everywhere?" said Sam, the calmest of the three of us.

"There was. It was on her clothes."

"I can't see any on the floor," said Matt, who up till then had been silent. "There don't appear to be signs of a struggle or a fight of any kind. To the naked eye, the area looks clean."

"Are you sure she was dead?"

I nodded. "Yes. No…I mean, yes. She was just staring at me blankly," I added weakly. "She looked dead, but I didn't check."

"How long ago did you find her?" asked Sam.

"I…I don't know. I got a message asking to meet for a clue. They said to meet immediately, so I left you guys and came straight here."

"You left us at about seven. It's now just after quarter past," said Sam. Jake was pacing behind him. I really wished he would stand still. The movement was making me feel even more agitated. If that was even possible.

"The informant!" I yelled, suddenly remembering I hadn't seen anybody. "I was supposed to meet someone under the stairs. Maybe they saw me running from the toilets and went in, found Faith first, and left to get help! They could have moved her before we got here."

Sam shook his head. "Alex, if that were true, there would be people everywhere. This is a television station. A reporter and camera crew would have been here the second word got out."

"But...but...you're the cameraman. And you were busy."

"There's more than one of us, Alex."

I felt the panic start again as I looked at the men around me. "You do believe me, don't you?" I cried. "I didn't make it up. Why would I make up something like that?"

"Because you hate me," spat Jake, pushing past Sam and getting into my face. "You're still angry about me dumping you years ago. Or maybe you were the one who hit her."

"What?" I shouted. Shock wore off as anger kicked in. "Oh my God, Jake, you moron. I wouldn't do something like this! Why would I hit her? And why would I run to you saying I'd found her dead if I had? Someone had to have found her and moved her. Or maybe she wasn't dead. Maybe she got up and left."

Sam rubbed his chin, and I heard the scratching as his hand ran over his stubble. "Maybe. But if she was bleeding the way you said she was, she would have dripped blood everywhere. I've seen accidents like that—and they are not tidy."

"Well, where is she?" yelled Jake, jabbing at his phone, turning his back, and storming out of the room. Silence followed him.

"Do you believe me?" I asked Sam quietly, forgetting Matt was even there.

I heard his sigh. "I believe you wouldn't make something like that up. But I don't know what the hell is going on."

The tears stung my eyelids as the adrenaline wore off, and the cold crept in. I didn't want Faith to be dead, of course. In fact, I was hoping she *had* gotten up and walked away. After all, I never did check her pulse.

Sam pulled me into him as tears escaped my lashes. His body heat seeped through my thin jacket, and suddenly, the world felt safe. He shouldn't have this effect on me, but right now, I wasn't questioning it.

"I think we should call the police," said Sam.

"Let's call Rachel first," suggested Matt, pulling his phone from his pocket and jabbing at it. "She might know something about it." As he spoke, the PA pinged to life, and Rachel's voice announced the entrée was being served in the marquee. After a few seconds of listening to his phone, he shut it down and put it away. "No bloody signal. Let's go to the marquee and find her."

"Do you think it's just part of the game?" asked Sam, his expression turning to curiosity.

My heart skipped as hope flooded in. "Could it be?"

"Are you *sure* she was dead?" Matt asked, looking at me.

I straightened up and tried to clear my mind enough to remember exactly what I'd seen. "No." I shook my head, hoping that would reboot my brain. It didn't help. "She looked dead, but I didn't touch her to check. I had no reason to think she could be faking it."

"Well, Rachel did tell us to sabotage our opposition."

"But Faith was on *our* team."

Sam sighed. "Let's go and find Rachel. We can ask her. If she knows nothing about it, then we'll call the police."

Sam and Matt looked at each other seriously. As the lights dimmed from the power drop-outs caused by the storm, I couldn't tell whether they believed Faith to be dead or not.

CHAPTER 5

*L*ightning flashed, and the rain fell in heavy sheets as we ran toward the marquee. The storm was definitely getting closer.

The marquee erected for tonight's dinner wasn't one of those gorgeous white ones you saw at weddings. This one was dark blue vinyl and advertised the Westport Television Network from the days long gone. I initially thought whoever erected it was being sentimental, but maybe they were just being cheap.

The vinyl sides didn't quite reach the ground, so the pouring rain splashed in, making the grass floor wet. And with fifty or so pairs of feet walking over it, it hadn't taken long for it to become muddy.

As the thunder rumbled, I looked around for Jake, but he was nowhere in sight. However, I did spot Georgie. She sat with her teammate Todd, smiling up at him as if he were a god.

I ran over to her. Matt and Sam followed me. "Georgie!" I squealed, grabbing her and pulling her in for a hug.

"Oh," she said, surprised. She wasn't used to my show of affection. I promptly burst into tears.

"I'm so...so...g...glad to see you."

Georgie pulled away and looked closer at me. "Have you been drinking?" she asked.

"No! Oh my god, you have no idea what's happened." I wiped at my tears, sniffed in a very unladylike way, and quickly brought her up to speed with the events of the last hour or so. As I spoke, I noted Matt scanning the room. Georgie's face paled as I told her the news of Faith.

"Who would want to hurt Faith?" she asked, her big gray eyes filling with tears. "She's so lovely."

That definitely seemed to be the general consensus. I, for one, hadn't bought into it though. There was something about Faith that didn't sit well with me. However, I still didn't understand why someone would want to hurt her so badly.

"There's Rachel," said Matt, pointing toward the food table. "Let's go and talk to her."

Georgie left Todd and followed us. "I can't believe it," she said to me as we all crossed the room. "I just can't believe it. Are you sure that's what happened?"

"I don't know, but that's what I saw. Honest."

"I believe *you*," she said, linking her arm through mine and squeezing it tightly. I just can't believe someone would hurt her. Where's Jake now?"

"I don't know. He was really upset, yelling at me and saying I was lying."

"I guess you can't blame him for being upset," said Georgie.

No, I couldn't.

Reaching Rachel, it didn't take a genius to figure she had consumed more alcohol than a regular person. The smell of Scotch hit me the second we stepped into her zone. I watched her closely as Sam filled her in on what had happened.

"Well, that's not part of the murder mystery," she said, annoyed. She then turned to me. "Are you sure that's what you saw, Alex?"

I was getting tired of that question already. "Yes," I answered.

"And she's not there now?"

"No."

"And nobody else has seen her?"

"Umm…"

"Well, have you asked anyone else?"

I shook my head. What did she want me to say: *Hey, everyone, has anybody seen Faith's body lying around?*

Rachel sighed. She then turned and stood—sorry, *swayed*—onto a chair, dinging her glass to get everyone's attention. "Excuse me. Has anyone seen Faith at all?"

"Who's Faith?" shouted Marty.

"Jake's wife. She's blonde, skinny, gorgeous."

Immediately everyone nodded then they shook their heads. They hadn't seen her.

Katie swallowed the mini-quiche she'd popped into her mouth and put her hand in the air.

"I saw her in the toilet earlier this evening," she said.

"How long ago?"

"Ummm, about an hour maybe."

"Why?" called Brent. "Why are you asking?"

"It seems she's missing," explained Rachel, probably not wanting to scare people with the fact there was possibly a murderer amongst us. "Alex says she found her in the toilet, dead, but her body seems to have disappeared."

Okay, I guess we weren't going with the *not* wanting to scare everyone bit. I heard the small screams and murmurs speed around the makeshift room.

"Don't worry," said Rachel, smiling. "Alex is just trying to sabotage the rest of you and distract you from finding the real murderer here tonight!" She laughed. "Well done, Alex!" She lifted her glass and toasted me.

What? I wasn't trying to sabotage anybody.

"So if anybody sees Faith, let me know, okay?" Rachel got down from the chair and smiled back at me, swigging the remaining alcohol in the glass. I got the impression she didn't believe my story. I looked around the room to see if anybody was taking this seriously. Not too many people seemed concerned about Faith but more than a few were glaring at me accusingly.

"I'm not lying," I hissed, turning to Rachel. "We need to get the police."

She sighed. Wes, who was standing close by, stepped over to us. "Rachel, we should call them. Just in case this is real."

"Wes, Alex is clearly making this up."

He looked at me skeptically.

"Think about it," continued Rachel. "Why would anyone murder Faith? No one even knows her. And where is her body? Hmm?" Rachel put her hand on her hips and glared at Wes, daring him to argue.

"Okay, but maybe we should look for her."

"Where's Jake?" asked Rachel. "Shouldn't he be the one looking for her? She is his wife."

"He walked off," explained Sam, who, like the rest of our group, stood silently assessing the situation. "I think we should go and look for him. I can only imagine what he's going through right now."

Sam grabbed my elbow and pulled me away from Rachel. Which was a good thing as I was about to shake her.

"Come on," he said to me. "Let's look for them both."

As we made our way toward the exit, Sally stepped over to us. "I'll definitely keep my eye open for Faith," she said, touching my arm soothingly. "She's a sweetie, but she gets a bit jealous sometimes. I wouldn't worry too much about her, Alex. She's probably stirring you up, giving herself some time out after finding out about the history you and Jake share."

Sally's words should have settled me, and to some extent, they did, but I knew the anxiety swirling in the pit of my stomach would only settle once we'd found Faith alive and well.

Once we'd moved away from the crowd, we stopped in a huddle to argue a plan.

"Whatever happened to Faith, we need to find her. I'm also worried about Jake. He shouldn't be alone at a time like this," said Sam.

I pulled my jacket closer around my body as the wind picked up and whipped under the marquee. "Yeah, but where do we start looking?"

We were standing around scratching our heads, trying to come up with a good plan, when Wes stepped up.

"Excuse me," he said, tapping Sam on the shoulder. "I was just chatting with Rachel, and we've decided to call in the police and get them to come up and have a look around. See what they can find. I'm not sure if what you think you saw was correct or not, Alex, but as Faith clearly isn't here, something is going on that Rachel and I know nothing about it, so it obviously isn't anything to do with tonight's event."

"Do you think someone is trying to sabotage us?" I asked.

"I have no idea. But if the police get here and find nothing, then no harm has been done." Wes shrugged and gave me a small smile. "Don't worry. I'm sure this is all just a prank."

God, I hoped so.

Wes turned and walked out of the marquee. Matt watched him until he was out of sight then pulled his notebook from his pocket and started to scribble.

"BEFORE WE START OUR SEARCH, I'm going back to the production booth for my camera. I'm grabbing something to eat on the way though," said Sam.

I looked at him, my eyebrows arched.

"What?" he asked, looking at me curiously.

"How can you eat at a time like this?"

"Well, I didn't see her, did I? Anyway, I'm a news cameraman, so not much ruins my appetite anymore."

I sighed. "Be quick then," I replied. I stood back on my heels as Matt followed Sam, obviously agreeing with him. Personally, I wondered if I'd ever be hungry again.

See? There is an upside to everything. At least my arse might get smaller.

Georgie gave me a quick hug. "Come and get me before you go, okay? I'll help you look for them." With that, she went back to Todd.

I think she also thought Faith was pulling a prank. I looked around the room, wondering if I could get a cup of hot cocoa. I wasn't hungry, but I needed something warm in my stomach. Maybe that would stop the shaking that had taken hold of me. I spotted the hot beverage stand on the opposite side of the marquee and pushed my way through the crowd toward it.

People whispered among themselves as I passed. Some snippets of their conversations included: *What kind of person makes something like that up?* and *She just wants to put us off our game.* My personal favorite and the one that made me want to scream was: *Of course she's making it up. They were the rules of the game, remember? Anyway, Alex was always competitive, so I'm not surprised.*

Tears stung my eyes as I tried to ignore them and stared ahead, keeping the cocoa in my sight. I knew I hadn't worked with these people in a long time, but I would have thought they had a higher opinion of me than that.

I swiped at my lashes as a flash of clothing slipping through a gap in the vinyl tarp caught my eye. I could have sworn it was the station manager Bernie, but why would he be hanging around the edges of the room? Why wasn't he in the mix of people? He was a pretty big personality, and attention was something he loved, but maybe I'd just missed him being here, my mind preoccupied by Faith.

I was just adding two heaped teaspoons of sugar when Katie,

the woman I didn't recognize but who obviously knew me, stepped up next to me.

"Oh, that looks good," she said, smiling. "I think I might have one of those too." She picked up a plastic cup and dropped two spoons of cocoa into it. As she poured in the milk, she looked over her shoulder at me.

"Sounds like you've had an eventful evening," she said.

I nodded and took a sip of my steaming drink. *Ouch, too hot.* "You could say that. Even though it seems Rachel doesn't believe me. But then, she never liked me much."

Katie nodded in agreement. "Yeah, she never liked me much either. Honestly, I don't think she likes anybody. Unless you're a guy. Then she's your best friend."

I smiled for the first time since finding Faith.

"Not much has changed then," I said, referring to how Rachel was now hanging off Brent's arm, pushing her ample bust into him.

"Actually, if I remember correctly, I think a lot about her has changed."

"Really? Like what?" I asked, intrigued.

"I reckon she's had some work done," whispered Katie, her eyes twinkling as she spoke.

"No way!"

"Next time you stand next to her, have a look around her ears. There's definitely some scarring there. Also, I was looking at some old photos of her, and her nose is different now."

I sucked in my breath, shocked at what Katie had told me, but then I thought about it for a second. She was right. Rachel did look different now. It didn't surprise me that she was vain enough to get work done. Rachel was in her early thirties, which I thought was a bit young for that kind of thing, but I guess she saw some signs of aging I'd yet to get.

"Huh," I said, taking a tentative sip of my cocoa, looking around for Sam and Matt. I couldn't see them, so I figured Sam had gone for his camera. I shifted uncomfortably as Katie refused to take her eyes off me. I moved mine to meet hers. They were an extraordinary green. "You have amazing eyes," I said, my mouth working faster than my brain. I gave her a half-smile, hoping she didn't think that was a pickup line. Not that I'm against that kind of thing. It's just not for me.

Katie smiled at me, and I sucked in my breath with the devotion I saw. I wish I remembered her, because she obviously thought we'd had a great relationship.

"Thank you," she said, leaning in close. "They're contacts. They're a gorgeous color though, right? Really natural looking." I nodded and smiled back at her.

After a minute of her staring adoringly at me, I asked, "Do we know each other?" I hated to be rude, but there seemed no other way of getting around the fact that she seemed to think we were friends.

"Yes, of course we do." She sunk back onto her heels and laughed. I was still none the wiser. In fact, I was starting to wonder if she wasn't just a little bit crazy.

"We used to work together, but I now live in the same apartment block as you."

She did? "Oh, sorry. I have a really bad memory." For names but not generally for faces.

"That's okay. I haven't lived in the apartment complex for that long. And I don't expect you to remember me from here. I'm just the cleaner." She shrugged.

A memory flashed of the lady who used to clean our department. She looked nothing like Katie. The lady I remembered had dark hair and freckles and walked with a limp.

"Really? I remember her looking very different. And wasn't her name Joan?"

Katie laughed. "You're thinking of the lady I worked for. Yes, her name was Joan. I was the girl who worked with her. She retired the same year you were all made redundant. I got promoted to head cleaner and moved to the newsroom. Still the cleaner, but it's a pretty interesting place to work."

I thought back to the girl who'd worked with Joan. She'd been skinny, had mousy brown hair, and even though I was no style icon, this girl needed some serious help when it came to her wardrobe. "I still wouldn't have recognized you. You look different now."

"Thank you. I've worked really hard over the years to better myself. It's amazing what a good gym and hairdresser can do." She laughed.

"The gym, hey? Wow. I'm impressed."

"Yeah. I can bench press eighty kilos now. Look, I'll show you my muscles." With that, she pulled her jacket off and showed me her biceps that were indeed bulging through the sleeves of her tight top.

Okay. I quickly changed the subject before she showed me any other muscles. "Hey, did you ever hear anything about what happened to Dean?" I asked. Dean was a middle-aged guy who lived in the apartment below me. Two weeks ago, he'd disappeared off the face of the earth.

"Dean?" she asked, her brow creasing.

"Yeah. Middle-aged, red hair, old-school moustache. Twirled it a lot."

Katie shook her head.

"He always wore sweatpants, even in the middle of summer. He went missing a couple of weeks ago."

"I'm sorry. I really don't know who you're talking about."

I sighed. "Well, you must know Nadine. Everyone knows Nadine." Nadine was my ground floor neighbor. She was mid-fifties and dressed like a retired hooker.

Katie shook her head. I was beginning to wonder if she wasn't just a little bit confused. Is twenty-something too young for dementia?

"She's in unit 104. If you know Nadine, you know everything that goes on."

"Sorry, I don't know her," explained Katie.

I stood back and studied Katie. Everyone in our block knew Nadine. So was Katie lying, or did she live under a rock?

Katie saw me studying her. "You have very beautiful hair," she said, stroking my head as she spoke.

Goose bumps broke out all over me at her touch. "Ummm… thank you."

I really wanted to extricate myself from this conversation, and thankfully, Georgie walked over to me, a purpose in her step.

"Hey, they found Jake," she said, concern etched across her brow.

"Where was he?"

"Outside, walking around in the rain. Sam's gone to try to get him to come inside."

Poor Jake. I couldn't imagine what he was feeling right now. His ex had just told him she'd found his wife dead, and yet, there was no body.

The more I thought about it, the more I figured it was all a ruse to sabotage our group. But why would Faith do that? And where was she hiding?

"Excuse me, Katie, but I'm going to help him," I said, dropping my cup into the nearest bin. "The quicker we find Faith, the sooner I'll be able to breathe easier again."

I pushed my way back through the crowd toward the exit and stepped into the rain.

eorgie followed me as I put my jacket over my head and ran toward Sam and Matt. Thankfully, they had managed to drag Jake out of the rain, but they were all taking shelter on the porch of the old house. I shivered as I ran the thirty or so meters toward them. I actually think that had more to do with the spooky old house than the cold rain.

We called it the old house because that's exactly what it was. It was now about a hundred years old and looked every bit its age. It once belonged to the first mayor of Westport and sat large and proud on top of the hill, overseeing the town, but about fifty years ago it was purchased for the television station as it had the highest spot for the transmitters. Since then, the house had only been maintained enough to store some props and keep it standing. Looking at it now, I wasn't sure how much longer that would be. Rumor had it that the house was haunted, but I was going for that just being a rumor. I will admit to the hair on my neck standing to attention the second I stepped onto the porch.

"Jake, what were you doing walking around in the rain?" asked Georgie, jumping onto the porch beside me. The rain pelted the tin roof and spilled over the old, rusted gutters, splashing onto the grass behind us.

"I was looking for Faith. She's not dead," he said, shaking his head. "I know it." His head hung low. "I wondered if she'd taken a walk and gotten too close to the edge of the mountain. In this weather, it's easy to slip, and if she had, then she would need me."

The only light came from the marquee. In it, Jake looked beaten. His black hair stuck to his face, and his hoodie was soaked. He shivered as a bolt of forked lightning struck a tree in the forestry surrounding the mountain. I screamed and jumped, grabbing hold of Sam's arm.

"For goodness sake, it's only lightning!" chastised Georgie. "It won't hurt you!"

I wasn't quite sure that was right.

"Umm, sorry to remind you, but a guy died on the golf course last week when he was struck by lightning," said Matt.

"Really?" said Georgie. "Are you sure? I didn't hear about that."

"I'm positive. I covered the story."

"Yeah, I had the job of taking the photos of the body for the police," said Sam. "It wasn't pretty. There were holes in his shoes, and his toes had been blown off."

"Why were you taking photos?" asked Georgie.

"Because I'm a good guy, and I help the police like that some-times," said Sam. "Also, the freelance work gives me a bit of extra cash, and that's always a bonus," he added with a grin.

"Did anybody hear that?" asked Jake, turning to face the house.

I shook my head. "All I heard was the thunder. And it came a hell of a lot faster this time. That storm is definitely getting closer."

"It wasn't thunder. It came from inside. I bet it was Faith." Jake quickly moved to the front door and turned the handle to get in.

Unfortunately for him, it was locked. Unfortunately for the old house, that didn't stop him. He pulled his arm into his hoodie and used his fist to smash the glass panel. Georgie jumped. I screamed. One click later, the door unlocked, and Jake opened the door.

"Man, you can't do that!" yelled Matt. "For one thing, there are laws against it, and for another, you could get fired."

Only Jake wasn't listening. He'd already moved into the hallway and into the darkness beyond.

The four of us looked at one another, waiting to see what we should do. Sam was the first to move, following Jake. Matt sighed and followed him, mumbling something about getting the glass fixed first thing Monday morning. I looked at Georgie. She was obviously thinking the same thing I was—would they notice if we didn't follow? A second later, Sam reappeared and grabbed my arm, pulling me along behind him. I guess he would have noticed.

The stale smell of damp wood poured out over us as Georgie flipped the light switch and illuminated the long hallway. I looked at the scarred floorboards and noted two sets of footprints in the dust. Someone had been here before us tonight.

"Even when I worked here and needed to store something in this house, I never came in this entrance," commented Georgie. I actually didn't want to go in there *now*.

"It's usually kept locked. Bernie, our almighty boss, is worried the ceiling in this room may come down and hurt someone," explained Sam, motioning for us all to look up to the ceiling. Sure enough, the old timber looked like it was about to collapse right on top of us. "He prefers we use the back door."

"Then why didn't we use the back door?" I asked, fearing for my life.

"Because Jake decided this was the quicker option."

I figured I couldn't blame him.

"It looks like someone has been in here recently," said Matt as Jake pushed ahead of us, ignoring all dangers.

"Not too many people have keys for that door," said Sam.

He'd obviously been to the production booth and retrieved his camera, as he now switched it on and put it on his shoulder.

The light illuminated the hallway far better than the sixty-watt bulb dangling from the ceiling.

He turned the camera to point straight at me.

"Sam, please turn that thing off. I hate having my photo taken," I whined, spinning away from it.

"That's true. You should see some of the footage of her running from the cameras. It's hysterical," said Georgie, giggling.

I could say nothing to defend myself here. What she was saying was one hundred percent true and correct.

"Can we hurry up, please?" I said, ignoring the comments altogether. "It's freezing in here," I added, pulling my jacket closer around my body, as the temperature had just dropped a good ten degrees.

"It's the ghost," said Sam, turning his head to look back into the viewfinder.

"It is not the ghost," I snapped. "There's no such thing." I hoped.

"I don't care. Can we please hurry up? Jake has already left us behind, and we should stay with him," said Georgie. "I don't think Faith is in here, but we should stay together."

Matt led the way down the hallway after Jake, through a door into a room that once upon a time was a kitchen. The light from Sam's camera illuminated the room, reminding me of every horror movie I'd ever seen.

We huddled closer to each other and moved further into the room. Thankfully, we spotted Jake standing near the back wall. We hurriedly moved toward him, as Georgie attempted to switch the overhead light on. Nothing happened.

Once again, the hair on my neck stood to attention, my gypsy-like intuition kicking in. One day, I'd actually remember to listen to it.

I LOOKED around our group as lightning flashed and lit the room once again. In that flash, I could see the remains of the kitchen—the scarred cupboards running along the adjacent wall, the wallpaper hanging from the wall above them. A small open window, just big enough to give large rodents entry, allowed the wind to howl in as the storm kicked up a notch, and the thunder rolled. Goose bumps raised the hair on my arms as Georgie let out a small scream. Everybody felt the charge of electricity in the air.

"Sam, stop being an idiot, please," she said, turning her attention to Sam. My eyes had adjusted to the shadows created by Sam's light, and I could now make out my friends quite easily, even when they weren't illuminated.

"I'm not doing anything," he replied.

"Well, who's tickling my back?" she asked, turning around to face Sam.

"You're just imaging things," he replied, trying to calm her nerves.

"Let's have a quick look around for Faith and get the hell out of here," said Matt, moving away from our group and toward a door on the left that led off the kitchen.

"Fantastic idea," I said, following him. I didn't want to freak anybody else out, but I had also felt the tickling on my back.

"The back door's still locked," said Jake. "If she came in here, she must have locked the door behind her."

"Seriously, why would she come in here?" I asked.

"She's trying to freak me out," he replied quietly. "She's done it before when we've had arguments. Last time she did it, I couldn't find her for two days. When she eventually came home, she told me she did it to punish me and make me realize what life would be like without her."

She sounded like a manipulative cow to me. My irritation kicked up a notch, and anger toward Faith started to brew.

"So, do you believe me when I told you I found her in the toilet?" I asked. If Jake was right and Faith had faked her own death, for whatever reason, then she needed a serious mental health check.

The lightning flashed and illuminated his face. He took a minute to stare back at me before answering. "I don't know," he said, shaking his head. "She's never taken it this far before, but I wouldn't put it past her. I love her, but she really knows how to hurt me." Anger stirred in my belly.

Georgie moved away from us and followed Matt and Sam through the doorway into an adjoining room, leaving the two of us alone. I took one last look at Jake, my memory flicking back to when we'd been together. I would never have hurt him like that. So why did he leave me and later marry someone like her?

Sadness replaced fear for a moment as nostalgia swamped me. I looked back at Jake and thought he'd changed a lot in the years we'd been apart. Jake looked at me and sighed as we followed the others into the room.

Sam swung his camera around, the light revealing the room to us.

My memories of this room were limited. I could only remember ever being this far into this house on one occasion, when I'd been helping set up an outside broadcast, and we needed some props that were stored in here. It had freaked me out almost as much then.

The room was large, the once ornate ceiling now falling down in places, damp leaving its mark on the walls. The old carpet smelled moldy and dusty as there were no windows to allow airflow. I moved in closer to Sam.

"Where do those doors lead?" I asked, nodding toward the three doors on the opposite wall.

"Two are old bedrooms, and one is now a bathroom," he replied. "This house was elaborate for Westport when it was built, but the original toilet was a drop box outside with a washroom attached. They converted one of the bedrooms into an inside bathroom back in the forties."

Jake tapped Sam on the shoulder. "Shine the light on that door, will you? I want to have a look in there." With that, he made his way across the empty room toward the nearest door. Sam followed him. The rest of us followed Sam. None of us wanted to be left alone in the dark.

The door creaked as Jake pushed it open and made his way into the room, dust rising up and filling my nostrils. Georgie coughed as she followed him.

It was reasonably empty, only containing some old props from a sitcom produced here years ago, some pieces of the old set, and a stack of about ten boxes all with *Liquorland* written across them. I figured that was Bernie's stash. A wardrobe was pushed against the wall in the corner. I held my breath as Jake opened the door to it, hoping Faith's body wouldn't fall out. Thankfully, there was nothing in it.

We made our way to the bathroom only to find it empty too. We moved to the third door.

Matt attempted to open it. "It's locked. Sam, come over here, will you?"

Before Sam even had a chance to move his feet, Jake pushed past Matt and rattled the door. He used his shoulder to push against it. For such an old, rickety house, this particular door was solid and not budging.

"Faith!" he called. *"Faith! If you're in there, answer me!"*

We all held our breath waiting for an answer.

The wind picked up and whistled through the timber walls, causing the dust to pick up even more.

"I think we should get the hell out of here," coughed Georgie once we were all satisfied Faith hadn't replied. "I'll ask Dad what's in there. Maybe he'll come and check it for you. And he can fix some bloody lights while he's here." Georgie's dad, Stuart, was a jack-of-all-trades and responsible for most of the maintenance. If there were a key to that lock, he would have it.

All except Jake agreed. He wasn't convinced Faith wasn't in

there, but he accepted that Stuart had a better chance of opening the door, so Matt grabbed his arm and pulled him along as we made our way back to the kitchen, ready to get out as quickly as possible.

Once again, lightning flashed, and the curtain on the open window moved in the wind. I screamed as something blew up, hit me in the face, and got caught in my hair. I only stopped screaming as Jake reached out and pulled the offending material from me.

"Arghh… It's soaking wet," I screamed, dancing on the spot as if that would chase the heebie-jeebies away.

"Yeah, well, it *is* raining!" he scoffed.

Sam turned his camera to Jake's hand and allowed the light to show us what had hit me.

The world swayed as the heebie-jeebies threatened to swallow me whole. There, in Jake's hand, was Faith's scarf—dripping with water and stained with what looked like blood.

Sam's camera turned to me, and in the glow, I saw the faces of my group look back at me in horror. I reached up with my hand and touched my face. I heard Georgie's strangled scream as I felt the moisture on my fingers and held them out to the light, only to find they were now red with blood. My knees buckled as the nausea swirled in my stomach.

"It's just a prop," said Sam. "It'll be part of the prank."

"Really?" I croaked, my voice fleeing the crime scene, my stomach cramping involuntarily.

"Of course it is. You don't think it's real, do you?"

Judging by his tone, I think he believed it to be just as real as I did, but I clung to those words like they were gospel. Everyone else in the group remained silent. Jake stared at the scarf, his jaw hardening.

Georgie put her hand on his arm. "Are you okay?" she asked.

He turned to look at her, his mouth tight. "I don't know."

"Do you think it's real?"

"I just know I need to find her."

I think everyone agreed with that sentiment.

"And I need to get into that room."

"Let's find Stuart and get him to open the door," said Sam.

I shivered and wiped my face as best I could, using my jeans to dry my hands. I *really* didn't want that to be Faith's blood, but the more I thought about it, the more I realized that if this was a prank then this old house would be the perfect place for Faith to hide. And if it wasn't a prank... Well, I didn't want to think about that.

I felt the tears pool behind my lashes as goose bumps broke out all over me. I wanted to distance myself, get a drink stronger than cocoa, and let the boys do all the investigating from now on.

Turning back to the hallway, Georgie opened the door as Sam's light illuminated a face staring back at us. Our screams drowned out the sound of the thunder that shook the walls.

CHAPTER 7

"Oh my God, Katie! You scared the shit out of us!" yelled Georgie, as Katie calmly looked back at us.

"Well, I'm sorry. I never meant to. I was just looking for the dog," she explained.

"What?"

"The dog. I was looking for it. I saw it run over here, and when I saw the open door, I thought maybe it had come in here."

"What dog?"

"It's medium-sized, light brown, short hair. I don't know whose dog it is, but it's been hanging around the marquee. I think maybe it escaped from its home because of the storm and ran away. It looked scared and wet."

My heart rate picked up again as I listened to her story. I hated the idea of a dog lost in a storm.

"Well, sorry, it's not in here," explained Georgie.

She moved forward, forcing Katie to back out of the hallway and onto the front veranda. Katie didn't look too happy about not being able to search the house, but I didn't think Georgie believed the story of the dog. I knew Georgie well enough to know she thought Katie was just being nosy.

Thankfully, though, Katie didn't argue, and we all made our way out to the veranda, Matt carefully closing the front door behind us.

"I don't know about the rest of you, but I never expected tonight to be so damned scary," I said quietly.

"Me either. I thought it would be fun," replied Georgie, holding my arm and giving it a squeeze.

"It is fun," said Sam, his smile back in place. "Except for Faith being missing, that is," he finished as he ran out into the rain and across the concrete back to the main building. Katie followed him, but she ran to the marquee.

Lightning flashed. I counted the seconds before the thunder rumbled. Three seconds. Shit. That meant it wasn't very far away at all. I looked back at the old house, took a deep breath, and ran into the rain.

We stopped to catch our breath in the hall outside the toilets. I shuddered.

"I want to wash my face," I said, thinking of the blood-like liquid that had dripped from Faith's scarf. Stepping toward the toilets, I took a deep breath, my hand stopping on the door, refusing to push it open. Memories of Faith filled my vision, the nausea once again churning in my stomach.

Georgie placed her hand on my shoulder.

"Maybe I can use the men's toilet instead?"

"That's disgusting," she said. "Come on. I'll come with you."

I turned my head to look at Georgie, my heart beating erratically in my chest. Her eyes were filled with compassion as she placed her hand next to mine on the door and pushed it open.

"We'll go and find Stuart," said Matt, watching Jake's back as he continued down the hall.

"Oh…" I looked back at the door that Georgie had just pushed open. "Can one of you stay here? You know, just in case we need you."

"Sure. Matt, you go with Jake. I'll wait for the girls," said Sam, reassuring me as I followed Georgie into the ladies'.

The room was empty, but Georgie tentatively checked the cubicles just in case Faith had miraculously reappeared. I stood by the mirror and checked my reflection, barely recognizing the person who looked back at me. My complexion was pale, my eyes were huge, and red liquid dripped from my chin to my shirt.

"Oh my God," I said, dropping my forehead into my shaking hands.

"It's okay, Alex. Remember, it's fake."

"Really? Do you really believe that?"

"Yes. I bet Faith is hiding in that locked room and she just dropped her scarf on the way in."

"But why would she do that?"

"I'm sure Jake told her the two of you used to be a couple, so maybe she's just upset with you. We're all guilty of a little jealousy at times." Georgie sounded so convinced that Faith was still sweet and innocent.

"But if that's true, she must have planned it all before tonight."

"What do you mean?"

"You didn't see her, Georgie. It looked real! If what you're saying is true, then she must have come here with fake blood and everything."

"Look, I don't know Faith *that* well, but if she's doing this to sabotage you and your team, then she must have a good reason. Whatever that reasons is, remember, Jake's production manager now, so she's spent a lot of time hanging around. She knows this place pretty well. And there are still plenty of props lying around waiting to be used. Remember the old vampire sitcom they made here? I bet the blood she used was left over from that. She'll be doing it to scare you, to give you a fright. But she obviously didn't think it through."

I sighed. "I guess so, but how did she know I'd be the one to find her?"

Georgie went quiet, thinking. "I bet she sent you that message."

"That's pretty convenient though, isn't it? I mean, I wasn't asked to meet in the toilet. I just decided to pop in here before meeting whoever I was supposed to meet."

Georgie sighed again. "I don't know, Alex. Let's just hope Dad unlocks that door and finds her inside—alive—and that she's done this as a prank."

I straightened and turned back toward the mirror, turning the tap on as I did so. Except for the part where Georgie couldn't explain how Faith knew I'd find her, Georgie's theory sounded plausible, which gave me hope that what was dripping from my face to my shirt was corn syrup and food coloring.

"What is that in your hair?" asked Georgie, pulling at strands of my hair as she spoke. Turning her hand around under the dim overhead bulb, colored light danced back at her.

"I think it's glitter from the headband I got as team leader."

Georgie laughed. "That's right. I forgot about that thing. Where is it anyway?"

I shrugged. "I probably dropped it. Damned ugly thing it was."

Wherever the headband went was the least of my worries.

BY THE TIME we emerged from the toilets, I felt a little bit better. At least my face was clean. Just not my jeans. Apparently blood—fake or otherwise—stained. Matt and Jake had disappeared completely. I figured they had found Stuart and had gone back to the old house. We just needed to wait and see what they found.

Sam decided he needed to change batteries on his camera, so we followed him to the newsroom. Walking down the long hall past the studio, I looked at all the photos of the on-air staff. I stopped at Matt's photo and smiled. Matt was actually really good-looking, and I could see why he was popular on air. Seeing him in action tonight, I could understand why he was also a good reporter. Not much had escaped a mention in his notebook.

The newsroom wasn't large—only holding six desks, all crammed close together and forming two perfect rows. Sam moved to the back of the room and took a minute to swap his battery.

I used the time to have a look at Matt's notice board. My attention turned to the photo of a woman I knew. Her name was Stacey, and she was my dentist.

A few weeks ago, she had gone missing from her workplace after all dental records had been erased from her computers. Her body had later turned up on the beach, a few body parts missing, presumably eaten by sharks.

At the time, it was rumored she had destroyed the records and then killed herself by throwing herself into the ocean. That rumor stopped when police found out she was a volunteer life-guard. Not only was she an exceptional swimmer, but she knew better than to go swimming in the ocean in her work clothes.

"Hey, Sam, what's the latest on Stacey's case?" I asked, turning back to him.

He stopped what he was doing and looked up at me, the over-head lighting causing his dark lashes to cast shadows on his cheeks. My stomach gave a little flip, apparently excited by that.

"Umm… They believe she was murdered, but so far, there are no suspects."

"How can that be? Surely they would have some suspects?"

"None that they're telling us about," he replied, shrugging. "Matt's having lunch with Sergeant Ed Helms on Monday. Hopefully, he'll have some info he can share. There was something really weird going on there, though."

"What do you mean?"

"She had a drawing on her torso the coroner thought was done after her death."

"How the hell does he know that?" asked Georgie.

"Something to do with the skin and how it reacts." Sam shrugged.

"Why would someone draw on her after they killed her?"

"I have no idea, but the coroner, Bill Gamble, is really good and isn't known for getting things wrong."

"What was the drawing of?" I asked, my skin crawling as Sam spoke.

"A butterfly."

I shuddered, thinking of the dead butterflies mailed to me in the invitation for this evening.

"Did you know her?" asked Sam, his blue eyes filled with compassion as he gazed at me.

"Yeah. It's just so sad."

"There've been a few murders in Westport lately," continued Sam. "They found the body of a middle-aged man this morning. I had to take the photos. Police weren't saying much, but there were murmurs that it could be a serial killer on the loose."

I heard Georgie suck in her breath. "What?"

"Why do they think it's a serial killer?" I whispered, my heart missing a couple of beats.

"The man they found had a dead butterfly stuck in his pocket."

"Have they named him yet?"

"Yeah, it was Dean-something," said Sam. He moved to Matt's computer and clicked a few keys. "Dean Jones," he said, looking up from the computer screen.

I felt the world sway at his words. Dean Jones was my downstairs neighbor. He'd gone missing the same day Stacey was found dead. The same day my apartment had been broken into.

"Where did they find him?" I asked, sitting down on a chair.

"He was found in bushland near his home. Bill still has to do a complete autopsy, but he thinks Dean died from a blow to the head. Stacey's autopsy showed the same cause of death."

"Oh my God," I said, sinking my head between my knees as my breath came in short, sharp spurts.

"Alex, are you okay?" asked Sam.

Georgie came around, crouched down, and put her arm around my shoulder, rubbing my back as she did so.

"Dean was Alex's neighbor."

"It...it... Dean..." I sucked in some air, trying to slow my breathing before I hyperventilated. "The butterfly was mine." I felt the tears sting my eyes as I blinked and sat up straighter. "I threw them on him."

Sam looked back at me like I was crazy.

"I didn't mean to," I explained. "The invitation I received for tonight contained ten butterflies. Nine were dead by the time I got the package, so I threw them over my balcony. Unfortunately, the wind picked up at that moment and blew them onto Dean, who was standing on his balcony below. I'm sure one of them just got stuck on his clothing."

Sam grinned. "You threw dead butterflies all over your neighbor?"

"It's not like I meant to do it!"

"But Alex," said Georgie. "You told me the police found a box of dead butterflies in his apartment?"

"Yeah, but he probably missed one of them."

"I don't think so. This butterfly was deep in his pocket. And it doesn't explain why Stacey had one drawn on her wrist," said Sam.

"It's probably just a coincidence."

"Matt says there's no such thing as coincidence," said Sam.

We were contemplating that as Matt and Jake walked into the room. They both looked at me, surprised.

"What?" I asked.

"You got here quickly," said Matt, frowning back at me. "How did you do that?"

"What are you talking about?"

"We just saw you out near your car."

"I've been here the whole time," I explained.

Matt looked at Jake. "It looked like you. You drive that yellow Mazda, right?"

"Yeah, but there's another one the same as mine here tonight. Honestly, I never knew they were so popular."

"But it was you getting into it. I was going to call to you, but the rain's coming down pretty hard. The storm's not far away."

"Sorry, not me. I've been here the entire time."

Matt shrugged, but confusion filled his eyes. At that moment, lightning struck somewhere close by, causing the building to shake as the thunder crashed through the night air. The lights flickered off, and we were plunged into darkness, the only noise was my heart beating loud in my ears.

"Bloody storm," I heard Sam curse.

His voice was reassuring as the hair on my neck stood to attention and my gypsy-like intuition told me to go home.

Sam picked up his camera and shone the light around the room.

"Did you find Stuart? Did he unlock that door for you?"

"Yeah, we found Stuart, and he's going to have a look in that room for us. He had to check the generators first, and then he'll let me know what he finds."

Jake's shoulders slumped.

"I thought you were going with him?" I asked Jake.

"I wanted to, but Matt said I would be more useful here. Stuart is apparently very capable of opening a room without me. If there's any sign of Faith at all, he'll let me know straight away."

Jake didn't look happy about that decision, but I figured, on some level, he could see the logic behind it.

"Did you check to see if your car is still there? Maybe Faith pulled the prank and went home," suggested Sam.

"It's still there," said Jake, his voice void of emotion.

"Someone didn't drop her home?"

"Who knows?"

"Sam, get away from the window, will you?" I begged as Sam stepped up to the window, watching lightning flash around us.

"I thought I saw somebody looking in," he commented. In the glow from his camera, I could see his puzzled expression.

"It's probably Stuart on his way to the generator."

"No, that's out the back of the building."

Matt moved to stand next to him at the window, looking out into the night lit only by flashes of lightning. "Only an idiot would go out in this," he said.

"Yeah, I must have imagined it," said Sam, turning back to the room.

"How long till the generators kick in?" I didn't like storms at the best of times, but with no power and uncertain about what really happened to Faith, it just felt really, really scary.

"As soon as Stuart gets out there and gets them running," explained Matt. "He was on his way to them when we left him, so it shouldn't be too long." He pulled his phone from his jeans pocket and switched on the flashlight. Using it, he scribbled some notes in a notebook, his face eerie in the glow.

Thankfully, the lights didn't take long to come back on. Stuart had obviously gotten the generators going. I blinked as my eyes adjusted to the light.

"I wonder if Wes got in contact with the police?" asked Georgie.

Her complexion looked pale, and I had a feeling she just wanted to go home too.

"Well, we can't do anything else, so maybe we should go look for him and find out," suggested Matt, pushing his notebook into the back pocket of his jeans. "There're a couple of questions I'd like to ask him anyway."

Looking for Wes was actually a really good idea. Hopefully,

we'd find the police, they would take control of the whole situation, and I could finally relax.

Following him out the door, Georgie linked her arm through Jake's and put her head on his shoulder. We all needed to remember his wife was still missing.

I said a silent prayer that she was okay and just being mean.

CHAPTER 8

*W*es no longer worked at the station, so he didn't have an office of his own. We thought he would probably be out in the marquee with Rachel. Heading in that direction and checking in a few offices along the way, we bumped into Sally coming in the back door near the toilets. She was wandering around on her own, looking wet and lost.

"Hey, Sally. You haven't seen Wes, have you?" I asked, approaching her.

"Wes? No, sorry," she replied. "Why do you want him?"

"He was going to call the police about Faith, and we want to know what's happening."

"You still haven't found her?"

"No," said Jake, his jaw flexing.

"Oh, I'm sorry, Jake. I'm sure she's okay though. This storm is pretty intense, so I reckon she's hiding somewhere and doesn't want to get her hair wet." Sally's expression was pained. I got the impression she really *did* feel for Jake. She was such a sweetheart.

"Are you okay? You look wet," said Georgie, stopping in front of her.

"I've lost my team. I was just out in the marquee looking for them," she replied, sounding sad. "I think they've ditched me."

"Oh, we were just going to check the marquee."

"Don't bother. No one is out there. Dinner has been moved to the studio because of the storm, so I guess you'll probably find Wes or Rachel in there," explained Sally.

"I bet your team just got caught up in the game and hasn't realized you're not with them," said Georgie kindly.

Sally smiled. "Thanks, Georgie. None of you have seen them by any chance, have you?"

"Yeah, I did," said Sam. "I just saw them upstairs in the old traffic department."

I looked at Sam and glared.

"Oh, thanks, Sam," she said, a smile spreading to her eyes. "You're a legend." With that, she squeezed Jake's arm affectionately and moved in the direction of the nearest set of stairs.

Once she was out of sight, I turned to Sam. "You didn't just see her team upstairs. We haven't seen her team since entrée."

"Yeah, I know, but remember, Rachel told us to sabotage our opposition." His dimple flashed as a smile lit up his face.

"That's mean."

"Nah, Sally loves me. She'll see the funny side of it." I hoped for his sake she did.

On our way to the studio, we asked everybody we saw if they had found Faith and if they knew where Wes was. By the time we reached it, all we'd found out was that almost everyone had forgotten about Faith, and those who hadn't, thought she was still playing the game. But it appeared they were all still having a great time, following the clues as to whom the fake murderer could be, the storm only adding to the effect. So far, nobody had solved it, but whispers suggested that Arthur might have something to do with it.

Personally, I'd forgotten we were here for the game. It all seemed too real. Looking at Jake, I wasn't alone in thinking that.

Anxiety swirled again, but I reminded myself that even *he* thought she was hiding. We just needed to find out where. I still had my fingers crossed Stuart would find her sulking in the old house.

Entering the room, we found Georgie's mum, Dawn, making sure the caterers were doing their jobs. Tables and chairs had been relocated, and mountains of food covered every surface I could see. The smell of spit-roasted pork filled the air as my stomach grumbled. I remembered I hadn't eaten since lunch. I looked at my watch. It was eight-thirty.

"Thank goodness we had entrée," said Sam, rubbing his stomach as he spoke.

"Yeah, I'd be starving by now if we hadn't," agreed Matt.

Jake pulled up the nearest chair and sank into it, his head hanging low as he contemplated his feet. He'd been trying to phone Faith ever since she went missing, but it seemed that even when he could get a signal and connect, wherever she was, her phone was either switched off or not in a cell service area. Well, at least that's what the recorded message on the other end of the phone was telling him.

Katie walked past me and smiled.

"Did you find the dog?" I asked her, hoping it wasn't running around in this storm. We might not be able to help Jake, but hopefully someone helped that poor scared animal. She looked back at me perplexed.

"The dog?"

"Yeah, when we saw you over at the old house you were looking for a dog," I explained.

Recognition flashed. "Oh, no, I didn't. Hopefully, he's gone home."

I hoped so too.

Georgie's mum walked over to us. Dawn was four foot eight and skinny as a rake. Her gray hair was pulled into a bun, and she looked at us through her oversized glasses.

"Are you having a good night?" she asked.

Georgie and I shook our heads.

"Have you seen Wes at all?" asked Georgie.

"Wes? No, sorry. Should I have?"

"He went to call the police." We quickly brought Dawn up to speed with what had happened throughout our evening.

"Goodness, that's quite a story," she said, frowning at us. "I'm sure Faith is just making it up though. She always seemed like a drama queen."

I liked Dawn's thinking.

"Georgie, have you seen your father?" she asked, changing gears, only half-interested in what we were telling her.

"No, but he was going to unlock a door in the old house for us. I'm not sure what he was doing after that."

Dawn gave a disgusted sigh. "Bloody men. Never around when you need them."

"I'll help you," said Matt.

"Thank you, Matthew," said Dawn, visibly relaxing. "That would be amazing." She glared at the rest of us.

I shivered as Rachel's voice drifted toward us.

"Dawn," she said, stopping in front of us. "Is dinner ready to go?"

"Yes. Announce it whenever you're ready."

Rachel looked at me, her brows furrowed. "What the hell happened to your hair?" she asked, crinkling her nose. "God, you look terrible."

I reached up and touched my head, suddenly feeling self-conscious. I'd done my very best earlier to remove the (hopefully) fake blood from my hair, but without shampoo and a hair dryer, I wasn't about to get amazing results. I thought I'd done okay but obviously not.

"Are you okay?" Dawn asked Rachel.

"Why wouldn't I be okay?" she responded, shaking her head at me and turning her attention back to Dawn.

"You just look upset."

Rachel clicked her tongue. "Don't be ridiculous. Why would I be upset?"

"I have no idea. Your eyes just look bloodshot, that's all."

"Probably because I'm bloody stressed!" shouted Rachel, looking around us as her mood changed dramatically. The word bipolar came to mind. "Georgie, go and make the PA announcement for dinner!" she demanded, her gaze stopping on Georgie.

"Why me?"

"Because I'm needed somewhere else, and I have no one to help me." She turned to point at me. "And it's all your fault!" she snapped.

"My fault?" I asked, shocked at her tone.

"Yes, you made up that ridiculous story about Faith, and Wes went to call the police. I haven't seen him since then. If it hadn't been for you, he'd be here helping me!"

"But did he get on to the police?"

"I guess so. But I told you, I haven't seen him."

"But the police aren't here yet?"

"Do they look like they're here?"

"Well, where's Wes?"

"I don't know."

"So he's not here?"

"Of course not! *Do you think I'd say he wasn't here if he was?*"

I actually thought Rachel was a little bit insane, but it didn't feel like now was the right time to vocalize that.

"Sorry," I sang, not really meaning it.

Rachel shook her head and gave me a disgusted look. Turning her attention to Georgie, she said, "Well? Are you going?"

"Oh! Sure." Georgie hurried off toward the nearest phone, ready to bring the PA to life and announce that dinner was served.

Rachel glared back at me, and I thought that Dawn was right. Her eyes did look bloodshot, and if I wasn't mistaken, that was the start of a bruise on her cheek. Plus, she'd changed her shirt. This one was black. She was wearing red earlier. I wondered about it as the PA dinged and dinner was announced.

Within minutes, the studio filled with the sounds of chatter as the groups packed the room.

I thought of Wes. The police force in Westport wasn't that large, so maybe he'd had to wait for someone to be free to come up and chat with us. After all, we didn't even know exactly what was going on here. The police couldn't leave a real crime in order to look for a woman who may or may not be missing. At least, that's what I hoped had happened.

I looked up as a commotion started on the opposite side of the room. Dawn wore a good portion of tonight's dessert as Matt stood in front of her, holding the empty bowl. I could see his face glowing from here.

"Matthew!" I heard her scream.

"I'm...I'm so, so sorry," he said, as Sam let out a snort of laughter.

Poor Matt. He had good intentions at heart.

Dawn didn't seem to know what to do. She looked at Matt, baffled. "How do you manage it?" she asked him.

He stood scratching his head, also unsure of what to do.

Sam leaned in to me. "Watching Matt is the highlight of my life. You could make a sitcom out of his clumsiness alone."

When he'd managed to placate Dawn and attempted to clean the mess he'd made, the caterers gave him a reprieve and sent him away. He walked toward us, wiping the remains of the tiramisu from his shirt, licking his fingers.

"I'm going for another look around to see if I can find Wes," said Matt, defeat in his eyes. "I'd like to know what he found out from the police and when they're coming. I'm also curious as to what he was doing in Bernie's office earlier this evening."

"He was probably checking up to see what we were doing in there," I replied.

"Maybe, but he seemed surprised to see us. It felt off to me," explained Matt. "After you've had something to eat, I think we should keep looking for Faith, but we need a plan. We won't achieve anything the way we've been going."

I nodded in agreement.

"Can I come with you?" Georgie asked Matt. "I'd really like to get out of here for a while."

"The storm's still hanging around."

"I know, but storms don't really bother me."

Matt flashed a smile. "Sure. I'd love the company." Matt was clumsier than most. Maybe he wasn't the best person to be wandering around in a storm. Thank God Georgie was going with him.

"You'll be okay here, won't you?" she asked, turning her attention to me. "Sam'll take care of you."

Sam's smile was wicked.

"Why can't I go and look for Wes?" I asked, thinking alone time with Sam might not be a good idea.

"In case we miss him and he turns up with the police whilst we're gone."

"I'll take extra special care of you. I won't take my eyes off you," said Sam, pulling me in for a hug.

That was what I was afraid of.

With that, they left me with Sam and a very sad-looking Jake. "Hey, Jake," I yelled, pulling away from Sam. "Why don't you go with Georgie and Matt? It'll give you something to do, and it'll be better than sitting here."

He looked back at me, his face strained. "No. I'll stay. I'm waiting for Stuart. Plus, Faith might turn up, and I want to be here if she does."

"Fair enough. Can I get you something to eat?"

He shook his head and looked back at his feet. I sighed. At least I'd tried.

"You can get me something to eat." Sam grinned.

I narrowed my eyes and glared at him. He laughed, a deep masculine sound that caused goose bumps to break out all over me. I sighed again, disgusted with myself for having such inappropriate thoughts when Jake was in so much despair. Then again, it was his wife causing all this drama, so why shouldn't I enjoy the night a little?

Sam linked his arm through mine and dragged me toward the food. "You haven't eaten anything tonight," he said. "You must be starving."

My stomach gave a very well-timed growl as the smell of the cooked pork drifted toward me.

The knot of anxiety in my stomach meant that even though I thought I was hungry, I didn't really feel like eating, but I filled my plate with roast meat and veg anyway, hoping the smell of it might trigger my appetite.

I looked around at the groups of people. Everyone else in the room seemed to be enjoying themselves. At least, they were laughing. Even though, on closer inspection, I could see the tension within the groups.

Brent's girlfriend, Deanne, seemed completely pissed off as she death-stared his old fling, Jane. Marty, the voice-over guy, was completely drunk, leering at Deanne as Brent ignored him completely. Brent, who had joined the party, was too wrapped up in Sheryl, his other old fling from sales, to notice.

Wes's wife, Kelly, had no food on her plate, but she was holding a very large glass of Coke. Judging by the way she was swaying, I thought there was more in that glass than Coke alone.

Continuing my scan of the room, I quickly realized there was someone in every group who seemed unhappy. I glanced at Rachel to see how she was enjoying what she'd created. She stood with her back to the wall, eyeing everyone in the room. Her gaze stopped on Katie. I noticed an unspoken communication pass between them and wondered about it. Earlier Katie had told me she didn't get along with Rachel.

Sam grabbed my elbow and moved me away from the table. "Hey, you're hogging the food," he said, humor in his voice.

I looked over my shoulder and realized that whilst I'd surveyed the room, I'd been standing in front of the roast veggies, making everyone reach around me to get what they wanted.

Oops. "Sorry," I said, smiling back at him.

"No need to apologize to me. I filled my plate." He wasn't kidding. His plate was almost overflowing.

"How can you eat that much?" I asked as we made our way to a table set up in the far corner of the room.

"I'm a growing man. I need my food."

Sam used his free hand to pull out the chair for me. I blushed, uncomfortable with the gesture. I'd never had anyone hold out a chair for me before. Thankfully, the lighting on this side of the room was dull, so hopefully Sam couldn't see my red cheeks. If he did, he didn't say anything. I sat my plate on the table and put my knife and fork in the correct position, fiddling uncomfortably.

"It doesn't feel right to be eating," I said.

Sam put his plate on the table and sat opposite me, his expression full of compassion. "I know, but I've covered a lot of stories around the local state emergency service, and one thing I know for sure is that the rescuers always need to look after themselves. What good are they to the person who's lost if they pass out from lack of food or get dehydrated?"

"I don't think this is the same thing. We're hardly going to die from dehydration."

"Speak for yourself," replied Sam, smiling. "Anyway, I think what Jake said earlier about Faith faking this is right. I've been here when he's been distraught because she disappears. I've seen what she does to him."

"Then why does he stay with her?"

"I guess he really loves her."

I sat quietly and watched Sam eat, his words about Jake and Faith playing slowly through my mind. He knew them better than I did, so if he wasn't worried, why should I be? The rational side of my brain knew what he said was sensible. So why wouldn't my anxiety listen?

"So," I finally said to Sam, doing my best to ignore the anxiety. "How did someone like you end up working here for all these years?"

"Someone like me?"

"Yeah. You look like you should be on a beach somewhere, riding a wave, not stuck with your nose behind a camera."

"It's a job that pays the bills. I surf in my spare time. What about you? What's the history between you and Rachel?"

"Why do you think there's a history between us?"

"Because cute as you looked in it, surely that team leader headband would only be given to someone she wanted revenge on."

I smiled at his comments about how cute I looked.

"When I first started working here, which was a few months before you started, Rachel was my manager. She was always shouting at me for no reason."

Sam nodded as he took a bite of food. My thoughts stuttered as he licked his lips.

"Anyway," I continued, shaking myself, my anxiety completely forgotten, "she scared me a little, so I tended to keep my mouth shut, but one day, she went too far. I decided I should stand up for myself. Rachel flipped right the hell out and left."

Sam raised his eyebrows. "What did you do?"

"Burst into tears. And then I ran into Bernie's office. I figured I had to fess up and tell him what I'd done and maybe he could convince her to come back. Instead, he flipped the hell out and told her that she needed to get back to work immediately. Or else!"

"So he liked you more than Rachel, hey?"

I shrugged. "More like he didn't like being dictated to." I took

87

a bite of potato and looked at Sam. "I never did ask you what you did before you worked here?" I said in between mouthfuls.

"That's because you would never talk to me then."

I blushed again at his comment. "I would so. I remember many conversations we had."

"Really?" Sam looked skeptical. "Name one of them."

My blush kicked up a notch as I racked my brain. "Umm... I remember you always asking me what I was doing that night."

It was Sam's turn to blush. "Yeah... Well, I was nosy." He smiled.

Sam looked closer at me, and the intensity increased in my stomach as the butterflies burst from their cocoons. I shifted uncomfortably on my chair, breaking eye contact. Which was a good thing. Sam's blue eyes had the ability to suck me right in, and if he weren't careful, I would leap over the table and kiss that full bottom lip of his.

"So," I said, my voice croaky, "what *did* you do before you started work here?"

Sam grinned that boyish grin and said, "I bummed around a bit and did the surfing thing. I wasn't good enough to make pro, but I always seemed to struggle with a proper job. My mum heard about this job and told me about it. She pulled in a few favors to get me here. Luckily, it turns out I quite like it!"

I smiled at his enthusiasm. I hadn't enjoyed a job that much since I'd been made redundant from Traffic five years ago.

"What do you love most about it?" I asked.

"Being outside most of the time. News cameramen cover all sorts of things from big news items like the recent murders to little things like that guy who married his dog last week."

It was my turn to raise my eyebrows.

"What? You missed that exciting bit of news?" Sam asked me.

"Was he clinically insane?"

"Apparently not," said Sam, laughing. "It was purely a platonic relationship."

Hey, I loved animals, but I couldn't imagine marrying a dog.

"I guess there are worse things," continued Sam, forking a piece of meat. "My sister has a dog, and he's great. Sure, he's caused her a few troubles, but I bet it's a lot less than a wife would cause this guy. Look at poor Jake, for instance. A dog would never cause you the kind of pain Faith's causing him."

Sam and I sat in silence for a few minutes as we dug into the food on our plates, both of us contemplating Faith's fate.

My gaze moved to Sam as he took a forkful of meat and put it in his mouth.

The saliva in my mouth dried up as I watched his lips move around the fork, holding it between his teeth. As he slid the fork back out, I groaned, wishing I was that fork. As I licked my lips, attempting to put some moisture back onto them, I moved to look at his eyes. A wicked glint shone back at me as Sam ran his tongue over his own lips suggestively, catching me watching him.

Shit. I really needed to get a grip. I mean, it's not like I hadn't had sex in a while. In fact, it was only…hmm. When was it? Oh, for goodness sake, it wasn't that long ago, was it?

Actually, it was. I remembered the one-night stand Georgie had set me up with. He was a guy from her work, and I'd been pretty keen for a date with him. You'd think at the age of twenty-seven—yes, it was a year ago—I would have been a bit wiser and made him wait at least until the third date, wouldn't you? But no, I think I was desperate even then.

Screams filled the silence between us and broke me out of my dream state. Now, don't get alarmed, these weren't blood-curdling screams that chilled you to the bone. They were more annoyed, *get the hell away from me* kind of screams.

Sam dropped his fork to his plate and stood, trying to see through the crowd as a dog ran between people's legs with what looked like a pork bone between his teeth. I guessed the dog Katie had seen earlier was real. Brent ran after the dog, stopping it and grabbing at the meaty bone in its jaw. A tussle followed, which Brent won. However, as the dog lost its grip on the bone, the force propelled Brent backward into the table, holding tonight's smorgasbord. The table broke, and Brent and the remaining food crashed to the floor. The contents of the gravy bowl, however, went skyward.

The occupants in the room stopped what they were doing to watch the gravy reach a pinnacle before gravity took hold and brought it back down to Earth in a hurry.

Unfortunately for Brent, it seemed he was between the gravy and Earth, so he was now the wearer of all the leftover meat and vegetables, as well as a liter of gravy. He did still have the bone clenched in his hand, though. Until the dog turned to see what was happening and took the opportunity fate had given him. He ran back toward the table, up Brent's prone body, and grabbed the bone out of his hand. Then he leaped from his position on Brent's chest and hightailed it out of the room.

I saw Deanne's face as it passed her, and I think if she could have, she would have given the dog an award. I guess she'd found out about Brent's relationship with the rest of his group.

As the dog ran past us toward the door and back into the hall, Sam turned to me and said, "I guess dogs are a bit like women, then. They'll knock you over to take your food every chance they get."

"Geez, what kind of women have you been with? I've *never* knocked a guy over to take his food."

"Maybe you haven't been with the right guy?"

"Maybe you should date a different kind of woman."

"Hmm, I'm thinking about it," he said, giving me a very suggestive smile.

I shifted uncomfortably under his stare. "Oh well, at least he won't be hungry," I mumbled, attempting to bring the conversation back to the dog.

Sam laughed and turned his attention back to his plate.

CHAPTER 9

J sat back in my chair, satisfied I had eaten all I possibly could, which I'd admit, wasn't much. I looked at Sam's plate still half-full and his enthusiasm not waning.

The studio had started to empty out as people finished their meals and excitedly wanted to get on with their sleuthing. I had listened in on conversations around me, and it seemed they were all wrong about Arthur fake-killing Rachel. He apparently had an alibi.

Word on the street now had it that Tiffany, the new station receptionist, was the favorite suspect. She fake-hated Rachel and wanted her dead after Rachel announced to the world that Tiffany was a thief. I wasn't sure what she'd stolen, but that was the rumor.

I was just contemplating this as Georgie and Matt walked over to us, pulled over two spare seats, and sat down.

"You didn't take long," said Sam, in between mouthfuls.

"No. We had a good look around but couldn't find him."

"What about Bernie's office? Did you find out what he was doing in there?"

Matt shook his head. "Not really, but I checked Bernie's

computer again, and all the history has been wiped. You didn't do that, did you, Sam?"

"Nope, I was going to delete the history of what we were looking at tonight, but I didn't have time."

"Hmm, I wonder if Wes did it?"

"Why would Wes do it?" I asked.

"Maybe he suspected we'd been looking at it and wanted to delete it before anybody else could," suggested Georgie.

"How many people know his password?"

"I wouldn't think too many. I mean, that's the point of passwords, isn't it?"

"Then why would Wes bother?"

"Maybe he was looking at something himself," said Sam.

"Like checking up on Bernie? Or just surfing the web?" I chipped in.

"Checking up on Bernie."

Matt pulled out the paper I'd found next to Bernie's shredder from his pocket and unfolded it. His brows knit together as he concentrated on what was in front of him. "Well, what should we do now?"

Matt shook his head, as if clearing his thoughts. "I think we should check every room and cupboard for Faith systematically. If she's hiding, we'll find her. We'll look out for Wes along the way to see what's happening with the police. If we follow a plan, surely we'll find one of them."

I felt slightly unsettled. I was hoping the police would have been here by now and would have found Faith hiding.

"Where's Jake?" asked Georgie.

"Don't know. He *was* sitting over there. Marty had hold of him, and they seemed to be in a deep conversation about something."

"What happened to the food table?"

Georgie laughed as I recounted the story.

"Shame I didn't have the camera on him," said Sam, laughing with her.

A thought hit me. "Sam, you've had that thing on most of the evening, haven't you?" I asked.

He nodded.

"I wonder if you got any footage that might help us."

"Hmmm...not a bad thought." He picked up the camera and pressed a few buttons. "Come on," he said, standing up. "Let's take this to the production booth and put it on the big screen. We might see something insightful."

———

THE PRODUCTION BOOTH was upstairs above the studio. It was reasonably small, held an awful lot of equipment I had no idea how to use, and was dark even when in full use.

Sam moved ahead of us and plugged the camera into a lead. Within seconds, the monitor in front of him flashed to life, and we were faced with an image of the studio from earlier this evening.

Georgie and Matt pulled chairs up to the desk. I stood behind them, and Sam came to join me. Matt seemed to know his way around a camera, so Sam stood back and let him drive the show.

It was comforting to have Sam close as my intuition buzzed. I had no idea what it was trying to tell me, though. In fact, the only thing I knew for certain at that moment was that I really wouldn't become president of the *Blondes Aren't Dumb* club.

I twisted my hair around my fingers, thinking how little I knew, when my face filled the screen. I was standing with Georgie, and we were talking to Wes as we had only just arrived in the studio. The crowd milled around us as the chatter poured from the speakers hidden in the production booth walls. The sound moved in to us as Marty walked over and gave Georgie a hug capable of breaking bones.

"Georgie!" he boomed. "How are you?"

"Good, thanks, Marty," she said, grimacing from his hug.

He let go of her and turned to me, his smile freezing in place. It was surreal watching myself on screen. I wanted to look away but was compelled to watch in case I saw myself doing something embarrassing.

"Hi, Marty," my screen-self said, smiling and giving him a little wave. I noticed how crooked my two front teeth looked and thought about booking an appointment with my dentist to enquire about braces. Oh, hang on, that's right. She was half-eaten by sharks. My stomach churned as I watched myself smile at Marty.

"Oh...umm. Hi." He held out his hand for me to shake. You could see the confusion cross his face. He had no idea who I was.

"Alex... I worked with Georgie in Traffic," I explained.

"Oh, yes, of course. Now I remember."

Liar. He still didn't have a clue. I watched as Wes leaned forward and whispered in his ear. Wherever Sam had been standing with the camera, the microphone picked up every word he said.

"Christmas party, 2009. Remember, we had to call the ambulance?" Marty's face lit up with recognition.

"Oh, Alex! Now I remember. Sorry, you look quite different now." He rocked back on his heels and smiled.

My screen-self blushed. Sitting in the production booth, I scowled. Okay, I had one night where I'd had a few too many drinks and *may* have fallen off the stage dancing "The Time Warp." Who hadn't done that?

True, an ambulance had to be called as I thought I'd broken my ankle, and of course, it had all been caught on camera. That was the absolutely worst thing about working at a television station. Everywhere you turned, there was a bloody camera. Actually, scratch that. Tonight that might be a good thing. I hoped.

The four of us sat in front of the monitor, searching every bit of footage Sam had captured in the studio, when Georgie turned in her chair.

"God, for someone who doesn't like the camera, you sure get in front of it a lot," she said to me.

I blushed. "I do not!"

But I had to admit, she was right. There seemed to be an awful lot of footage of me in this show.

I turned to look at Sam, questioningly, but his attention was on the screen.

"Has anyone else noticed Katie is in every shot I have of Alex?"

She was?

"Yeah," mumbled Matt, his pen in between his lips. He flipped back a page in his notebook. "I had noticed that."

"Why?" I asked.

Sam and Matt shrugged.

"There are a lot of people in that room," said Georgie. "It's probably just a coincidence."

"I don't believe in coincidence," said Matt.

"There's Faith," said Sam, his words snapping everyone's attention back to the screen.

Matt paused the footage on Rachel talking to Faith. He pressed play and zoomed the image in closer on the two of them.

Rachel had her back to the camera, so we couldn't make out what was being said, but Faith appeared annoyed with her. No surprises there. Most people seemed annoyed at Rachel tonight.

There was something about the picture that seemed wrong to me, but I couldn't put my finger on *what*. My intuition screamed. Sometimes I wished intuition would just write it on a wall or something. You would think if the Universe were to give a gift like intuition to someone, it would give it to someone who understood exactly what the hell it was on about, wouldn't you? I sighed, thinking I must be a great disappointment to the Universe.

On screen, Rachel flicked her hair over her shoulder and spun on her heel. She faced the camera, and the four of us saw the smirk that sat happily on her face.

"What was that about?" I asked, hoping someone else had picked up on what I'd missed.

"Probably some drama she was cooking up."

"They seemed pretty chummy," commented Georgie. "I didn't know they knew each other that well."

"What does it matter anyway?" asked Sam. "Unless you think Rachel has something to do with her disappearance?"

Georgie gave no comment.

We watched the footage for another half hour, Matt pausing at several places so we could get a closer look, but at the end of it, we were really none the wiser.

Matt was just turning off the camera when Brent walked into the room, dragging Sheryl behind him.

"Oh, what are you all doing in here?" he asked, looking around our group. "Alex!" he said, turning to me, surprised.

"Yes?"

"How did you get here so fast?"

"Umm, I came in here about a half hour ago with these guys."

"Really?" asked Sheryl. If she was embarrassed at being caught holding Brent's hand, she wasn't showing it. "I could have sworn it was you going into the traffic department before."

"Why would I go in there?"

Sheryl shrugged. "How would I know?"

"So, it wasn't you?" asked Brent. "But it looked like you. Are you sure it wasn't you?"

Brent was actually quite intelligent. Right now, you wouldn't have known it.

"Nope. Been here the whole time."

"Huh," Brent and Sheryl said in unison.

"But seriously, what *are* you guys doing in here?" finished

Brent. My question was what were *they* doing in here? I shook myself. I knew exactly what they were doing.

"We've been checking video footage of this evening to see if we can find any clues as to what happened to Faith."

"Oh, haven't you heard? Faith's in the studio. Apparently someone locked her in the old dub room. It's Jake they can't find."

SHOCK AND RELIEF swept the room.

"Why didn't someone tell us?" asked Georgie.

I didn't care why no one had told us, I just wanted to see for myself that Faith was okay. I pushed past Sam and hurriedly moved to the door that opened to the spiral staircase leading directly to the studio.

Rushing through it, I shivered as a dark shadow moved from the bottom stair tread and disappeared into the darkness behind the set.

"Who was that?" asked Georgie.

"I don't know."

I ran down the stairs as quickly as I could, Georgie hot on my heels, hoping to see whoever it was, but by the time I got to the bottom, whoever it was had disappeared. I looked around, wondering where they could have disappeared to. The boys bounded down behind me.

I blinked as my eyes adjusted to the dim light. Things were much messier behind the scenes with sets, props, and mountains of cardboard boxes cluttering the area. Remembering that they still made commercials here, I noticed the billboard for a local mattress company. I'd noticed none of this earlier this evening when I was running for help after finding Faith. Matt rounded the set, Sam right behind him. I was torn between wanting to search the area for whomever I'd seen and wanting to question Faith. Wanting to question Faith won out.

I followed the boys and found Faith sitting on a chair in the middle of the room, a plate of food balanced on her lap, whilst she nibbled on a bread roll, a very big bandage stuck to her temple. Dawn must have had some leftovers in the kitchen as I clearly remembered Brent wearing tonight's dinner.

I marched over to her and stopped, my hands on my hips.

"What the hell are you playing at?" I asked.

Faith looked back at me, her eyes large and innocent. "I don't know what you mean."

"The whole toilet death scene!" I could feel my blood pressure rising as anger set in. Unfortunately for me, when I'm angry, I usually cry. Tears welled behind my lashes as all the emotions I'd been through tonight came to the surface. Sam put his hand on my lower back. Another emotion started in my belly, but that emotion would have to wait because, right now, it was not appropriate.

Dawn glared at me like only a mother can. "Alex! Leave the poor girl alone. She's been through a lot."

"She's been through a lot? What about us? What about Jake?"

"You have no right to yell at me, Alex," said Faith, dropping the bread roll onto her plate, anger flicking in her eyes. I took a quick look at the roll and noticed the tiny little nibbles she'd taken. "I should be yelling at you. Why did you hit me?"

I sucked in a lungful of air and tried to slow my breathing. "I'm sorry, what?" I asked, my lips trembling as my anger still simmered. "What the hell are you talking about?" I asked, the quietness in my tone forced.

"I have no idea why you did it, but you did. I know it was you. You were wearing that stupid headband. I was minding my own business in the toilet when I stepped out of the cubicle, and there you were. You had your back to me, and when you turned, you hit me. That was the last thing I remembered until I woke up in the dub room." With those words, the tears spilled over her lashes. Within seconds, she was sobbing.

Dawn looked at me accusingly. "Alex! *Why* would you hit her?"

"What?" I asked, shaking my head, hoping the pieces would fit together that way. "I didn't hit you!"

I felt all eyes turn to me as Faith sat sobbing innocently.

"I found you in the toilet. And yes, someone had hit you, but it wasn't me. I wouldn't do that. *Why* would I do that?"

"Because you're jealous of me," whispered Faith, imitating a timid mouse.

"I'm not jealous of you. Why would I be jealous?"

"Because you still love Jake."

"I...I do not love Jake!" I stammered, shocked by her accusation. Thankfully, Sam still had his hand on my lower back, his warmth seeping in and comforting me. "Honestly. I don't." I looked around the faces that had gathered around us.

"Y...you...you're making it all up," Faith said, between sobs. "You wanted me out of the picture so you could win him back. But he doesn't love you anymore. He loves me!"

I was about to turn on her, the full wrath of my anger (yes, I know, I'm not really that scary) when the studio door burst open, and Rachel stormed into the room.

"Georgie!" she yelled.

Georgie jumped.

"Call everybody to the studio. Now! I have an important announcement to make."

She was obviously in a don't-mess-with-me mood, so Georgie jumped up and almost ran to the PA. Rachel's anger was obviously much scarier than mine.

I wanted to say more to Faith, but Sam grabbed my arm and pulled me backward. I stumbled on my feet and fell into him. Thankfully, his big strong arms saved me from the embarrassment of falling on my arse.

I did feel the hitch in my stomach as I was pressed into his hard abdomen, but I tried my very best to ignore it. I was angry at Faith, and nothing would stop me.

Okay, that was a total lie. The feeling of Sam's arm around my waist *may* have momentarily made me forget all about Faith, but you could understand the situation, right?

Sam held tight until he sat me on the chair as far away from Faith as he could find. He obviously had no real understanding of my anger. I was honestly not a threat to anyone.

He sat down opposite me as Georgie pressed the appropriate buttons for the PA to come to life. After she called everyone back to the studio, we waited. She moved back to me as Matt pulled up a chair, and I stared at Faith, questions zipping through my mind.

Sam raised his eyebrows at me, obviously thinking the same thing. Within minutes, people started to fill the room. I tapped my fingers on the table impatiently. I wanted Rachel to hurry up with the announcement so I could get back to questioning Faith.

And where the hell was Jake? I looked at the clock on the wall and noted it was now nearly ten o'clock. No wonder I was tired. It was nearly my bedtime.

The lost dog wandered across the studio floor, dripping water as it went. It came and sat at my feet. I didn't know why it picked me. I wasn't the biggest animal lover in the room. It looked up at me with big eyes, hair soaking wet, and a shoe in clenched in its jaw. I put my hand to its head to give it a pat, and it shivered. Instantly, my anger dissolved as my heart melted. It dropped the wet shoe at my feet.

Rachel walked over to me.

"Oh my god! Get that thing out of here. It's already caused enough problems for one night!"

"He's not causing any trouble now," I said, rubbing his head, as the smell of wet dog wafted up to my nostrils and stung my eyes.

He licked my hand. Now, I'd admit to liking dogs, but I couldn't admit to liking stray dog tongue touching my hand. I didn't want Rachel to see that, so I sat smiling at her, all the time telling the dog what a good boy he was.

"Get it out!" she yelled, pointing to the door.

I sighed and grabbed at its collar, checking its identity tag. The tag said his name was Baxter, but there was no phone number engraved on the back of it. Poor Baxter.

"Faith!" said Rachel, suddenly realizing Faith sat in the middle of the room. "You're alive. What a shock." Rachel turned to me and glared. "Alex, didn't your mother ever tell you not to tell lies?"

I felt my cheeks heat up as the crowd gathering in the room all looked at Faith sitting innocently, nibbling her bread roll, reminding everybody of a scared rabbit.

I wasn't sure what shocked them the most though—the fact that she was alive and well or the fact that she was eating bread. Looking at her figure, I figured carbs were never on her radar. They then all turned to me, glaring.

"I didn't lie," I said, ready to defend myself. I realized that years ago, I'd been scared of Rachel, but I guess with time we all change.

"Whatever," she said, rolling her eyes as she spoke.

I still had some questions for Faith, but the room was filling fast, and I was forced to bite my tongue and wait.

Faith picked up her plate and moved to a table opposite us. I looked around the room, wondering where Jake was and if he'd heard about Faith yet.

"Where's Jake?" I asked, spinning on my chair to Georgie.

Georgie shrugged. I added it to my mental list of questions for Faith.

As I turned back to face the front, Faith was staring at me. Suddenly, I didn't see the scared rabbit.

"Where's Jake?" I mouthed across the room.

"I have no idea," she mouthed back, tears brimming behind her lashes. I rolled my eyes.

"Is anybody else taken in by her act?" I mumbled to my group.

Sam looked at me, his thoughts unreadable. Georgie (always the sweetie) didn't respond, but it was Matt who surprised me.

"I don't believe it for a second," he said.

I'd come to realize that Matt was the quiet observer of the group. He didn't always say a lot, but he was definitely taking everything in. "She's missing her scarf, for starters."

"But we found that in the old house."

"Yes, but how did it get there? We know for a fact Alex didn't have it, so someone took it there."

"If someone took Faith to the dub room, she could have just dropped it on the way though," said Georgie quietly.

"It still doesn't explain how it got to the old house," I said, jumping on Matt's train of thought.

Matt was stopped from responding as Rachel stepped up to the microphone and addressed her audience.

"Can I have everyone's attention?" she called, very impolitely.

Chatter amongst the groups quieted. "Now, as I'm sure you're all aware, we've been having one of the worst storms to hit Westport in years. Of course, we were prepared. Our wonderful weatherman, Tony, did predict it. I also know that not all of you were planning on staying the night, but it looks like river is up, and the road is cut, so guess what? Now you are."

Our invitation had prepared us for a whole night of festivities, but I had assumed not everyone would have stayed for the duration. I looked at Arthur's group, thinking they'd all be upset not to be returning to their comfortable beds tonight, but surprisingly, they didn't seem bothered. In fact, they appeared to be cheered by the news. On closer inspection, they did seem to have consumed quite a bit of alcohol. Apparently, the older you got, the harder you could party. Who knew?

"Where are we all going to sleep?" asked Sally. She did appear to be upset by the news.

Rachel sighed. "Well, if you were prepared to stay for the entire night's events and had not made excuses to leave early, you would have been prepared, wouldn't you?"

Sally blushed.

"So, I guess you'll be sleeping on the floor."

"I wasn't making excuses," said Sally, quietly. "I really do need to get home. Mum needs me."

"Well, whoever is with her now will just have to stay. It's not like I can do anything about it, you know! It's not my damned fault the river is up. And anyway, had *you* listened to Tony, you would have known the river would cut us off. It always does!"

Okay, someone needed to get Rachel another drink. Her alcoholic good humor seemed to be wearing off.

Sally shrank back into her chair. Rachel straightened her shoulders and smoothed her shirt, attempting to regain control once more.

"Now," she continued—only Wes's wife, Kelly, interrupted her.

"That's Wes's shoe," she yelled. I looked at the shoe Baxter had dropped at my feet. "What's his shoe doing *here*?"

Matt picked up the brown leather loafer and inspected it. Not sure what he was looking for but whatever it was, he obviously couldn't find it. He passed it to Kelly.

"It's Wes's all right. Look—he wears orthotics. That's his orthotic." Her voice rose several octaves. "Why is he not wearing it?" She looked wildly around the room, her eyes stopping on me.

Like I knew the answer.

Everyone's eyes stopped on me. "I...I don't know. This isn't my dog."

"Well, whose dog is it?"

"I have no idea. I think he's just lost in the storm."

"Where did he find that shoe?"

"I'm sorry, but how would I know?"

"What happened to Wes?" asked Tiffany.

"You've probably got him stashed somewhere with everything else you've collected," sneered Rachel.

Tiffany blushed. I could only imagine Rachel was referring to the fake-thieving Tiffany was rumored to do.

"He went to call the police after we couldn't find Faith," explained Matt. "We haven't seen him since."

Kelly gave a small scream. "You don't think he went out in this storm, do you?"

The room fell silent.

"I bet he just took his shoes off so he didn't get them wet," said Sam, reassuringly.

I'm not sure how many people in the room believed that to be the truth, but I, for one, wasn't one of them.

"But Sam, why would he do that?" asked Matt.

Sam shrugged his shoulders in a *how the hell would I know? I was just trying to calm Kelly down* kind of way.

"Oh my God! You think something bad has happened to him!" screamed Kelly, standing.

"No, I don't. I think he's busy somewhere."

I took the shoe from Kelly and had a closer look at it. Rain water dripped to the floor. "It's pretty wet," I said, looking at Georgie.

Georgie looked at me. I knew what she was thinking. Wes hadn't been seen for quite some time now. "Maybe he got locked in a room like Faith did," she suggested.

"Yes!" cried Faith. "Alex hit me and then locked me in there!" Everyone's eyes turned to me. "And now the dog gives her the shoe belonging to Wes, who's missing," she continued. *Cow.* "She probably did the same thing to him!"

"Don't blame me! I had nothing to do with any of it. Sam has been with me the whole night. He can vouch for me."

Sam nodded.

"Well, maybe someone needs to go and look for Wes," suggested Brent.

Should I have told him we kind of had been? No, maybe not. That would just upset Kelly even more.

"That's a good idea. Why don't you go, Brent?" said his girl-friend, Deanne.

Brent shifted uncomfortably in his chair. "Okay. Sure. But

someone needs to come with me. It's not safe to go out in a storm like this alone."

I was glad everyone else seemed to be taking this a lot more seriously now.

"I'll come," volunteered Matt.

"Stuart's missing also," added Dawn, quietly. "Can someone look for him too, please?"

Stuart was missing?

"And Jake," piped in Faith. "Even though I would think Alex knows where he is."

I sighed. Faith was really pushing my buttons. "I do not know where Jake is. Nor do I want to know."

Actually that bit wasn't quite true. I figured Jake had probably found a corner and was worrying about Faith, but my intuition was prickling, and I didn't like it very much.

"Jake is your husband, Faith, so please, keep your insecurities to yourself." Did I sound grown-up or what?

Faith replied by glaring at me as she gently touched the bandage on her temple, her way of reminding everyone she thought I'd hit her.

"Don't worry, ladies. We'll find them all. This storm is pretty wild, so my guess is they are all sitting it out somewhere safe," added Brent. "In fact, why don't we wait until the storm has subsided a bit before we head out with the search party? We wouldn't want to get stuck in it too, would we?"

"Take the four-wheel drive," suggested Dawn.

"Why do we need to drive?"

"It's much sturdier against the wind. You can drive around the building with the spotlights on. It'll be much safer than walking."

"Yeah, that's a good idea," added Marty. "Wes probably went down to the storage shed to check on the drink supplies. I'm sure he's sitting down there waiting for someone to pick him up. I'll get you the keys, Brent. I'm pretty sure they keep them in reception."

With that, Marty almost ran from the room. Brent stuttered a bit, obviously trying to come up with another reason not to go out in the storm. By the time four people had patted him on the back and told him how good they thought he was, he really had no other option but to follow Marty for the keys.

Sam swiveled on his seat to face me. "I've been assuming all night that Wes called the police and we were waiting for them to arrive."

I nodded. I'd assumed that too.

"But what if he didn't? What if something happened to him before he got to call them?"

"What do you mean?" I asked, my skin prickling. I didn't like what Sam was insinuating.

"I don't know." He sighed and sat back in his chair.

"I've been wondering the same thing," said Matt, picking up Sam's conversation. "If Wes called them, why didn't they arrive?"

"Maybe they tried, but the river was up, so they couldn't get through. I know Rachel has just told us about the river crossing, but it probably went up a few hours ago," I added.

"Maybe I should give them a call and see if Wes ever contacted them," said Matt, standing and pulling his phone from his pocket.

Matt walked from the room, obviously looking for a better phone signal.

I watched Rachel talking to Faith and could almost feel the animosity between them. My guess was Faith thought Jake and Rachel had some sort of relationship, and she didn't like it much. It was only as Rachel turned and smirked at me that I felt my skin prickle. I didn't know what she told Faith, but I did not need the two of them causing me any more trouble tonight than I'd already had.

It felt like an eternity, but eventually Matt returned, his expression confused.

"Well?" asked Sam.

Matt sat heavily on the nearest chair and shook his head. Water droplets flew through the air, landing on my arm.

"Well, it's really strange."

"What is? Did Wes call them?"

"I still don't know. I had some trouble with my cell phone signal, so I wandered around, trying to get a better signal. I gave up and went to use the phone in the newsroom. The line was dead. And I don't mean just a monotonous tone, I mean there was nothing. No sound, no dial tone, nothing. So I had a look around reception and found someone had removed all the cables leading from the wall sockets into the main phone exchange. Without it, no phone in the station will either receive or make an outside call."

"They hadn't just fallen out of the socket?" I asked.

"No. They're gone completely. There are no longer any cables connecting the phone system to the outside phone lines."

Now that *was* strange.

"So then I decided to use the two-way radio in the newsroom. This time, the handset was missing. Same in the news vans. All handsets are missing. Unless I can get a cell signal—which is dodgy at the best of times in this building—I can't contact the outside world."

"But why?" I asked, completely confused as to who and why anyone would do that.

"Well, this building is made of cement. Even the internal walls. Add to that all the cabling and insulation running through the walls, it makes cell signals hard to get through. However, usually if you step outside you can get at least one bar of reception. But not tonight. Not with the storm around. It's just dropping out too much."

"No, I understand that bit," I said, half-smiling at Matt's explanation of cell signals and why I couldn't get a very good one tonight. "I don't understand why someone has removed the handsets and cables. And this is a television station. Surely we have a spare phone cable lying around!"

"We probably do. We'll just have to find it."

"I still don't get it. Why are the handsets for the radios missing?"

"Yeah," said Matt. "I've been thinking about those too. What if whoever hit Faith panicked and didn't want the police called? Like I said before, cell signal is dodgy around here at the best of times. In a storm like we've had tonight, it almost drops out altogether. I know my phone is nearly flat because it's been searching for a signal all night."

"Yeah," said Sam. "That would make sense. If I'd done it, I would want to remove any way Wes could call them."

"Do you think the attack on Faith was pre-planned?" I asked, a lump forming in my throat.

Sam and Matt looked at one another. "I don't know. Maybe. Or maybe whoever did it just panicked because they thought they'd killed her."

"But why did they look like Alex?" asked Sam, his brow creased.

"Oh my God, do you think they tried to frame me?" I felt the panic start in my chest, but I took a deep, calming breath and waited for Sam or Matt to tell me that was ridiculous.

"Only if it was pre-planned."

Okay, that caused the palpitations to kick up a notch. "Guys, you're not helping!" I cried.

"It's okay, Alex. You just stay with me all night, and I'll keep the camera on you. That way we have proof you were with us and couldn't do anything. If it happens, of course."

All right, that made me feel slightly better. "But who hates me enough to frame me for something like that?"

"Who hates Faith enough to want to kill her?"

Georgie, who'd been sitting quietly until that point, took a deep breath. "Well, it's funny how Jake is missing now."

"And Wes."

"And Stuart."

"Do you think any of them could have done it?"

"I don't know. I'm positive it wasn't Dad," said Georgie. "I don't know Wes well enough, and I never thought Jake would hit a woman, but he and Faith did argue before she went missing, and she was pretty upset about it. I heard her in the toilets earlier, and she was crying."

We all thought about what Georgie had just said. I thought back to the days when Jake and I were a couple. The Jake I knew would never have hit me, no matter how hard I pushed him. But that *was* years ago.

"Maybe Wes's disappearance is related to whatever he was doing in Bernie's office," I said, liking that idea far better.

Matt looked at me silently, his mind obviously going over the options. "Hmmm, maybe. Wes was definitely doing something in there he didn't want anyone to know about."

"Remember, we don't know that anything has happened to Wes," Georgie reminded us. "Or Jake, or Dad." I saw her swallow hard.

"I think we should look for a cable for the phone or the handsets that belong to the radios," said Sam. "No matter what, we need to call the police and at least find out if Wes called them. Even though they can't get through the river to us now, we still might know more than we do already."

"Shouldn't we be looking for Wes, Jake, and Stuart?" I added.

"Brent and Matt are on it. I trust Matt. If there are any clues out there, he'll find them. For now, I think we should concentrate our efforts on finding something that will help us contact the police."

"If we're not sure anything bad has happened to them, do we need the police?" I asked.

"Yeah, it'll be good to get their opinion on what's really going on around here tonight. After all, someone attacked Faith, and that *someone* was dressed like you."

I nodded in agreement. We definitely needed the police. And anyway, looking for the equipment gave us something constructive to do and was a far better option than sitting here with everyone thinking I hit Faith or me sitting here wondering who in this crowd could have wanted to frame me for doing something so horrible.

CHAPTER 10

*M*att left with Brent for a drive to once again check for any sign of Wes, Stuart, or Jake. Georgie had decided to stay with her mum, hoping to give her some comfort until Stuart reappeared, and Sam and I started our search of the station, looking for the handsets or some cabling or whatever we could find that would give us all some answers.

The rest of the groups had debated what they should do. Some argued that sitting around doing nothing wasn't helping anyone, and they should also start a search. Others argued that the three missing men were probably all sitting out the storm somewhere safe.

In the end, they agreed to continue on with solving the murder mystery. At least it gave them something to do, and they could keep their eyes open for Jake, Stuart, and Wes, wherever they believed the three men were sitting out the storm. It appeared that most of them believed that I'd hit Faith, and other than a shoe, what evidence was there to suggest anything suspicious had happened to the men?

I noticed Arthur whispering something to Sam. When I questioned Sam, he explained that a few people were worried about my temper and the notion that I'd hit poor Faith because I was jealous of her.

He told them he would keep an eye on me, which appeased them enough to not lock me in the dub room. Sam placated *me* by saying that those who'd suggested I'd do such a thing didn't know me at all. They'd worked here long before I'd started, and if they did know me, they would know I wasn't capable of harming anyone. Well, at least he knew me well enough.

My intuition still buzzed about the missing men, but I had no real reason to think anything awful had happened to them, so I took a few more calming breaths and followed Sam. All I had to do was stay within the view of his camera, and all would be okay.

Oh, and in case you're wondering, I did ask Georgie and Dawn to stay with Faith. If the earlier attack on her was pre-planned, there was a small possibility the attacker would try again. As much as Faith and I didn't really like each other, I would hate to see her hurt.

"Where should we start?" I asked, admiring the view of Sam's backside walking ahead of me.

"I think reception. We'll work our way down the offices and into the boardroom. If we don't find anyone or anything there, we can go back up the hallway and search the storage room and the area under the stairs." Sam had his camera on his shoulder, pointing ahead of him. I guess you'd be able to hear my voice in the footage, so that was enough proof I was with him.

"Hopefully, we'll find them before then."

We made a left turn into reception. For a television station, the reception area was pretty ordinary. The latest receptionist, Tiffany, had pretty cramped quarters. The front of her long timber desk faced a small foyer that held two black leather chairs and a glass coffee table. The six-month-old copies of *Vogue* and *Australian Photography* sitting on top of it proved this area didn't get too much new traffic through its doors.

I sat in her high-backed, black leather chair and spun around, looking at Sam as he placed the camera on the desk. I played my fingernails in the cracks in the leather as he opened the first of the timber-clad cupboards lining the wall behind the desk.

It revealed a lot about Tiffany. On the surface, her work area appeared pristine and organized, but her cupboards revealed the mess underneath. Good to know. I'd only met her for the first time tonight. She looked all of nineteen, gorgeous figure, flawless skin, and massive brown eyes that sparkled as her tinkling laughter floated through the air. It was a relief to know that underneath her perfect exterior lived a very normal person. It gave hope to the rest of us.

I stood and moved to the cupboard on the opposite end of the wall and opened it. I looked at mounds of envelopes and reams of paper, all stacked haphazardly. I was actually a very organized, neat person when it came to my work and living areas. Seeing this, I felt an itch start around the back of my neck, but I reminded myself why we were here and ignored the urge to tidy.

Sighing, I moved things aside, looking for a phone cable or the handsets. I didn't think Stuart, Wes, or Jake would fit in this cupboard, so at this point in time, they were off my radar.

"Why such a big sigh?" asked Sam, smiling at me.

"I just wish we could hurry up and find what we are looking for."

"But we've only just started."

"It'll be in the last place we look."

"Of course it will. If it wasn't, we would keep looking, and then it wouldn't be the last place, would it?" That actually made sense.

"I hate this. I just want to get to the finish line."

"Alex, life is about the journey. One must enjoy the journey, or what's the point?"

"Not for me, sorry. I'm more of a destination kind of girl."

Sam stopped what he was doing and smiled a wicked smile. "I bet I could make you enjoy the journey."

Oh boy. I bet he could.

Blood rushed to areas I am definitely not naming, so I quickly turned back to the cupboard. I heard Sam's chuckle, and the blood rush kicked up a notch.

I cleared my throat and forced my mind to move to other areas. After a minute of awkward silence, Sam moved toward me, stopping way too far into my personal space for me to feel comfortable.

"Sorry," he said. "I can be inappropriate at times. I didn't mean to make you uncomfortable."

I looked up into his sparkling blue eyes and saw a softness and compassion that actually took my breath away. Wow, this man was gorgeous. And I couldn't remember the last time a gorgeous man had been this close.

I gulped in an attempt to swallow the saliva threatening to drown me. "It...it's okay. I...I don't mind. I know you're only joking."

The world stopped for a beat whilst he looked deep into my eyes. I heard his breathing deepen and become more rapid. My heart beat erratically behind my ribs, causing my breath to shallow. When I couldn't handle it anymore, I looked away. I'd never had a man make me feel like that before, and it was pretty intense.

Thankfully, Sam moved back to his end of the cupboards as lightning flashed through the glass facade behind us. I racked my brain to think of something clever to say that would make me look worldly and smart.

"Can't believe this weather!" Okay. That wasn't clever, worldly, or smart, but it was out there now. What could I do?

"Yeah, it's full-on, but summer storms are often like this."

"I hope the dog is okay," I added, thinking of Baxter and how Rachel had taken him away.

"He'll be fine. If he turns up again, we'll take him to the pound tomorrow and see if he's microchipped."

"The pound?" My heart raced for a whole different reason.

"Yeah, they have a scanner there, so they can check if he's microchipped. If he is, they'll contact his owner."

"But, if he's not microchipped, won't they put him to sleep?"

"No, if he has no chip they will keep him for a couple of weeks to see if his owner calls looking for him."

"What happens after the two weeks?"

"Well…"

"Sam! You can't do that to him!"

"Well, what do you suggest?"

"Maybe we can take him there, but if he's not microchipped maybe they'll let us keep him."

"I thought you lived in an apartment?"

"I do."

"Can you have a dog that size in your apartment?"

No, I couldn't. Unless it had gills or feathers, my body corporate wouldn't allow it. I know this for a fact because my downstairs neighbor, Dean, had spoken to them when I dog sat for my mum. True, that could have had more to do with the fact that a Saint Bernard was a little large for my one-bedroom apartment, but I think they meant it when they said *absolutely no dogs!* I sighed.

"Don't worry, Alex. We'll sort it out. I'm sure its owner will come looking for him."

"I don't understand why people can't lock their dogs up properly in a storm. I mean, it's not like they don't know. The RSPCA advertise it all the bloody time." Thinking of poor Baxter made me agitated. Or that could have been the two large glasses of Coke I'd downed before leaving the studio. "Do you have a dog, Sam? Maybe you could have him if his owner doesn't come forward?"

"Let's see what tomorrow brings, okay?" said Sam, smiling at me.

"Didn't you say earlier your sister has a dog?"

"Yeah, he's a bit smaller than Baxter though."

"Maybe she can have another one?" I felt a need to protect Baxter. I didn't know why. I didn't think maternal instincts covered animals, but maybe I was wrong.

"Maybe."

"Does your sister work, or does she stay at home all day with kids or something?"

"She works for the post office."

"Really? What does she do there?"

"Delivers parcels." Sam had moved on to the next cupboard and was now pulling out boxes of pens, pencils, and erasers. I looked at the piles he placed on the desk behind him and wondered how a workplace could need that much stock of stationery and how Tiffany actually functioned in the chaos.

"I used to work for the post office delivering parcels," I commented, shaking my head.

"Really? She used to work for Gary. Do you know Gary?" he asked.

"Yes! I worked for Gary. What's your sister's name?"

"Chloe."

"Chloe?"

"Yep. That's her name."

"Is she really pretty, dimple, and at the moment, her hair is light blonde?"

"Yeah, that's her. Do you know her?"

"Yes," I replied, unable to form any other words.

Chloe was always trying to set me up with her brother, but I'd had a lot of bad experiences with being set up with brothers, so all I'd ever done was change the subject when she mentioned it. I looked at Sam and sighed. I really needed to start listening to people.

"That doesn't sound like a good sigh," said Sam, stopping what he was doing to look closer at me.

I really wished he wouldn't. It now seemed that every time he even so much as glanced my way, my stomach did somersaults.

"Oh, Chloe's...ummm...lovely. She still delivers my parcels, so I...ummm...I see her quite a bit," I said, shaking my head again.

I couldn't believe that Sam was her brother. I'd never connected the Sam I used to know with the surname he shared with Chloe.

"I...ummm...definitely put her in the...umm...friend category."

"Wait a minute. She didn't try to set you up with me, did she?"

Oh crap. "Ahh...maybe," I answered as I busied myself looking through a box of envelopes. Yes, I knew that half a dozen radio handsets wouldn't fit in a box of DL-sized envelopes, but it was the closest thing to me.

"And you said *no*."

I felt the heat start around my ears as blood flooded my face. *Why did I say no?* Sam was so incredibly hot! But I didn't know that then. Every friend I'd had, at one time or another, had tried to set me up with her brother. And some I had gone out with. I learned pretty quickly there was usually a reason they needed their sisters' help. I looked at Sam out of the corner of my eye and figured he wouldn't have trouble getting a date, so Chloe must have had another reason for setting us up. Damn. If only I'd listened to her. Better late than never, though, right?

I turned to face him, resisting the urge to fan myself to cool my burning cheeks and maybe ask if now was too late to agree to a date, when I noticed he seemed a bit red in the face too. "You said no, didn't you, Alex?"

"Ummm..." I felt the air around us change with Sam's mood. Lightning flashed as I saw the disappointment in his eyes.

"Well...yes, but..."

"Okay. Understood." Sam picked up a box of pens and threw it back into the cupboard.

"Sam, I didn't know..."

"It's okay," he said, cutting me off before I could say anymore. "Chloe has a really bad habit of setting me up with her friends. I keep telling her not to, but she doesn't listen. She means well enough, but really...why would I want to go out with one of her friends? I'm not desperate. I *can* get my own date."

Sam then scooped the remaining boxes up into his arms and almost threw them back into the cupboard.

"I don't doubt that," I said.

"What does that mean?"

"What?"

"You don't doubt I can get a date? Do you think I pick up women all the time?" he asked, his eyes challenging me. The jovial Sam who had stood so close to me before now seemed annoyed. "I'll have you know I'm not like that...well, not anymore."

"You don't have to explain anything to me," I added, quietly.

"No, you're right, I don't. And please ignore my sister. I would never go out on a date she set up." With that, he slammed the cupboard door shut, turned his back on me, and stomped off toward the nearest office.

I felt the lump form in my throat. Did this mean Sam wouldn't flirt with me anymore? I kind of liked that he flirted. And I kind of liked him. Yes, he was gorgeous, but there seemed to be more to him than that. He radiated goodness and kindness. And compassion. Oh, and humility. And if I was completely honest, I'd admit that he radiated an enormous amount of sex appeal. An amount that was causing all sorts of emotional reactions in me tonight.

I quickly picked up the envelopes and pushed them back on the shelf, shivering with the desire to clean. At least that's what I thought the desire was about. It definitely wasn't a desire to run after Sam and kiss him. No, it was definitely a desire to clean. I hoped.

I quickly closed the cupboard door, pushed the chair back

under the desk, and ran after Sam. His long legs managed to cover a lot more ground a lot quicker than mine could.

I found him in the nearest office. The nameplate on the door said it belonged to Vanessa Tompkins, Program Manager. I didn't know Vanessa, but I'd heard someone talking about her earlier this evening. And if I was right in my assumptions, she was the lady who was nine months pregnant. I wondered if her job would be available shortly.

Walking in, I found Sam with his head down, rummaging through the drawers of her desk. I stood at the door and watched him.

He didn't seem angry. I figured he was more upset. His shoulders hunched forward, his eyebrows pulled close together in a frown, and a sadness shone in his eyes.

"Are you okay?" I asked. "I didn't mean to upset you."

He stopped what he was doing and sighed. When he looked up at me, he smiled. Only it stopped at his lips. Sure, I'd only reconnected with this man—what, five hours ago now—but I knew that when he smiled, his eyes couldn't help but join in. And when they did, they sparkled. Right now, his eyes looked dull.

"It's all good, Alex. You haven't upset me. I'm just tired."

Fair enough. The clock now read ten forty-five pm.

"Yeah, me too."

"We need to hurry up and find these cables. How about you take the next office over? That way we can speed up the process?"

I'd enjoyed spending time with Sam. Now, it felt like all he wanted was distance. As he turned his back on me to open the cabinet behind him, I felt the disappointment sit heavily in my stomach.

Bloody Chloe. Why did she always have to be setting him up? I guess it was as humiliating for him as it was for me.

I DECIDED to start in the boardroom at the opposite end of the hallway and work my way back toward Sam. Eventually, we would meet in the middle and wouldn't overlap.

I shivered against the cool night. Thank goodness the lighting was bright, and for the first time since finding Faith, I didn't feel like I was being watched.

My mind flicked to Sam's sister, Chloe. Now I knew they were brother and sister, I could see the family resemblance. They both had twinkling blue eyes and an adorable dimple in their right cheek. Not that I thought it was adorable on Chloe. No, that wasn't really my thing, but it was definitely adorable on Sam.

I shook my head, hoping to clear thoughts of Sam's dimple, but it only served to give me a headache. Although the headache could have been because I was so damn tired.

I often thought I could have been closer friends with Chloe. We were alike in a lot of ways, and when I'd worked at the post office, she was the reason I'd stuck it out for as long as I had. Sure, that had only been a month. Apparently, people were picky about getting their own parcels and not someone else's. My boss, Gary, had suggested the job probably wasn't for me.

Fine by me. It was damned hard work. And with the weather in Westport, it was either extremely hot or raining. Neither of which were the best conditions to be running around delivering parcels.

I yawned and rolled my neck, reaching the boardroom door. Unlike the rest of the station, this door was painted high-gloss black, just like the other doors that ran the length of this hall. It was showy and meant to make visitors and important business executives believe the station was high-class and affluent. *Ha.* If only they walked a few meters past the newsroom, they would soon see that the walls changed to whitewashed cement, and the doors were basic and white. No excess money spent on the workers.

Placing my hand on the door, I pushed it open, taking a step to walk through it. Immediately, it slammed shut in my face, hitting my nose as it came back on me. I let out a small squeal, my heart rate instantly picking up. I took a step back, rubbing my nose and looked at the closed door, wondering who was on the inside, and hoping it was Jake, Wes, or Stuart.

As my heart rate settled, I looked at the door. I could hear murmured voices on the inside, so I gently knocked and called, "Hello."

A second later, the door opened slightly, and Rachel stuck her head out.

"What?" she snapped. "Oh, it's you," she said, disdain dripping from every syllable.

"Rachel!" I said, stunned.

I didn't know why I was stunned, but I thought we'd left her in the studio. I'd thought wrong.

"What do you want?" she asked.

"Ummm… I wanted to check the boardroom. We're looking for a phone cable we can use to get the main switchboard up and running. Or maybe a radio handset."

"Well, there're none of those in here."

"How about Wes, Jake, or Stuart?" I asked hopefully. If Wes were in there, Kelly would be pissed.

Rachel sighed and looked at me like I was an idiot. "No, they are not here," she snapped.

"What are you doing? Can I come in and look?"

"No, you cannot! Go and do something useful, like solving the murder mystery. That's what you are supposed to be doing. I didn't go to all this trouble to make tonight a success for you to just ignore it and go wandering about the station like you own the bloody place!"

"But…" I stuttered.

Rachel still had the ability to make me lose my train of thought. That was her tactic. Yell at people so that they retreat, and then she gets what she wants. Well, I was past that.

"Sorry, Rachel, but I'd really like to have a look around." Plus, I wanted to know whom she had in there.

"Go away, Alex," she yelled, closing the door in my face. I heard the lock tumble.

Sighing, I placed my ear to the door and listened. Once my heartbeat slowed enough so that the only sound of it was in my chest and not in my ears, I could hear Rachel.

Her voice was too low for me to work out what she was saying or whom she was with. I figured she wasn't on the phone, as I still had no cell service, so she wouldn't either. So what she was doing? I'm sure it had nothing to do with coordinating tonight's event.

She'd been acting strange all evening, but then, strange was pretty normal for Rachel. Should I be concerned about her? I had no reason to be. Maybe she'd removed the cables and handsets to stop people contacting the outside world. But then they all had cell phones, so what good would that have done?

I pulled my phone from my bag and checked my signal again. It flickered between one bar and none but mostly on none. If I tried to use it to make a call, I wouldn't even get it to connect.

I sighed and pushed it into the pocket of my jeans. Then I thought about the radiation so close to my body, pulled it out, and pushed it back into my bag.

Turning, I was about to move to the next office, making a mental note to talk to Sam about her, when I heard a cough coming from behind the boardroom door. And my guess was, it belonged to a man.

I quickly turned back and put my ear to the door—that secret part of me that loved office gossip excited. I strained to listen, but all I got was silence. *Damn.*

Curiosity got the better of me. I really wanted to see if the door would open, but did I dare? No. After hearing what Matt and Sam said she got up to with WTN employees in her spare time, I could only imagine what she was doing in there. That was definitely not something I wanted to see. I'd loved to have known who she was doing it with, though.

I smiled and turned to the next office off the hallway—Bernie's. Wes's earlier warning about not being in there rang in my ears, but this was necessary, right? I turned the handle and pushed on the door. Flicking on the light switch, I looked around the room. Everything seemed just the way it had been earlier this evening. Yet something screamed at me. Something wasn't right in this picture.

I entered the room and took a slow look around. The cabinets gleamed with their polished mahogany. The desk was still tidy, the chair pushed under it. The pictures on the wall were the same. So what was wrong? Probably nothing other than my tired brain causing my imagination to run wild.

I moved to Bernie's desk and opened the one and only drawer. It was very tidy, and it only took a second to realize it didn't hold a phone cable or radio handset. I checked the cupboards with the same result.

Spinning back, ready to give up and move to the next room, I took a moment to look at Bernie's desktop, thinking of how Matt had said the computer history had been wiped.

I moved to the computer and wiggled the mouse. The screen sprang to life, asking me for a password. Guilt swamped me as I remembered telling the boys off for doing this exact same thing. I snatched my fingers away from the keyboard and used them to rub my face. Tiredness made me do stupid things, things I would have never normally done.

I quickly straightened the keyboard and mouse, ready to make a quick exit, and then I noticed it. I saw what was wrong with this picture. The photo of Bernie's family, the one in the ugly crystal frame, was missing.

Where could it have gone? Who had taken it? I thought of Wes. He'd been in here. Maybe he'd taken it. Maybe Bernie had caught him, and they'd had a fight.

My imagination took off at a million miles an hour, thinking of all the scenarios that could have happened. In the end, I only gave myself a bigger headache, so I pushed the chair back in and added it to my list of things to talk to Sam about. Providing he was still comfortable enough talking to me.

I closed Bernie's door and made my way into the hallway. I'd found nothing really useful, but my fingers were crossed that Sam had found what we were looking for.

I looked into the next office off the hall, expecting to see him, but instead, I found it empty. The lightning still flashed, making the night feel creepier than normal, but the rain had eased to a light patter against the window behind me, so I figured the storm was on the move.

I turned, ready to move down the hall in search of Sam, then let out a small squeal as a large, hard body blocked my way. I guess I found him.

"Sorry, didn't mean to scare you," he said, taking a step backward.

"Oh, that's okay. What did you find?"

"Nothing."

"Crap. I was hoping you'd found them. Like, you know, cables, handsets, Wes, Jake...Stuart. Maybe then we could have some fun."

"Yeah, I guess we just keep looking."

We turned and moved back toward reception, the distance between Sam and me much larger than before. A door behind us slammed shut, and Rachel stormed her way down the hallway, almost knocking me over as she passed me. Obviously, her meeting hadn't had a happy ending. Sam looked after her.

"What was that about?" he asked.

I quickly filled him in on my earlier interaction with Rachel.

"Hmmm," he said when I finished telling him my story. "There's only one door out of the boardroom, so whoever was in there with her will still be there. Do you want to go and check it out?" he asked me, a wicked glint in his eye.

He loved office gossip as much as I did. "Is that a silly question or what?" I replied, smiling.

We retraced our steps and made our way back to the boardroom. I thought the door would be locked, but it wasn't. Sam opened it silently and stepped inside, flicking the lights on as he moved.

I followed him in, expecting to see Rachel's companion sitting in the dark. Only the room was empty. Well, that was strange.

Sam raised his eyebrows then moved around the room, checking in all the cupboards. I moved to check all the windows. Whoever had been in here with Rachel had left somehow. However, I found all windows closed, and Sam found all the cupboards empty. Well, empty of a person anyway.

"Are you sure she was talking to someone?" he asked.

"Yep."

"Maybe she was talking on the phone."

"I definitely heard a man cough."

I sat my bottom on the windowsill and wondered what Rachel had been up to.

"Sam, this windowsill is wet," I said as the moisture soaked into my jeans. "I guess whoever was in here jumped out of it."

Sam moved to me and felt around the sill. Nodding his head, he said, "Well, I guess we'll never know what was going on in here."

"We've got a pretty good idea."

"Yeah, but who was she with, though?"

I thought about that for a second. "It could be anyone. Rachel obviously isn't picky."

Sam chuckled. "Come on. There's nothing in here for us to see. Let's check the storerooms."

I followed Sam as he led the way back toward reception. Passing the floor-to-ceiling glass window, I noticed the lost dog

Baxter running up to the door. Even though the rain had slowed to a fine mist, he was soaked from head to toe and shivering. I moved to the door to let him in.

"Rachel's going to kill you if you let him back in," said Sam.

"Look at him. He's cold and scared. I can't leave him out there."

I opened the door, and in ran Baxter, rubbing his wet body against the leg of my jeans. It was my turn to shiver. Sam smiled.

"What's in his mouth?" he asked, crouching down to take a closer look. He tried to get whatever it was away from Baxter, but Baxter seemed a little attached. I heard Sam sigh as Baxter growled his warning. Sam gave up and stood back up.

I stroked Baxter's head, hoping to alleviate any anxiety that he would be feeling. He stopped growling at Sam and looked up at me, his eyes huge. My heart melted as he dropped his winnings at my feet.

"Awwww, that's so adorable," I said, kneeling down to his height. I picked up what he'd dropped and had a closer look at it. It was some sort of fabric, and it looked familiar.

"I think that's part of Wes's shirt," said Sam, his forehead creasing.

Suddenly, I didn't think it was so adorable. I squealed and dropped the fabric, making Baxter jump in fright. Then I felt bad as he cowered down in front of me.

"Oh no, it's okay, Baxter. I'm not angry at you," I said reassuringly as I patted his head. It didn't take long for him to look bright-eyed once again.

"I wonder where he got it?" asked Sam.

"Are you sure it's Wes's?"

"How many people tonight wore yellow hibiscus flowers on their clothing?"

Not many. Only one, in fact.

I looked down at Baxter, who was now looking up at me adoringly. His shivering had stopped, but he'd left a big puddle of water on the floor. At least, I hoped it was water. My eyes hadn't been on him the whole time he'd been standing there, but boy dogs didn't squat, did they? So it had to be water, right?

"Where did you get this, Bax?" I asked him. Sam laughed beside me. "What?" I asked.

"He can't exactly tell you, can he?"

Humph. "I guess not."

Baxter stood up and ran to the door. Part of me didn't want to let him back out into the dark night, but the other part of me wondered if he either wanted to empty his bladder or if he might find his way home now that the storm was passing.

Either way, he didn't belong to me, so I felt the only option I had was to let him out again. Baxter ran past my legs and outside, disappearing into the dark night. My heart squeezed, hoping he would be all right. No need to worry though, a second later he reappeared and stopped in front of me, barking. He then turned and ran away from me again.

Was this some sort of game he wanted to play?

"I think he wants you to follow him," said Sam, stepping close behind me for the first time in the last half hour. I felt the warmth of his body, even though he wasn't touching me.

"Really?"

Baxter reappeared. *Woof.*

"Come on," said Sam, moving past me. "Grab an umbrella from the stand over there. Tiffany always keeps them there for any important visitors."

"You get important visitors up here now?" I asked skeptically.

Sam flashed a smile. "Nah, mostly she uses them herself when she wants to go out to the lunch van on the rare occasion it shows up."

I smiled and grabbed the bright yellow umbrella from the pot near the door. Sam waited for me and then lifted his camera back onto his shoulder, using its light to show the way.

CHAPTER 11

*I*t was hard keeping up with Baxter. I figured he could see better in the dark than we could. Sam's light gave us a path to follow, but the path was only so wide, which meant I tripped over every little thing.

In hindsight, I should have grabbed two umbrellas. As I was the shorter of the two of us, it was quite a stretch for me to hold it high enough to clear Sam's head. Hence the many curse words he mumbled along the way.

I heard Baxter's barks as he ran into the darkness, the rain pattering on the umbrella, my feet wet as I failed to negotiate the puddles in my high-heeled pumps.

We made our way away from the building and the security of light toward the helipad out the back of the old house. The helipad sat on the edge of the mountain overlooking Westport. The drop off the edge wasn't severe at first, but from memory, you wouldn't be able to walk too far down the slope before it got dangerous. From there it was a very big fall, if the many large trees on the way didn't stop you.

My stomach flipped with anxiety. Why would Baxter bring us here? I hoped it was just a game he liked to play, but the fact that he'd been carrying a piece of fabric that was the exact match to Wes's shirt had me thinking the worst.

Thankfully, Sam stopped as we got closer to the edge. Baxter ran ahead down the first part of the slope into the long grass. The lightning still flashed in the distance, giving me the occasional glimpse of where Baxter had disappeared to.

"Stay here, and hold the camera, please," said Sam, turning off the light, lifting the camera from his shoulder, and handing it to me.

As the house blocked the main building and any light it may have cast, and the clouds blocked the moon, darkness surrounded us. I heard Sam's breathing as he stood close.

"What are you doing?" My own breathing kicked up a notch.

"I'm going to where Baxter has gone. He seems pretty intent on showing us something."

"But it's pitch black."

"I'll use the flashlight on my phone."

"Okay, but Sam," I said, reaching and grabbing his arm, "be careful."

I felt Sam smile as he leaned closer and gave me a feather-light kiss on the top of my head. "I will." He flipped the phone flashlight on and stepped away from me toward the long grass.

I shivered as his light faded, and he moved after Baxter. I pulled my phone from my bag and switched my flashlight on. I didn't want to be left alone in the dark. I didn't know how far Sam got down the hill, but it felt like an eternity he was gone. His camera was heavy in my arms as I cradled it, attempting to keep it dry from the light rain as I balanced the umbrella in the same hand.

My intuition buzzed again as the feeling that someone was watching me ran over my skin. I spun around, shining the light in every direction to see if anyone was there. However, my phone wasn't the greatest light, only shining a few feet into the dark, revealing no one.

I shivered again, figuring I had an overactive imagination, when I heard the distinct snap of a branch breaking as someone stood on it. And the noise came from behind me.

I spun fast on my heel again. "Hello! Who's there?" I called, my voice shaking as fear crept in. "Hello!"

My ears strained as my eyes grew wide, taking in anything my senses could grab hold of. Logic told me it couldn't be Sam. He'd gone in the opposite direction.

I looked down at the news camera and wondered how to switch the light on. There were quite a few buttons I could see in my limited light, but I had absolutely no idea which one I needed. I took a deep, calming breath and told myself the noise was probably just a kangaroo hopping through the bush. Even though I didn't really want to come face to face with one of those either. A male roo could be huge.

"*Sam*," I called again.

"I'm here," his voice said from behind me.

I screamed and jumped, almost dropping his camera in the process. My heart beat hard against my ribs as I spun around to face him. I'd been so preoccupied with what was in the bush, I hadn't even heard him sneak up behind me. *Shit*.

"God, you scared me," I said, dropping my phone as Sam reached out to take his camera from me. "What did you find? Where's Baxter?"

I needed my heart rate to slow down before I had a heart attack, but until I had answers, it probably wouldn't happen.

"Baxter stayed behind. Alex, listen to me." He sounded serious. God, that couldn't be good. I swallowed the lump in my throat. "I need you to go into the station, and find help."

"What? Why? What did you find? Never mind... Don't tell me. I don't want to know. Actually, yes, I do. *What was it?*" Okay, I knew I was babbling, but I couldn't seem to stop it.

"Alex," said Sam, taking hold of my shoulder. "I need you to do as I asked. Okay?"

I took a deep breath. "Okay. Did you find Wes?" I asked, quietly. The light from my phone shone up from the ground, illuminating Sam. In the glow, he looked eerily pale.

"Yes," he replied. "Yes, but I need you to go and get help. I'm going to stay here so you know exactly where to come back to. Okay. Can you do that?"

I felt the uncontrollable shaking start the second I heard he'd found Wes. "Is he…?" I couldn't bring myself to say the word.

Sam used his free arm to pull me in close. My knees were shaking so hard I was unsure they would hold me up.

I felt his kiss on top of my head as he replied, "He's dead. I'm sorry, Alex."

I heard his words, but my mind just wasn't keeping up. Tears pricked my lashes as Sam held me tight. He moved and cradled my face with his hand. "I need you to go and get some help. We need to get him out of there. Can you do that? Can you get me some help, please?" He looked down at me, eerie shadows dancing across his face. My stomach clenched, and I wondered if I was going to throw up, but then I looked up at Sam and knew he needed me. And I needed to get some help.

"Yes. Yes. I'm okay. I'll find whoever I can."

"Good. Tell whoever you can find to meet me here on the helipad."

I bent to pick up my phone and sprinted for the main building. Thunder rumbled in the distance as my heart pounded in my chest, and my tears fell down my cheeks. Tonight was supposed to be fun, yet this was the second time I was running for help, thinking someone had died.

Only this time it was real.

I FOUND Georgie in the studio, sitting quietly with her mum. Other than the two of them, the studio was empty. I tripped in my hurry to get to her. Tears stung my eyes. I desperately tried to hold them in, but panic made it difficult.

Before tonight, I'd never been in a situation anything like this. I'd never had to tell anyone I'd helped find a dead body. And even though I hadn't seen Wes for a long time, my heart ached for him and his family.

Sam hadn't explained what had happened to Wes, so I was going with maybe he'd walked too close to the edge of the mountain and slipped. It would have been easy for him to hit his head as he fell.

"G…Georgie," I stuttered, my lips trembling and my hands shaking.

"Oh God, Alex. What's wrong? You look like you've seen a ghost."

She was close. I felt the trembling move from my hands into the rest of my body.

Georgie stood and helped me sit in the chair next to the one she'd vacated. She sat and put her arm around my shoulder. Her warmth was comforting, and for a selfish moment, I wanted to stay in close and allow the sobbing to take over. But that wouldn't help Sam. And right now, he needed me.

"We…we f…found Wes," I cried, using my jacket sleeve to wipe at my tears. Georgie paled.

"Oh. Judging by how much you're shaking, it can't be good."

I shook my head. "He fell. Outside…down the hill. Sam needs help. Georgie, Sam needs help."

"Okay. Help. That's something we can do." She jumped up and used the PA to call Rachel.

The second I'd entered the studio, shaking and stuttering, Dawn had stood to get me a hot drink. She was just returning as Georgie finished the PA announcement.

"What's happened?" Dawn asked.

Georgie quickly brought her up to date.

"We have a first aid kit. I'll get it. I know the river is up, and no ambulance can get here, but hopefully we'll have enough to help him." Before I had the chance to correct her, she spun on her heel and made her way out of the studio.

I turned to Georgie. "No...no...you don't understand," I stuttered. "Wes, he's...he's dead."

Georgie sat heavily in the chair next to me, staring back at me. No words passed between us, but a thousand things were said. She slowly nodded her head as tears ran from behind her lashes.

The studio door opened with a slam, and in stormed Rachel.

"This better be important!" she yelled, walking toward us. She stopped in front of me, her hands on her hips.

I brought her up to date.

Rachel's assertive nature came in handy as she sprang to life, calling for Marty and his teammate, John, to meet her in the studio immediately.

Whilst she waited, she moved to the bar and poured herself a very large glass of wine. She didn't talk to us—she just drank. That was fine by me. I didn't have anything to say anyway. My words seemed to have dried up.

The silence in the room was broken as Dawn hurried back into the studio, closely followed by Marty and John. Georgie swiftly moved to her mum, ready for Dawn to hear the bad news.

Rachel's voice was quiet as she filled the men in on what had happened and told them to follow me to wherever they were needed. I'd never seen Rachel soften, and the impact hit me hard.

Marty and John's first instinct was not to believe what she'd said. This wasn't the first time tonight I'd found a *dead* body, but they silently followed me outside to where I'd left Sam.

Thankfully, Sam efficiently took control of the situation, pointing Marty and John to the spot where he'd found Wes.

"Alex, why don't you go back inside and wait?" said Sam. "There's nothing you can do to help out here."

His look was compassionate in the limited light, and not for the first time, the selfish part of me wanted him to hold me tight until tonight was over. But he didn't. He turned his back and followed the men. As they disappeared from view, the cold night air crept through my jacket and chilled me to the bone.

Strangling the sob in my throat, I made my way back inside, figuring alcohol would be the next best thing at this stage. If nothing else, it should warm me up.

IT DIDN'T TAKE LONG for the news about Wes to get around. Dawn was panicking because Stuart still hadn't turned up, and now that Wes had, she was scared something bad had happened to him too.

"Mum," said Georgie, "I'm sure Wes just slipped on the wet grass and fell. That wouldn't have happened to Dad because he knows better than to go too close to the edge in weather like this."

I liked her thinking, but I figured Wes would have known that too.

"Yes, I know that. But where is he?"

I had no idea. To be honest, I was starting to panic about Stuart too. I just didn't want Georgie or Dawn to know that. So I downed glass number three of the really bad wine and hoped the alcohol would kick in quickly.

It took another hour, but finally, the men helping Wes trickled into the studio. I was reorganizing my bag as Sam moved toward me. Only then did my anxiety drop slightly. Now *that* was something I would have to address later.

Something about Sam drew me to him. I told myself it was his incredibly sexy ass. To be honest, though, it felt like something deeper. But then I remembered how he'd reacted when he'd thought Chloe had tried to set us up, and my heart flipped. He obviously enjoyed the flirtation but wanted nothing more intimate than that.

"Did you get him okay?" I asked as he walked closer to me. I noted his wet, muddy clothing and swallowed the lump forming in my throat.

He nodded. "Yeah, it took a couple of us to reach him. He'd slipped down the hill a bit."

"What did you do with him?"

"What do you mean?"

"You know…his body." I felt weird just saying those words.

"Oh. We've put him in the boardroom. We probably shouldn't have moved him at all, but it just didn't feel right leaving him there. I made sure everything was filmed so the police can see it all for themselves though."

"Why shouldn't you have moved him?"

"The police are a bit picky about people interfering with a crime scene."

My heart missed a beat. "A crime scene?"

Sam nodded in response to my question.

"But didn't he just slip and hit his head?" I asked, panicking.

"No. There was nothing to hit his head on, only long grass."

"But why do you think it's a crime scene?"

"Well, I'm no expert on forensics or anything, but he had a very big wound to the back of his head. My guess is he died from that."

"You think someone hit him?"

"Yeah, it looks like it."

I took a minute to look around the room. The noise level had picked up as people nervously discussed what had happened to Wes, the fake murder of Rachel long forgotten.

"Everyone thinks he died from an accident," I whispered.

"Let's keep it that way for now."

"Who do you think could have done it?" I was impressed by how steady my voice sounded. I definitely didn't feel steady. In fact, fear screamed its way to the top of the list of my emotions. This was the second time tonight someone had been hit on the head, and Sam's words about the serial killer rang in my ears.

Sam shrugged. "I don't know. When I see Matt, I'll ask what he thinks. He's really good at solving things like this. I've always told him he should have been a detective instead of a journalist."

"But how will the police get here if the river has the road cut off?"

"We still have the helipad. Maybe they can get in that way. I think this will be a big enough crime for them to use it."

I looked over at Faith, who now sat on a chair in the corner of the room, her eyes huge and innocent, and I wondered about her. Wes died when he went to call the police to find her. Did she stage her own disappearance to get rid of Wes? Surely not. She had no reason to disappear. If she wanted him dead, she could have lured him away without anyone noticing. And where was Jake? He still hadn't surfaced. At least that I knew of.

I left Sam pouring himself a drink and made my way over to Faith. I stopped in front of her, looking down.

"Have you found Jake yet?" I asked.

"No. I haven't." She took a sip of the coffee she held. Her hand shook.

"Have you looked?"

"Yes, of course I have. Do you know where he is?" She looked at me challengingly.

"No, Faith, I don't. There is not now, nor has there been for many a year, anything between Jake and me. Tonight is the first time I have seen him since we split up."

Tears filled her eyes as she looked into her cup. I felt her surrender, so I sat on the vacant chair next to her. "I asked him earlier if there was anything between him and Rachel," she said quietly.

"Did he answer you?"

"He denied anything had ever happened."

"Do you believe him?"

Faith looked back at me. "Would you?"

I thought about her question, and then I thought about the Jake I used to know. "How long have you known Jake?"

"A long time," she answered quietly.

"How long is that exactly?"

Faith's face flushed with color. I should have been surprised, but I had a feeling there was more to her relationship with Jake than I was supposed to know about.

"Why is that even relevant?" she asked.

"Hmmm… I'd guess you've known him for at least five years. Would I be right?" I asked, completely ignoring her question. "In fact, I reckon you knew Jake when he and I were together." I was guessing, jumping to conclusions, but I had a feeling I was spot on.

Faith went quiet and looked down into her coffee cup.

"Are you the reason he left me?" I asked. At one point in time, I would have been holding my breath waiting for her to answer, but now, I was strangely okay with it.

I didn't think she was going to answer me, but finally, she replied. "Jake and I met through our parents. I'd known him for years before he met you. I always knew he was the man for me. I just needed to make him see that. But when he met you, he fell hard." She stopped, lost in her memories. "He really loved you. He still does."

I stopped listening, stuck on her saying he still loved *me*.

"I managed to seduce him one night when you were away visiting your grandparents. He felt really bad about it and told me it would never happen again, but I fell pregnant. That's when he ended it with you."

I thought I was ready for her answer, but I was unprepared for her to tell me about the pregnancy.

"You…you had a baby?" I asked, shock causing my throat to close and ringing to start in my ears.

"No. I lost it. And Jake."

"What?"

"He left me. He wanted to get back with you. To make you forgive him, but Georgie told him you were with someone else. Eventually, I managed to make him see we were right for each other. It took him another four years to marry me, though."

I did hear what Faith said, about how long it took Jake to ask her to marry him, but my mind was stuck on what she'd said about Georgie. Georgie was my best friend. She'd never mentioned to me that Jake had been looking for me and wanted to get back together. Best friends are supposed to tell each other things like that.

"I guess Georgie never told you about that?"

I shook my head, stunned at her words.

"Would it have changed anything if she had?"

I thought about that question, and back to when Jake and I split up. At the time, I thought he might have met someone else, but I never thought he'd slept with her. I never thought Jake was that kind of guy.

"I suppose I'd ask you if he was capable of having an affair with you then do you think he's capable of having one with Rachel?"

Faith's eyes filled with tears once again. "Where is Rachel?"

"I have no idea. I haven't seen her since she left to find Kelly and give her the bad news."

Personally, I didn't think Jake would have slept with Rachel, but I obviously didn't know him very well. I stood and looked down at Faith. "I'm sorry, Faith. I hope for your sake he's not with her, but karma's only a bitch if you are." I stood, turned my back on her, and walked away.

By the time I had crossed the room to the bar, my knees were knocking so badly, I thought they might just give out.

I pulled up a seat next to Sam and asked him to pour me a

drink. He took one look at me, frowned, and poured me a full glass of very bad wine. I thanked him and downed it in one go.

"Are you okay?" he asked.

I shook my head, pulling a face at the bitter taste. "I don't know. I just found out Jake cheated on me."

"How do you feel about that?"

"I don't know. I guess if I think about it, I always knew something was off. He never did give me a real reason for wanting to end things, but I never picked him to be a cheater."

"How did you find that out?"

"Faith told me. She was the one he cheated with."

"Are you still worried about where he is?"

"No. Not really. Let her worry about him. They deserve each other. Personally, I think she's a bit nutso, completely obsessed with her stupid jealousy. What have you got there?" I asked him, referring to a book he was holding.

"It's a book on the history of Westport."

I raised my eyebrows.

"It's actually really interesting. The land the station is built on was originally purchased for sugar cane farming, but turns out that sugar cane didn't grow too well up here, so they changed to cattle farming. And did you know that the mayor who built the old house was a bit eccentric? He was particularly wealthy for the time, owning three thousand acres of the land surrounding us, but he was a bit of a conspiracist. Always thinking people were trying to take his money. He did a lot for Westport, getting the first bank here. Not sure if he kept his money in it. Rumor says he used to bury it somewhere. Rumor also has it that after the First World War, he was obsessed with Westport being invaded, so he installed an early-day safe room."

I raised my eyebrows quizzically.

"You know," continued Sam, "a bit like the old priest holes they had in ancient houses where the occupants could hide the priests from the bad guys. Only this one was bigger and made to hide the occupants of the house, not priests."

"Really? Where in that house would you hide a room like that? It's not big enough."

Sam shrugged. "Traditionally, those types of rooms weren't that big, and this book doesn't actually specify how big it was. In fact, it says that the room is only a rumor since no one has ever found it. But, that's not the odd thing I found. This is." He handed me a photo. It was a photo of me at the beach on my twenty-first birthday.

"I don't get it."

"Neither do I. I found it stuck between the pages of this old book."

Okay, that gave me the heebie-jeebies.

I opened my mouth to say more, but I put it all on hold as Matt walked across the room and pulled up the chair next to me. He looked wet, muddy, and beat.

As it was now well after midnight, I figured I probably didn't look any better.

"You've been gone a long time," commented Sam. "I was starting to worry about you."

"Brent decided we should drive down and check the river. Just in case Wes went for a drive. Only Brent didn't stick to the road and drove too close to the riverbank. We got bogged in the mud. We only just got ourselves out."

Matt didn't look very happy about that. Not that I blamed him.

"What have I missed?"

Sam filled him in on how he found Wes, as Matt also downed a glass of wine. When Sam had finished, he put his empty glass back on the bar.

"Did you check Wes's body for any butterflies?" asked Matt, his jaw tense. My stomach flipped at his words.

Sam shook his head.

"Why would he do that?" I asked, my heart fluttering as I spoke.

"Westport doesn't have a huge crime rate. It's rare for people to be murdered. And the last two casualties died from a hit to the head. That's not a coincidence."

"But are we sure he didn't just fall? Maybe there was a rock nearby he hit his head on."

"I think I need to have a closer look at Wes."

"Rachel said we all had to stay in the studio until we knew what was happening," I said.

"Well, where *is* Rachel?"

I shrugged. "She left to find Kelly."

"If I see her, I'll tell her what I'm doing. Sam, will you come with me? You can witness that I'm not removing any evidence. If I find anything, I'll document it and leave it for the police. In the meantime, if there is a killer amongst us—and I think there is—we should do whatever we can to figure out who it is."

I felt the weight of Matt's words sit heavily in my stomach. I really hoped he was wrong, but the more I thought about it, the more it made sense. *Shit.*

CHAPTER 12

*W*aiting for Matt and Sam to return felt like an eternity. I sat on a stool, propping up the makeshift bar and drank another glass of wine. I flicked through the book Sam had left and crowd-watched. Sitting still doing nothing was killing me.

I looked back at the photo—the one Sam had found inside the book. I actually remembered the day it was taken really well. It was my twenty-first birthday, and my friends and I were celebrating at the beach. It was the day I got my tattoo, which turned out to be a really bad decision, as apparently you shouldn't get into salt water after getting a tattoo. Who knew? So I sat on the sand and sweltered as they poured bottled tap water over my head to cool me down.

I had no idea why this photo was found in a book about Westport. Maybe whoever was reading the book had used it as a bookmark. But whom did I know well enough to do that? I knew it wasn't a book I'd ever read, and even if I had, I wouldn't have left a photo of myself inside it.

I picked up the book and flicked through the pages once more, wondering where, exactly, the photo had been. As I did, something caught my eye. I stopped flicking and worked my way backward through the pages until I found what I'd seen.

A small piece of paper was neatly folded and pushed within the pages, close to the spine of the book. I carefully retrieved and unfolded it. It was a sketch, drawn by hand with colored pencil, of a purple butterfly bouncing on a spring, glued to a sparkly pink headband.

I felt the roll of nausea in my stomach as I put all these pieces of information together. Sam had told me that both Stacey and Dean had butterflies on them. That was a drawing of my headband. It was found inside a book with one of my old photos. Could it all be connected to me? No, surely not. I was overreacting, imagining things that weren't real. Yes, I knew Stacey and Dean, but my relationship with them definitely wasn't close. And as far as I knew, they didn't know each other, so it must have been a coincidence. But Matt said there was no such thing as a coincidence.

I reached into my handbag and pulled out the notepad and pen I'd received with tonight's invitation. Turning to the first clean page, I started to make a list. I suddenly understood why Matt made so many notes.

I wrote Murder Mystery and underlined it with two lines. Under that, I wrote Stacey's name and how a butterfly had been drawn on her wrist. I then wrote Dean's name and how he had a butterfly in his pocket. I also wrote a list of everything I could remember that had been taken from my apartment that day.

That in itself was a strange list. Nothing of value had gone missing, only personal stuff that meant something to me. Like my favorite gray sweater, my old jeans with the hole in the knee, my old WTN T-shirt, a photo album, and a really ugly necklace my grandma had given me. Oh, and some makeup and tampons, of all things. I couldn't see how any of that was related to Stacey and Dean.

I looked around the room again. Most people seemed upset

about Wes, some seemed a little freaked out, and some just looked tired. Rachel was still nowhere to be seen, and I wondered where she had taken Kelly. Was she still with her? And was she really the best person to be comforting Kelly at the moment?

I remembered Matt and Sam telling me how Rachel and Wes had had an affair. Could Kelly and Wes have fought about it tonight? Could Kelly have hit him and then panicked? That would actually make sense. But Kelly didn't look strong enough to have killed him. Maybe Rachel and Wes fought, and Rachel got angry and hit him. That seemed a much more realistic suggestion. Rachel was known for her temper. I made a note of my thoughts to ask Matt about when he got back.

My eyes flicked around the room, and I saw Georgie sitting with Dawn and Faith. I wondered about Faith's connection to what happened to Wes. He did go missing after he went to get the police. If Faith was somehow connected, maybe Jake had done something to protect her? Or maybe she hit Wes *and* Jake, and Jake was lying injured or killed somewhere too.

My stomach churned at that thought. I didn't really know why. Five years ago, Jake had hurt me a lot more than I thought he had, so why did I care what happened to him?

The photo Sam had found sat on the table in front of me, so I picked it up and had another look. It was taken from the sand dunes with my back to the water. I was laughing, my eyes bright and my smile large.

Who was the photographer? Was this a photo one of my friends had taken? If so, why was it placed inside this old book? I made a note of all of it and reminded myself to ask Sam exactly where in the book he'd found it. Maybe Matt was wrong about coincidences. Maybe they did happen.

Lost in thought, I missed Matt and Sam walking back into the room. I only noticed as Sam grabbed a new bottle of wine and unscrewed the lid.

"Well?" I asked, actually quite scared of their answer. "Did you find a butterfly?

"No. There was nothing on him I could find that would give us a clue as to who hit him," replied Matt, accepting the full glass from Sam. Sam then filled his own glass and downed it, only coming up for air once the glass was empty.

"Now what do we do?" I asked, quietly grateful that all butterflies were absent.

"We think," said Matt.

I handed the book to Matt. "I had some thoughts while you were gone. I'm not sure what they tell us though. I seem to have more questions than answers."

Matt silently read my notes as Sam poured another glass of wine, this time only sipping at the contents.

When Matt finished, he looked at me. "Do you think this is all connected to you?"

"No. I mean how could it be? I just thought it was odd, that's all."

Sam took the book from Matt and skimmed my notes. "You forgot to add that Faith was hit by someone who looked like you."

Shit. That was right. "That doesn't help my theory that it has nothing to do with me."

"Maybe whoever is doing this is doing it to frame you?" suggested Matt. "That would explain the break-in. They could have been stealing clothes to dress as you."

I didn't like the sound of that. My stomach flipped at his words. "W…why? Why?"

"Have you upset anyone lately?"

I shook my head. "No. I try my very best not to upset anybody."

We fell silent for a minute.

"Maybe it *is* Faith," I said. "She could have done all this to get back at me for having a relationship with Jake. She did say he still loved me."

"Do you think she's right?" asked Sam, his look piercing my soul.

"No, but it only matters that she thinks that. She could have locked herself in the dub room."

"But who hit her?"

"She could have done it to herself. I've heard of people doing that before. It happened to a friend of mine. His girlfriend was a bit psycho and threw herself down the stairs. She then told the police he pushed her. He only got off because he had twenty witnesses saying he was at the pub at the time."

"Why hit Wes?"

"Because he was going to get the police. Maybe she wanted to stop him." I was on a roll now. I had this thing solved. Somehow Matt and Sam didn't look as convinced about it as I was.

"I think I need to have a chat with Faith," said Matt, placing his glass on the table and standing. I immediately did the same and followed him across the room. Whatever she had to say, I wanted to hear.

"Hi, Faith," said Matt sweetly. "Do you mind if I ask you a few questions?"

"What about?" she asked.

Matt pulled up the chair next to her and gave me a look that said, *Bugger off. She'll talk better without you here*. I sighed and moved to sit next to Georgie.

"Are you okay?" I asked, noticing her eye makeup now smudged under her lashes. Dawn was laid across two chairs, her head on Georgie's lap, dozing.

"I made her take one of her anxiety pills," she explained, smoothing Dawn's hair as she spoke. "She won't help Dad in the state she was getting herself into."

"Is anyone looking for him now?" I asked, sitting on a chair next to her.

I knew that I also wanted to ask her about what happened

years ago when Jake spoke to her and why she didn't tell me, but now didn't feel like the right time.

She shook her head. "Rachel told us to all stay together here in the studio. Marty did look earlier but couldn't find him. I'm really worried, Alex. He's been gone for hours."

Georgie's big gray eyes filled with tears. I felt my heart squeeze. Georgie wasn't like me. She didn't cry easily. She looked down at her mum.

"If she wakes up, I don't know what to tell her."

"Don't worry, Georgie. I'll get Sam, and we'll go and look for him. Do you remember the last place anyone saw him?"

"It was when the boys asked him to check the old house. But Marty went out there and couldn't see him."

"Well, we'll check again, okay? It'll be all right, I promise."

I shouldn't have been making promises like that as I really had no idea what had happened to Stuart, but I needed to give Georgie some hope. She smiled back at me, unconvinced that I was right.

I stood and kissed her on the cheek, giving her an uncomfortable hug as Dawn was still asleep on her lap. I turned and crossed the room again, looking for Sam.

I found him talking to Sally. I waited for them to finish their conversation. "Hey, Sam," I said. "I was wondering if you'd help me with something."

"Sure."

"I want to go back to the old house and look for Stuart."

"But Marty has already done that," said Sally.

"Yes, I know, but it won't hurt to have another look. And even if we don't find him, we may find something that would suggest where he went after that. If he got there at all, that is."

"Why do you think he wouldn't have gotten there?"

"Well, I don't, I guess, but I think we should check just in case."

"It's better than standing here doing nothing," said Sam.

"But Rachel said we should all stay together, here in the

studio," said Sally, panic making her voice shaky. Sally was a sweetheart. "You shouldn't be wandering off on your own. You might get hurt."

I took a closer look at her and could see the genuine panic in her eyes.

"It's okay, Sally," said Sam, touching her arm as he spoke. "She has me. I won't let anything happen to her." He turned to me. "I'll just get my camera."

As Sam walked away to get his camera, Sally grabbed my arm. "Alex, please don't go. Stay here with everybody. You're safe here."

"Honestly, I'll be okay," I said, smiling reassuringly.

"But…but look what happened to Wes."

Everyone thought Wes had died from an accident. I wanted to keep it that way. No use scaring everyone.

"I'll be okay. Sam's a good guy. He won't let anything happen to me."

"Ready?" he asked, walking up behind me.

"Ready." With that, I smiled at Sally again and walked with Sam toward the door.

I FOLLOWED him back through the dark to the old house. I blinked, rubbing sleep from my eyes as they adjusted to the light coming from Sam's camera. I honestly didn't know what we would have done without it. Before tonight, I'd hated cameras, but being on this side of it, I realized that they weren't quite so bad.

The rain had stopped completely, leaving puddles on the concrete driveway. My shoes had only just dried out from their earlier cross-country run trying to get help for Wes. If I was careful and dodged all potholes and puddles, they might just stay dry. Ruined but dry.

Sam stepped up onto the porch, and I noticed him shiver. He turned to look at me over his shoulder. "Ready?"

Not really, but what could I say? "Ready."

He turned the handle and pushed the door open. The hallway didn't look any more appealing than last time we were in here, but thankfully, the ceiling was still where it was meant to be.

My senses were on high alert as we made our way down the hallway and into the kitchen. The wind still whistled through the open window, and I shivered at the memory of Faith's scarf hitting me in the face.

"Okay back there?" called Sam, maybe sensing my unease.

"Yes, but can we do this quickly? I really don't want to be in here any longer than necessary."

The timber creaked beneath our feet as the wind picked up, causing haunting sounds to echo around the empty room.

"Sure," said Sam. "I could have done this on my own, you know."

"That's okay. I'd rather be either seen or heard on the camera, so if any other attacks happen, everyone will know it couldn't have been me."

"I could have left you with witnesses."

Shit, I didn't think of that. I sighed.

Sam chuckled.

Making our way into the old lounge room, Sam shone his light toward the bedroom we couldn't get into earlier. We both immediately moved to the locked door. There was a key in the lock this time, and as Sam turned the handle, it opened.

I sucked in my breath as I realized the key proved that Stuart had at least made it this far. Then I coughed up a lung as a cloud of dust, caused by me dragging my feet, got sucked right in.

"Did you hear that?" asked Sam.

No. All I'd heard was my lung attempting to be expelled through my mouth. He moved into the room. Following him was better than standing here in the dark.

The room was small, only about two meters square, with one window on the opposite wall to us. That window was covered with a floral curtain that was pulled closed. A now-redundant fireplace was on the wall to our right with a crooked picture hanging on the wall above it, but other than that, the room was empty. I wondered what was so important in here that this door had been locked.

"I wish we had more light," said Sam, slowly spinning around the room so that his light gave us a good view of the room's contents.

"Don't worry. It'll be daylight soon, and then you'll have all the light you need."

Sam chuckled, spinning around once more.

"You know what's interesting?" said Sam.

"The strange feeling someone is watching us?"

"The floor's clean," he replied, ignoring my imagination. He turned his light toward the ground.

Indeed, he was correct. "Humph. Why?"

"I don't know, but someone cleaned it for a reason."

"Why do you think that?"

"Every other floor in this house is filthy."

"So what was in here that was so important?"

"Or what is *still* in here that is so important?"

I looked toward Sam, baffled. "Sam, there's nothing in here."

"Yes, there is. There must be, or that door would have been left unlocked. Matt told me that when he spoke to Stuart about it earlier this evening, Stuart didn't even know about it. He didn't know of any reason for it to be locked as no one ever came out here anymore. They haven't done for years. It's not exactly the safest place to hang out."

I thought about what Sam had said as he moved slowly around the room, filming every square inch of it. I couldn't see anything valuable enough to be locked in here. Other than a crooked picture, the room was clean.

As he stopped next to me, we heard an almighty crash.

I jumped, nearly knocking the camera out of his hand. Well, that would teach him not to stand so close to me. Even though I was enjoying it.

"What the..." I screamed as my heart rate spiked into the heart-attack zone.

"It's okay. I think it was just a tree branch falling onto the roof."

"Really?"

"Yes, but look, Stuart's definitely not here, so let's go back to the others. We can have a look at this footage and see if we notice any clues as to why this room was locked. I can't see any in here, but I often notice more when I watch it back."

Sam didn't need to say that twice. As soon as the words left his lips, I spun on my heel and hightailed it back to the front porch, not even looking at anything on the way. Stuart could have been standing in front of me, and I wouldn't have noticed. I was only focused on getting the hell out of there.

CHAPTER 13

*R*eentering the building, we walked past the old dub room, and Sam suddenly stopped. I slammed into his back.

"Faith got locked in there once already tonight. Maybe we should check it out."

Maybe *I* needed to pay a little bit more attention to what he was actually doing and not just his backside. When I was a kid, my anxiety had been so awful, Mum had sent me to a lady who specialized in mind training. She told me that whenever stress or anxiety reared its ugly head, I should focus on something happy, something that made me feel good. It appeared that tonight, it was Sam's ass.

The old dub room was housed in an area adjacent to the toilets. Before the age of digital media, commercials that advertisers wanted to have played would arrive on a spot spool or a dub, as we called it. These dubs were about eight inches round and kept in a small box. A label listing everything we needed to know about the commercial it held was stuck to the side. This room was where all those dubs were kept, waiting to be needed.

I remembered the room well. It was large, held six rows of

ceiling-high metal shelves all facing side-on to the door, creating aisles. Back in the day, these shelves were filled with small pizza-shaped boxes. Now they were filled with large cardboard boxes containing who knew what.

Sam stepped into the room, wanting to have a look around. I stepped in behind him, flipping the light switch as I went. The first thing I noticed was a stack of boxes scattered across the floor as if the pile had been knocked over.

Sam wandered around the aisles as I moved to the boxes and stacked them back into a standing position, ready to push them neatly back onto the shelf. I was just lifting the first box when Sam called me.

"Hey, Alex, come here."

Putting the box to the floor, I moved back past the door, toward Sam's voice. As I did, the door clicked closed behind me. I was about to quickly reopen it when Sam called again.

"Hurry up. Look at this."

Ignoring the door, I found Sam in the farthest aisle. He stood looking down and filming a pile of clothing. I walked up behind him and looked at what could be so interesting.

"What is it?" I asked.

"It's a sweater, but there's blood on it."

Instantly, my blood ran cold.

Sam pulled his arm into the sleeve of his jacket and used it to gently move the gray material for a better look. The soft fabric fell in folds to the floor, revealing the label to both of us.

My blood froze as I read the name written on the tag. It was mine. The one stolen from my apartment during my break-in, the one I took to the gym and had to write my name in because another girl had the exact same sweater.

"Are you okay?" asked Sam, looking at me with a concerned expression. "You're not going to throw up, are you?"

Probably not, but I definitely needed to sit down, as the world seemed to get darker. I pushed my back to the wall and sank my bottom to the floor. I pushed my head between my knees and took some deep, calming breaths. Sam crouched next to me, dropping his camera to the floor.

"Sorry. I know you said you didn't like blood, but I didn't realize you were that sensitive to it."

I shook my head and looked up at him. "No. It…it's the sweater. It…it's m…mine," I stammered, my lips trembling uncontrollably.

Sam's head whipped up as he looked back at the sweater. His eyes stopped on the label, and I saw shock reverberate through them. I knew what he was thinking. This proved someone was trying to frame me.

"It's the one I lost when my apartment was broken into."

The shakes had taken over my body as nausea crawled in my stomach.

"You need sugar. You have a chocolate bar in your bag, don't you?" said Sam, more as a statement than a question.

He stood up and moved around the aisle until he found where I'd dropped my bag. Bringing it back to me, he was about to hand it to me but had second thoughts. Instead, he opened it and found the Mars bar carefully pushed into one of the internal pockets so it wouldn't get squashed.

"Geez, you're organized," he said quietly.

I thought it was a compliment, but as he looked at me, I thought maybe not.

Ripping the wrapper open, he handed me the chocolate and demanded I eat. Only when the sugar kicked in and the shaking stopped did he help me to my feet.

"Come on. We need to get Matt and Rachel. They need to see this."

I allowed Sam to pull me along back to the door. I waited behind him as he turned the handle to let us back out. Only nothing happened. It was locked.

"What the hell?" he snapped.

"Humph. Maybe Faith did get locked in here."

"How can it be locked?" asked Sam. "There's no button. You need a key to lock it."

"It must be just jammed. Give it a shove with your shoulder. You're big, strong, and muscly."

The sugar hit had done a lot to calm me. I was still freaked-out by my sweater being here, covered in blood, but the panic attack had definitely stopped.

"Stand back," he said, nodding for me to get out of his way.

With that, he smashed the door with his shoulder. It didn't budge. Not even a millimeter.

Then I remembered. "When the station was built, this room was made as a strong room. A kind of safe. The walls are thick concrete, and the door is reinforced with steel. That's why it's so heavy." I too had read a book on the history of the station earlier this evening.

Sam rubbed his shoulder and cursed under his breath. I couldn't repeat what he cursed, as it wasn't very nice. In fact, his mood now just seemed grumpy.

"You couldn't have told me that before I rammed it?"

"Sorry, I only just remembered." I cringed. "Maybe banging on it with your fist and screaming will work better. You know, get someone's attention."

"Whose attention are we getting? Isn't everyone supposed to be staying in the studio?"

"Well, yes, but we're out here wandering around. Surely we can't be the only ones."

"Do you have any more chocolate bars in that bag?" asked Sam, not impressed with my suggestion.

I opened my bag and looked. I did, at one point in time, have another chocolate bar in there, but I was pretty sure I'd eaten that earlier this evening when I'd been left alone and bored in the studio. Probably best just to say—*No, I don't.* But then I spotted a Midori bottle I'd found at the makeshift bar.

"I have something better," I said, smiling. Breaking the seal, I handed the bottle to Sam.

"That's nowhere near big enough," he said but accepted my offer anyway.

Downing half of the contents, he handed the rest to me and moved to sit on the floor, checking his phone for a signal. I looked at his scowl and sat, leaning against the wall opposite him. Sometimes a bit of distance was the best solution.

I DIDN'T CHECK the time, but it felt like hours that we sat there. Sam informed me it was probably only ten minutes, and could I please not keep mentioning it. I figured the time to be well after one in the morning and put his mood down to tiredness. I knew I was feeling it.

He sat up against the wall, his head slumped backward, his eyes closed. I noticed the shadows on his cheeks from his eyelashes, his lips slightly parted, and how his face was now covered with whiskers. As I watched, his breathing slowed, and his features relaxed. My stomach flipped, and my heart fluttered.

I mentally slapped myself for having such feelings. Sam clearly wasn't interested in me in that way. Yes, earlier he'd been flirting with me, but he flirted with everyone. And even though it made me feel special, I figured he didn't mean it to. It was just his way.

I felt the tears prickle my eyelids at that thought. Geez, I really needed to get some sleep myself. Fatigue was definitely affecting my tear ducts. At least, that was what I put it down to. It definitely couldn't be disappointment that Sam wasn't falling for me the way I seemed to be falling for him.

I dropped my head to the floor and used my arm as a pillow. We really needed to get out of here, and I *was* keeping my ears open for any sounds indicating someone would be on the other side of the door, but a part of me didn't want to leave. It felt safe in here with Sam. Judging by his mood, I did wonder if maybe it was a little bit too intimate for him, and he was uncomfortable.

He had no reason to be. It's not like I was going to launch myself across the room and rip his clothes off. Okay, in my head I was doing that, but I would never have the courage to *actually* do it. I didn't even have the courage to initiate that kind of thing when I was in a committed relationship. I always left that up to the guy to start.

I sniffed and wiped at my eyes. A minute later, I heard the rustle of clothing as Sam stood. I didn't open my eyes. I was already desperately trying to keep the tears in. His rubber-soled joggers squeaked on the vinyl flooring as he crossed the room. I felt him sit down next to me, lift my head, and place it on his leg. He then gently wiped my hair back from my face. He obviously wasn't worried about personal space or me jumping him.

His leg felt warm and hard under my cheek, and the smell of Sam filled my senses. Sure, his clothing wasn't as clean as it had been when the reunion started, but he still smelled good. It was a mixture of laundry detergent, Gucci's *Guilty* aftershave, and what I could only describe as *Sam*.

"I'm sorry," I whispered.

"What for?" he asked, his voice filled with curiosity, and his grumpy mood gone.

"Getting us into this mess."

"Alex, you didn't get us into this mess. It just happened. The door closed."

"No, I mean all of it. Like earlier, if I had taken you guys with me to meet whoever sent me that message, you would have been there when I found Faith, and we would have known she was alive. Then Wes never would have left to call the police."

"We don't know those two things are connected."

"No, but it's pretty coincidental, isn't it?"

Sam sighed. "What I've been trying to figure out is why you're connected to it all. Have you had any contact with these people since you finished working here?"

"No, only Georgie and her family."

"You said earlier Faith believes Jake still loves you."

"So?"

"Why would she think that? Have you had any contact with him over the years?"

I sat up and used both my hands to wipe my face, pulling my hair back. God only knew what I looked like. "No. Jake dumped me with no real explanation other than he wasn't in a good place for a relationship. At the time, I asked him for more information than that, but he left and would never return my calls. Eventually, Georgie convinced me to forget about him and move on."

"Did you?"

"Sam, what are you suggesting?"

"Nothing. I'm not suggesting anything. It's just…well…I think Faith may be right."

I rubbed my eyes, attempting to wake myself up. "Jake was not in love with me then, and he certainly isn't now."

"But I've seen the way he looks at you. It's like a pained *how did I let her get away* kind of look."

"He's probably got gas," I said, shaking my head at Sam's suggestion.

Sam laughed. It was good to hear. It made me feel warm inside.

"Anyway, it wouldn't matter," I continued. "I've moved on. He was my first love and will always be that, but I definitely don't want him to be my last."

"Your last?"

"Yeah, that spot is reserved for my soul mate, my forever man."

Sam's blue eyes looked deep into mine. I felt my heart stutter and wanted to say more, but the words just wouldn't form. His hand moved to cup my face, and my heart rate kicked up, causing my breath to become shallow. His thumb skimmed my lip, and time stood still as I waited, waited for his soft, full lips to touch mine.

"You've got chocolate stuck—there," he said, rubbing the corner of my lip.

So much for a romantic moment. He was just grooming me.

"Put your head back down. You should get some sleep." His voice was gruff as he moved his hand to guide my head back to his leg.

I felt the hitch in my throat. It wouldn't have mattered whether I'd listened to his sister, Chloe, or not. Even if I'd gone out with him before tonight, I obviously wasn't the girl for him. Then why did I feel that he was the guy for me? Tears pricked again as disappointment sat heavily in my chest.

We sat quietly. Sam's leg was warm under my head, his hand resting on my shoulder. I knew that I was supposed to sleep, but I couldn't. My hormones were racing. My mind was racing, and I generally just felt agitated. I sighed.

"I forgot to tell you about Bernie's office," I said, yawning.

"What about it?"

"When we were searching for the cables earlier, I went in there. Do you remember seeing the family photo on his desk?"

"Yeah, it's been there for years. He was strangely attached to the frame."

"Well, it was gone."

I felt the muscle in Sam's leg tense. "Hmmm, that's odd. I'll ask Matt if it was there when he searched the computer history the second time."

My eyelids felt heavy as I fidgeted and adjusted my position.

"Can you sit still please?" asked Sam, his voice husky.

"Sorry." I attempted to sit still and quiet. I wasn't great at it. Sure, my eyelids were heavy, and my yawning had turned up a few notches, but sleep wasn't anywhere on my radar. I had way too much running through my mind. And every bit of it created yet another loose end. I hated loose ends. They were messy.

"Why do I recognize Faith?" I asked, more to myself than to Sam.

"She looks like you."

I sat up straight, knocking Sam's arm away as I moved. "What?"

"She looks like you."

"She does not!"

"Yes, she does," he said. "And she knows it. So does Jake."

Now, sure she has blonde hair and sort of blue-green eyes, but that's where the resemblance stops. And anyway, even if we did share those characteristics, that's just a type. It didn't mean anything. All men have a type. Don't they?

I was about to question Sam more about it when we heard a noise coming from the other side of the door.

CHAPTER 14

$\mathcal{S}$am instantly jumped up, almost knocking me onto my back in the process. He ran to the door and started to do exactly what I had suggested earlier. He banged on the door and shouted to whoever was out there.

See, not such a stupid idea, was it?

"Hey!" called Sam. I jumped up and joined him.

It was Matt's voice we heard call back to us. "Sam? Alex?" he called.

"Yeah," replied Sam, rather loudly in my ear. "We're locked in. Can you get us out of here?"

I could imagine Matt scratching his head. "We need a key. Who has keys to this door?" His muffled voice came back.

We all went quiet, thinking of the answer. I was the one with the big idea. "Ask Dawn. She may have one," I yelled.

"Okay. I'll be back. Just sit tight."

I looked up at Sam. We had nothing else to do.

Thankfully, Dawn did have keys that would open the door. And after Matt dropped them twice, the door was open, and we stepped out to freedom.

"How the hell did you get yourselves locked in there?" asked Matt.

"The door swung closed. It must have locked automatically," I said. Both men turned to look at me.

"Alex," said Sam. "That's not possible. The only way that door can lock is with a key. People could get locked in there otherwise."

Well, of course I knew people could get locked in. That's what happened to us, but what exactly was Sam suggesting? The expression I wore must have said it all.

"Someone locked us in, Alex," continued Sam. "Did you not realize that?"

I was way too tired for my brain to comprehend this. "What?"

Sam reached out and pulled me close under his arm. "Come on. Let's go and get a hot drink. I don't know about you, but I'm freezing."

He didn't feel freezing. He felt warm and snuggly and safe.

"You need to show Matt the sweater," I said, enjoying the feeling of Sam's arm.

Sam shook his head. "I'm so tired I forgot about that."

He led Matt back into the room. I waited in the hallway, just in case we got locked in again. I was a quick learner. I wasn't falling for that twice.

Matt's expression was grim as he walked back out to me.

"How long were you in there?" he asked, walking ahead of us.

Sam shook his head. "What's the time now?"

"Just after two-thirty." Under the fluorescent lights, Matt looked as tired as I felt.

"Probably about an hour then," finished Sam.

"What are we doing about the sweater?" I asked.

"Leaving it where it is. We'll lock the door behind us so no one else can get in, and we'll leave it for the police to sort out."

"But they'll think I did it!" I protested, panicking.

"Didn't you say that you had reported it stolen?" asked Sam.

"Yes."

"Well, you'll be fine then. They'll know someone is trying to set you up."

Sam and Matt seemed happy with that solution as they locked the door and moved down the hallway. I wondered if they would feel the same if it were their sweater. I bet they wouldn't.

"What have you been doing? I thought you would have missed us before now," Sam asked Matt as I jogged to catch up with them.

"I've been busy. I wondered who sent you that message, Alex. You know the one that asked you to meet an informant under the stairs?"

That felt like years ago. In a time when murder was fun and alcohol was flowing.

"Well, I wondered what happened to whoever was supposed to meet you and who it was. Maybe they saw somebody else going into the toilets. That may give us a clue to who may be running around tonight dressed as you. Don't know whether that will help us solve what happened to Wes, but it may help if we know what happened to Faith."

Good idea. One I hadn't thought of.

"How do we find out who sent it?" asked Sam.

Matt smiled. "Well, I checked with Blake, our resident techie. If we take Alex's phone to him, he can trace who sent the call."

He could? *Wow.*

"Is Blake here tonight?" asked Sam.

"Yeah, he's here. I found him in the presentation department, asleep on one of the computers. I think he'd been gaming earlier this evening."

"Why was he here gaming? Couldn't he do that at home?" I asked.

"Of course he could, but why use his own internet when he can use the station's for free?"

Good point.

"Okay. Let's find him," said Sam, a renewed purpose giving him energy.

"He's upstairs in his office. I was actually on my way looking for you when I found you in the dub room."

"Okay. Lead the way."

"Can we still get that hot drink?" I asked, thinking a coffee might just reactivate my brain cells. Thankfully, both men agreed, so we made a quick stop at the studio.

As we entered, the lighting was on low, and people were camped everywhere. Some had been organized and had a blanket with them, others were using each other as pillows, and some were sitting up, backs against the wall, napping. I looked over at Georgie and saw her still sitting on the same chair, Dawn lying on her lap.

I wandered over to her as Sam and Matt went to the makeshift coffee stand, saying they would get me a cup whilst they were there.

"Hey," I said quietly, approaching Georgie. She opened her eyes. I noticed the strain and tiredness around them, and my heart squeezed. "Your dad hasn't turned up yet?" I asked, hoping he had just wandered in whilst Sam and I were locked in the dub room.

She shook her head. "Where is he, Alex?"

I felt the tears sting my eyelids. "I don't know, Georgie, but we're going to find him. I promised you that. And he'll be okay." He had to be.

She nodded her head. "Okay. Okay."

"Where's Faith?" I asked, looking around and not seeing her. "Has she found Jake yet?"

"No. She's asleep somewhere over there near Tiffany. She was pretty freaked-out, and it wasn't helping Mum. I felt really bad sending her away, but you know… I have to look after Mum first."

I nodded. "Of course you do." I smiled reassuringly at Georgie, but my heart flipped.

The storm had passed hours ago. Well, passed enough that if Jake and Stuart were sitting it out somewhere safe, then they should have been back by now. "Maybe they sat the storm out and fell asleep. The sun will be up in a few more hours, and I'm sure they're going to walk back in here, laughing at how silly they were."

"I hope so." I leaned over Dawn and gave Georgie a hug.

MATT LED the way to Blake's office, and I shuffled after him. Sam had left his camera in the studio with Georgie, and he walked behind me, sipping a cup of coffee. I'd finished mine in the studio.

I looked at Sam over my shoulder, getting the creepy feeling we were being watched.

"Did anybody ever get through to the police?" I asked, my brain cells waking as the coffee did its thing.

"Yes, I did," replied Matt. "I spoke to Blake about the phone situation here and how the cables were missing. He said he had spare ones in his office we could use. Thankfully, he did find one, and we got the phone system up and running quickly. I used it to call Sergeant Ed Helms and informed him about this evening's events. Wes never got through to him earlier. However, the Westport police have had a very eventful evening. There was a really bad accident on the highway, six cars and a truck involved. Sadly, quite a few deaths. But after telling him about Wes, he moved pretty quickly. He's getting in contact with the police in the city to see if they can get the helicopter up here. The road is still cut off, and there's no other way for him to get in. Apparently, he's quite happy with what we've done so far, but he's really concerned about everyone's safety. Especially when I told him Jake and Stuart were still missing."

I didn't like the sound of that. They had to be asleep somewhere. I didn't want to have to tell Georgie we'd found Stuart the same way we had Wes.

"How long until they get here?" asked Sam.

"I don't know. The helicopter was being used on the south coast, so it could take a while longer yet."

I sighed. Tonight had already been long enough.

Reaching Blake's office, we walked in. Well, walked in as far as the mess would allow. I did wonder what Fire Safety would have to say about it.

The office had no outside windows. There was a small desk. I think it was timber, but that was only because I could see a small piece of the leg. The surface of it held a computer, a keyboard and mouse, computer parts, cables, power leads… You name it, it was on the desk.

The room was tiny, only about two meters square. There was a small walkway to the desk that meant I could actually put one foot in front of the other, but otherwise, the room was overflowing with boxes and what I would describe as junk.

Blake was exactly what I had expected. He looked to be in his twenties, was short, like just-over-five-foot short. He had a mop of brown, curly hair, and his glasses were on the desk next to him. He wore jeans two sizes too big, a T-shirt that advertised *The Big Bang Theory*, and had the distinct imprint of a keyboard on his face. My guess was he'd fallen asleep at his desk again.

"Hi, Blake," said Sam, his earlier cheerful mood returning thanks to the coffee.

"Oh hi, Sam," replied Blake, rubbing his eyes awake.

"I was just telling these guys about how you can trace the message Alex was sent," explained Matt.

"Oh yeah, sure." Blake ran his hands through his hair, causing it to almost stand on end. "Do you have the phone?"

I reached into my bag and pulled my phone from its little pocket, handing it to Blake. As I did so, Blake's hand grabbed on to mine for a second longer than necessary. His eyes shot open, and a sleazy smile spread across his lips.

I snatched my hand away and smiled politely, attempting to cover the shiver that ran down my spine. "Hi," I said, wanting to wipe my hand on my jeans. I didn't want to insult the man who was about to help us, so I waited until he wasn't looking and then did it.

"Matt never told me how pretty you were," said Blake, awkwardly. I figured this guy needed to put his glasses on.

Sam moved next to me. "The phone, Blake," he snapped. Maybe Sam needed another cup of coffee. One wasn't having a lasting effect.

Blake jumped at Sam's tone and glared at him, but he did take the phone and turn back to his computer, picked up his glasses, and put them on. He then wiggled his mouse, clicked a few keys on the keyboard, and his computer sprung to life. He swiped at my phone, did some nosing around, and installed an app.

"This app will tell us who sent the message. Well, it will tell me the number, anyway. I can then reverse-check who it belongs to." It was that easy.

I moved to sit in a chair opposite him. I put my head in my hands and sighed. Why did I feel like my privacy was being invaded? And was there anything on that phone Blake shouldn't see?

Damn it! Yes, there was. It wasn't incriminating or anything, but judging from the way he looked at me before, I probably didn't want him seeing that photo I took in the change room the other day when I was trying on that new bra. I was really unsure whether I liked it or not and wanted Georgie's opinion, so I took a selfie in the mirror and texted it to her with the message, *What do you think? Too slutty?* But maybe he wouldn't see that. He was only tracing a message from an unknown texter. He shouldn't be looking at anything else, should he?

After a few minutes, Blake looked up at me and smiled. "Well, your anonymous tip off came from Tiffany Jones."

"Really?" I wondered why Tiffany would want to help me in this game. I didn't even know her. And how did she get my number?

"Really," he replied. I stood and took the outstretched phone from him, grateful for his help.

"Oh, and in my personal opinion—not too slutty," he said, cupping my hand as he spoke.

I blushed and snatched my hand away. Matt and Sam looked at him quizzically, but he grinned back, looking like all his Christmases had come at once. They probably just had.

Sam looked like he was about to ask Blake what he was talking about, so I quickly interjected.

"Let's find Tiffany."

"WHAT WAS HE TALKING ABOUT?" asked Sam in my ear as we walked through my old office space, following Matt back to the studio. I ignored him and studied Matt's backside as he walked ahead of me. I shook my head and wondered what the hell was wrong with me that every time a guy was in front of me, I was checking out his backside.

There was nothing wrong with me. This was not my usual behavior. I didn't know what it was about tonight, whether the storm had messed up my emotions or whether it was being back here that was stirring everything up.

Seeing Jake again initially didn't have the effect I thought it would, but after hearing about Faith's pregnancy, I definitely felt unrest.

Wes dying had thrown me. I hadn't had anything to do with him for a long time, but *anyone* dying upset me.

Then there was finding out Georgie had hidden things from me, old photos of me turning up in weird books, Stuart missing, Faith telling me she thought Jake was still in love with me, and to top everything off, there was Sam. He was the biggest thing affecting me tonight.

Guilt swept me as I thought how selfish and self-indulgent that seemed. A man had died here tonight, and the thing that affected me the most was a good looking man who influenced my hormones. *I'm a bad, bad person.*

"Alex," said Sam, leaning in way too close to my ear. "What was he talking about?"

My stomach flipped, and the guilt switched up another notch.

"It doesn't matter," I croaked in response.

"Yes, it does. He talked about you being slutty. Do I need to go back and have a severe word with him?"

Sam sounded in good humor. I just couldn't share that emotion. I had this awful feeling that the events of this evening were all my fault. Remember how I had mentioned my gypsy-like intuition? Well, this was one of those times I just knew something to be so. I had no idea how or why, but tonight was connected to me.

Entering the studio, we spotted Tiffany asleep in front of the news desk, right alongside Arthur. She'd found an old blanket and had used it as a pillow, and she looked as uncomfortable as a girl could get. I remembered Georgie telling me Faith was asleep near Tiffany. Funny thing was, I couldn't see her.

We quietly approached her.

"Tiffany," whispered Matt, tapping her on the shoulder. "Tiff."

She stirred and blinked up at him. "Huh?" she asked, rubbing her eyes and sitting up. "Is everything okay? What's wrong?" I could hear the urgency in her voice and needed to dispel her anxiety quickly.

"Nothing's wrong," I said. "Everything's okay. We just wanted to ask you a question."

She looked wearily back at us and nodded.

"We found out you sent the message to Alex earlier, telling her to meet you under the stairs. You had a clue for her," explained Matt.

Fear took the place of sleep in her eyes. *"Shhh!"* she said, louder than she probably should as Arthur stirred next to her. "Don't let Rachel hear you!"

I looked around me and couldn't see Rachel anywhere in sight. I wondered where she was.

"She's not here," I whispered, as Arthur rolled to his back and gently started to snore.

"Oh, okay. How did you find out I sent it anyway?"

"Blake," said Sam.

That was all the explanation she needed. He was obviously a wiz when it came to technology.

"What did you have to tell me?" I asked.

"I didn't send you a message," she said.

"Yes, you did. You said to meet you under the stairs and that you had a clue for me."

Understanding flashed in Tiffany's eyes. "Oooh, now I get it. I meant to send the message to Georgie but must have put in the wrong number. I wondered why she never turned up."

That was an easy mistake. Georgie and I had both signed up for our phones at the same time and thought it would be fun to choose phone numbers that were only one number apart. This wasn't the first time I'd received a message for her.

"I just wanted to give her a clue," continued Tiffany. "I was going to tell her to look closer at Brent."

Well, that didn't help us at all.

"Did you wait under the stairs closest to the toilets?" asked Matt, undeterred.

"Yes."

"Did you see anyone going in or out of the toilets?"

"Well, yes. Alex. I was waiting for Georgie to arrive when I saw Alex go into the toilet. She was in there for ages, and I did wonder what she was doing that took so long. I wondered if she was unwell, but then I saw her go in again."

"You didn't think that was strange? Me going in twice?"

"Well, yes, but I figured you must have walked out without me seeing you."

"Did you stop watching the toilets at any point?" asked Matt, who now had his handy-dandy notebook back out and was scribbling away.

"No, but there was no other way to explain it."

"How long was it between seeing Alex go in the first time and seeing her the second time?"

Tiffany thought carefully before answering. "Ummm...more than five minutes but less than ten. I remember the second time she went in because she made a lot of noise. Her handbag got caught in the door, and I laughed at the curse she let out."

I blushed at the memory.

"Anyway, that's when Rachel walked past and saw me. She started yelling at me because she said I was up to something and asked if I was cheating."

"So you never went into the toilets?"

"No, I left with Rachel yelling at me. I was supposed to be sabotaging my opposition, not helping them. She's a sick woman," Tiffany finished, whispering behind her hand.

I had to agree with her.

"And you never saw anyone leaving," finished Matt.

She shook her head. "Sorry."

"That's okay. Thanks anyway," I said, stepping away from her. "Well, that was a waste of time," I said, wondering what we should do next.

"No, it wasn't," said Matt. "We found out that Faith was telling the truth. You hit her."

I stared at him, unsure if I'd just heard him correctly. "No, I didn't. I never went into the toilets twice. I only went in once," I whispered in harsh tones.

"I know. Which means that someone who looked like you went in the first time and hit Faith. She wasn't lying."

"But the toilets were empty when I went in there."

Matt put his pen tip in his mouth and thought. He flipped backward through pages in his notebook. "When I checked the area after you told us about Faith, I couldn't find anything that suggested a struggle. The area was clean. A little bit too clean for my liking, actually."

He was just mentioning this now?

Sam grabbed my arm and said, "Let's go to the newsroom and talk. People are trying to sleep here."

Matt looked around and nodded.

Once in the newsroom, though, Matt moved to his white-board and cleaned an area. It was only a small area as he seemed to have a lot of information on that board, but I guessed it was big enough for this purpose.

He started writing names and places and notes. I saw Faith, toilets, polystyrene, clean, Wes, bush...the list went on. When he'd finished, he rubbed a few things out and put them in a different order. Personally, I was going cross-eyed already.

"What's the polystyrene note?" asked Sam.

"It was the only thing I found on the floor in the toilets," commented Matt as he continued to write.

"What was that doing on the floor?" I asked.

"I had no idea at first," said Matt. "It was small and looked like it came from a ceiling tile, but all the tiles were in place when I checked."

My heart stuttered. "A ceiling tile?"

"Yeah," said Matt, pointing upward. "Like those." I looked to where he was pointing. The ceiling in the newsroom was the same as all the others in the downstairs area of the station. They were falsely low, allowing for the air-conditioning ducts to run from one place to another, and were covered in polystyrene tiles about six hundred centimeters square.

"But they weren't," I continued, distinctly remembering sitting on the toilet and feeling like I was being watched. "One of the tiles was askew. I remember being creeped out by it."

Sam and Matt turned to look at one another.

"Maybe we should have another look," said Sam.

"What will it tell us?" I asked, standing quickly as they both turned to walk out of the room and back down the hall toward the toilets.

"I'm hoping it will give us a clue as to who has been dressing as you. If we can prove someone else hit Faith, it will throw suspicion on them for hitting Wes."

"How do you know the same person hit both people?" I asked, almost running to keep up with them.

"We don't for sure. At this stage anyway. But remember, I don't believe in coincidences. Two people were both hit the same way. The same way that both Stacey and Dean died."

Okay, *that* made chills run up my spine, but maybe that was the creepy feeling I was being watched again. "Does anyone else feel like they are being watched?" I asked.

Both men turned to look at me, shaking their heads. Sam stepped away from me and had a look around. "I can't see anyone, but stay close," he said, guiding me in front of him.

Matt opened the outside door to the toilets and then banged on the ladies. Turning to me, he said, "Maybe you should go ahead of us in case a lady is in there. I'll be right behind you." Pushing his body against the wall, I moved past him and opened the door. Matt held the door open whilst I checked the cubicle situation.

"All clear."

Matt and Sam entered the small room.

"Which tile was askew?" asked Sam, looking up at the now-perfect ceiling.

I thought about what he'd asked. "I think it's that one," I said, pointing to the one above his head. "Hang on, though." Moving into the cubicle I had earlier occupied, I took up the correct position and looked up. It was definitely the one above Sam's head.

I moved back out as Sam jumped up on the counter. He then pushed the ceiling tile up, flipped his phone to flashlight, and used his incredible arms to lift himself up into the ceiling space. Now that was something I would never be able to do. My arms were barely strong enough to carry the grocery bags, let alone my own body weight.

"Be careful, Sam," called Matt. "Not all of those beams are strong enough to hold you."

"And that's why I'm the one going up," said Sam. "I'll make sure I don't fall through." Matt's ears turned a little bit pink, but he was probably used to Sam teasing him about how clumsy he was.

"Can you see anything?" I asked.

"Yeah, I can," said Sam, sticking his head back down to us.

"What?"

"A blood-covered glass vase and a partial bloody handprint on the beam next to me."

CHAPTER 15

*S*am took lots of photos using his smartphone and then lowered himself back down to us. Personally, I was already sitting on the floor, hugging my knees to my chest.

Sam crouched down in front of me.

"This is good, Alex. We can now prove that someone else did it as we have a fingerprint in blood."

I nodded. I knew that, yet my body seemed to have started to shake and didn't want to stop, probably because it was creeped out as hell that someone had been watching me while I peed. I'd never trust another public toilet again. Ever.

"I want to phone Sergeant Helms again," said Matt. "Give him an update on what we've found and ask how long until the helicopter will be here."

"Okay," said Sam. "While you do that, I want to take another look at the footage. I want to watch the crowd to see if we can see anybody who looks like Alex in it. If we can zoom close enough, we'll maybe see who it is. Give the police as much information as we can."

"Okay, but only because I want this to be over," I said. "I really want to go to the studio and sleep. I don't want to be traipsing back and forth trying to figure out who did this. I live in a happy world! Not one where people *dress up as me* and go around *hitting and maybe killing people!*" I was close to hysteria. I knew that. But I couldn't seem to stop it.

Sam pulled me in close and held me tight. I only moved once his warmth had replaced the cold feeling in the pit of my stomach. I dried my tears, swallowed my pride, and took some deep breaths. Then I followed him to the studio to retrieve his camera. Once he'd done that, we went back to the production booth. Sam plugged the camera in, and we sat and watched this evening all over again.

This time, however, I was more focused on the crowd. It appeared everybody was having a great time, and if Wes hadn't died, it would have seemed that tonight was a success. Sam fast-forwarded to the point where Faith reappeared. I looked for the similarities in the two of us. Faith had blonde hair, I had blonde hair. She had green-blue eyes, I had green eyes. Tonight she wore a black top, but I'd worn a white one. It was only as she smiled that I saw what Sam was talking about. We didn't look identical, but we definitely could pass as sisters. *Shit.* Maybe Sam was right. Maybe this was more than a type.

I was just contemplating the implications of that when Matt entered the room.

"How did it go with the police?" I asked.

"I filled Ed in on what we'd found, and he said to sit tight and keep everyone in one place. The helicopter is on its way back from the south coast and is stopping in Westport to pick him up. They should be here in an hour or so."

I felt reassured at those words. Matt sat and looked at the screen.

"Who's that there?" he asked, pointing to the screen.

Sam stopped the footage, rewinding it slightly until Matt said, "Stop".

It was a point where Sam and I were checking the reception

for the phone cables or radio handsets. Sam had placed the camera on Tiffany's desk, but he'd left it recording. Standing in the hallway, peeking around at the corner at us, was Faith.

Sam pressed the play button and sped the video up, stopping whenever we could see someone hiding and watching us. We saw her three times. I knew someone had been following us.

"I thought she was supposed to be in the studio," said Matt.

I thought I'd asked Georgie to keep her with them.

"We need to ask her why she's been following us," I said, irritated.

Both men agreed, so we stood, ready to make our way back down the stairs to where Faith was supposed to be sleeping. Only we didn't need to go that far because, as we turned, we found Faith sneakily pulling her head back around the doorframe on the other side of the booth. She moved fast but not fast enough. Sam sprinted ahead of us and caught up with her, gently grabbing her arm and stopping her in her tracks.

"Why are you following me?" I demanded, catching up with them.

"Because you know where Jake is!" Hysteria shone in her eyes.

"No, I don't." I sighed. I really didn't want to go over this again.

"You have to know," said Faith, her shoulders slumping. "You're my only hope of finding him," she added quietly.

I looked at her expression. Her huge eyes were ringed with dark circles. Her makeup was now nonexistent, and her hair was messed. She'd lost her shoes somewhere along the way, and to me, she looked younger—almost childlike. I wondered about her grip on reality and if she was getting some sort of medical advice. I should have hated her for what she did to Jake and me all those years ago, but right now, that would be like hating a lost puppy. No one could do that. But I did make a mental note to talk to Jake when we found him and make sure he had her mental health assessed. That would be a fun conversation.

"I'm sorry, Faith. Believe me, if I knew where he was, I would tell you. I don't like the fact he's missing any more than you do."

Faith's head shot up at my words, and Sam stiffened.

"You do still love him, don't you?" she asked, her eyes filling with tears.

I took Faith's arm from Sam and turned her to face me. "I've had enough. I don't want to do this anymore. I'm tired. I'm cold, and I want to go home. But I can't. None of us can. All we can do is try to sort this mess out and make the most of what we have right now. When Jake turns up—and he will—you have to stop this. He married you. You won. Got it? Or do you really want to lose him? Because Jake is a good-looking guy, and I'm sure there will be a queue of women waiting to fill your shoes."

Faith's tears spilled over her lashes, and she fell forward into me, nearly knocking me over. Well, I hadn't expected that.

"I love him so much," she sobbed.

I patted her on the back awkwardly. "There, there," I said, in an attempt to comfort her.

"Are you sure he will turn up?" she asked in between sobs.

"Yes." I really needed to stop making promises I wasn't sure I could keep.

Sam and Matt seemed to be looking for the exits. I think this was all too much emotion for them.

"Ummm… Why don't you take Faith back to the studio, Alex," suggested Matt. "You can get some sleep too. I have something I want to chase up, and I can manage it without you."

"I'll help you," added Sam quickly, looking at Matt. "In fact, I think I should get my camera and change the battery again."

I didn't think either of them actually had anything they needed to do other than get some distance from a crying Faith.

"Okay," I said, letting them off the hook. "Will we be okay on our own, though?"

"You don't have far to go, so just stay together."

"All right. Come on, Faith. Let's get you some sleep."

I steered Faith away toward the nearest staircase, taking the shortcut back to the studio from where we were. I flashed Sam a grin as I left and stuck out my tongue. I meant it in good humor, but the look he gave me back was much more serious. I figured he would much rather be taking a nap as well.

The staircase we used brought us out at the front of the station, near reception. This was the closest to us, and it was the one I steered Faith toward.

Faith broke the silence. "I'm not the only one who has been following you all night," she said.

My heart skipped a beat. "Pardon?"

"Someone else has been following you as well. I tried to see who, but every time I got close, whoever it was saw me and disappeared—like a ghost or a phantom."

"Ghosts and phantoms don't exist."

"I'm just telling you what I know."

"Faith, you did believe me when I said I didn't hit you?"

"Yes. I didn't then, but I do now. I thought you'd done it to get rid of me and get close to Jake, but if that were true, then you would be with him."

As Faith stepped down the stairs ahead of me, I felt the hair on my neck rise. I grabbed her arm to make her stop. Halfway down, the stairs curved around a corner and continued in the opposite direction. Intuition screamed at me to go back up and not turn that corner.

"What?" asked Faith. "Why have we stopped?"

I heard the stairs creak. Faith's head snapped around to see who was coming, but I had an awful feeling I didn't want to see who it was. Why? I didn't really know. Maybe tonight had creeped me out way too much.

I made a quick decision to turn and go back the way we came. Faith followed behind me as I took the stairs two at a time. It was only as she screamed that I stopped.

I turned just in time to see her fly backward, landing against the far wall with a sickening thud. Her screams stopped as I felt the almighty blow hit my temple. My head exploded, and the world turned black.

IN THE DISTANCE, I could hear someone calling my name. I tried to open my eyes to see who it was, but the pain searing through my head made me close them tighter. I had no idea why my head was hurting so much or why someone was incessantly calling my name.

I felt the slap to my cheek and snapped my eyes open. *Ooh, that hurt.* I really wished I hadn't done that. I slammed them shut again and winced at the pain.

I put my hand up to where I'd been slapped and felt the warm sticky liquid on my fingers.

"Alex!" I heard my name being called. "*Alex!*"

I struggled to open my eyes, slowly this time, and moved to see who was calling me.

"Oh, thank God, you're alive. I thought you were dead for a minute there." The voice was deep and gravelly and belonged to Jake. *Jake!*

I sat up quickly, the world swaying as I did so. My stomach churned, and I had a moment where I thought I might throw up. I think Jake thought the same thing. He moved away from me pretty quickly then handed me a wastepaper bin.

I took some deep, calming breaths and slowed my heart rate back to somewhere around normal. Well, normal for tonight anyway.

"Jake! Where have you been? We've been worried about you."

Jake looked tired in the dim light. His clothes were dirty, and his eyes were dark.

"We couldn't find you, and we've been looking and looking!"

I felt the tears sting my eyes as they filled behind my lashes. I swiped at them with my fingers as they escaped and ran down my cheeks. I continued, ignoring the fact Jake was trying to stop me from wiping my tears. He stood, and I looked around the room for the first time. I had no idea where we were.

The room was small, less than three meters square. There was a single overhead bulb giving the room very limited light, a closed metal door, and a cement floor. The walls were covered in photos of I don't know what, and there was an armchair and a desk. Stuart was slumped in the armchair, his eyelids fluttering open and then closing again. Jake moved back toward me, carrying a tissue box from the desk.

"Stuart!" I said. "Oh my God! Is he okay?"

"Sort of," said Jake.

I noted the large gash on Jake's forehead, the dried blood crusting on his skin.

"He keeps dropping in and out of consciousness. I tried to stop the bleeding, but it's a bit hard to do when he's bleeding from the back of his head."

"What are you doing in here? Why don't you get him some help?"

Jake gently pulled a tissue from the box and used it to wipe my face. Only when he threw the tissue in the bin did I see it was covered in blood. My blood.

I felt the world sway once more, the smell filling my nostrils.

"We're stuck in here, Alex. There's no way out. I've looked."

"Where are we?"

"I don't really know. All I know is that I was hit on the head and woke up here. Stuart was lying on the floor in a pool of his own blood. I've been trying to help him, but we've been in here for hours."

I felt my own head and the lump that was now forming. My memory flicked to the stairs and someone hitting me.

"I don't know who hit me. I didn't see their face, but they

looked like me. Same hair, the same clothes. So at least we know it's a female."

Jake shrugged. "A damned strong female." He sounded frustrated. "I was wandering around the grounds looking for Faith when I saw a light coming from around the back of the old house. I made my way over to it. It was a flashlight, and it was shining straight into my eyes. I thought it was Faith, so I called to her. Then, whoever it was hit me."

"Why did you think it was Faith?"

"I shielded my eyes against the light, and I saw blonde hair. I couldn't see her face either though."

I moved to stand. Jake held my hand and helped me to my feet. The dizziness started, and my stomach rolled.

"Here, sit down," said Jake, reaching for the desk chair and rolling it toward me.

I gratefully sat. And that was when I noticed the walls and what exactly the photos were of. There were photos of me. There were photos of Jake. There were photos of us both together. *Everywhere*.

I sucked in my breath as my heart stuttered, and my mind tried to comprehend what I was looking at.

Jake sat on the edge of the desk. "Scary, hey?"

I couldn't speak. My mind just couldn't seem to find any words. Instead, I stood, Jake holding my hand to steady me, and looked around the room.

The walls were almost wallpapered with photos of us taken at various times, past *and* present. There were photos of me working in the traffic department, laughing with Georgie. There were photos of me getting into my car, at the beach, at the shops. There were even photos of me walking into the dentist.

The desk held my photo album, my MAC eye shadow, and my tampons. A plastic basket was filled with old pens, a broken mug, my old phone case with Minnie Mouse on the back—all of which I knew I had thrown in the garbage bin.

Over the back of the chair Stuart was slumped in were my old jeans with the hole in them, and three T-shirts I'd donated to charity. Stuart was covered with a blanket from my bed—the one I thought I'd lost.

In fact, looking around me, I could see a lot of things I thought I had lost. Mum always said I would lose my head if it wasn't screwed on. Well, she was wrong. All of this had been *taken*.

Then I looked at the photos of Jake. Some were of the two of us together. Some were much more recent. Some were taken when I'm sure he thought was alone. But the only photo he had with Faith was on their wedding day. And Faith's face had been cut out of the picture and mine glued in its place.

I was in shock. I shook my head, hoping this was all a bad dream and that I would wake up at home, and we'd all be safe. Instead, all the shaking did was kick my headache up a notch.

My knees buckled as I spun, looking around the small room. I picked up the stuffed teddy bear Jake had given me on our first date at the Westport Show. It still had the missing ear and wonky eye that had made me love it. I stroked its soft fur as I continued to look around.

I stopped when I saw the photo of my twenty-first birthday party. It was similar to the one I'd had earlier, except this one was of me standing in the middle of my group of friends. My head was back, and I was laughing like I didn't have a care in the world. *If only I could rewind time.*

Jake stepped up next to me and looked at the photo.

"You don't think I had anything to do with this, do you?" I asked, quietly.

He shook his head. "When I first saw it, I wondered. But Stuart has been mumbling a name all night. I can't make out what he's saying, but it's definitely not Alex. And if you'd done it, you wouldn't have been thrown in here after being hit on the head. I also don't think you would have plastered the walls with your own photo. You're not that conceited."

I nodded, relieved. Looking at that wedding photo, it would be easy for him to think I had.

"I don't know who's behind this, but I think they've been setting you up," he continued.

It sure looked that way. "But why keep all these things belonging to me? And if they're obsessed with you, then why glue my picture onto that photo? Why not their own?"

"I have no idea," he said, sinking to the floor.

"Are there any clues in here as to who did all of this? Is there any way out?" I asked, hysteria bubbling to the surface. I wasn't going to cry. It wouldn't change anything.

"Nope." Jake hung his head low. "I'm sorry, Alex," he said quietly.

I shook my head as the tears once again started, and I gave in to the emotion. This time, however, they quickly descended into deep heart-wrenching sobs. Within seconds, I could no longer breathe. Jake stood, pulled me back to the chair, and sat me down. Pushing my head down between my knees, he rubbed my back. It brought back memories of how he used to comfort me when I was sad.

Crouching down next to me, he encouraged me to slow my breathing while he continued to rub my back. Up and down. Up and down. The sensation calmed me, and it didn't take long for me to regain control of my breathing. Once I had that under control, he pulled me in close and held me tight.

CHAPTER 16

I wasn't sure how long we sat like that. It should have felt uncomfortable, but it didn't. It was only when I felt Jake kiss the top of my head that I stiffened. Sam's words came flooding back to me. *Faith thinks Jake's still in love with you.* Could he be?

I pulled away and looked at Jake. His dark eyes were no longer looking at me like I was his enemy. Not like they had earlier in the evening. Now they held compassion, friendliness. Maybe even regret.

"I'm sorry, Alex," he whispered.

"What for?"

"For the way I treated you all those years ago. It wasn't right, and I've never forgiven myself for what happened."

"All I wanted was an explanation as to why."

"I know. And I should have given you one. But Faith and I..." He turned away from me, unable to look me in the eye.

"I know what happened, Jake. I know about the baby," I said quietly.

He gulped, and I noticed his hand shake as he ran it through his hair. "I'm sorry, Alex. I'm so sorry. I didn't mean to...you

185

know. It just happened. And afterward I felt so guilty. When you came back from your grandparents', I couldn't even look at you. I knew that if I did, you would know what I'd done."

"I remember. At the time, I thought I was the one who'd done something wrong. And you wouldn't tell me what it was. I wanted to fix it. To make things right between us again." Old anger stirred in my belly. I tried to repress it as it wasn't doing me any good now.

Tears filled Jake's eyes as he nodded his head, looking only at the floor. "I was going to tell you. To find a way to make you forgive me, but Faith called and told me she was pregnant. I didn't know what else to do. I'd caused this mess. I couldn't leave her to handle it on her own, but I didn't want to leave you. In the end, I did what I thought was right."

"But you never told me why!" I yelled, making Stuart jump.

Jake moved to him and checked that he was okay. When he was satisfied Stuart was as comfortable as he could possibly be, he sat on the floor with his back against the metal door. Silence filled the air between us.

"Why are you telling me this now?" I asked, annoyed. Annoyed at Jake, annoyed at our situation, hell, I was just annoyed in general.

Jake stared at me, his eyes soft and vulnerable. "In case we don't get out."

His words felt like a blow to my chest. Yes, on a conscious level I knew we were stuck in here, but hearing those words made me realize Jake thought this was it. We were going to die. There was no way out of it for us.

I didn't like the sound of that, and the panic once again threatened to take over. I couldn't let that happen. If it did, Jake would be right. We would die in here tonight. I attempted some deep, calming breaths and tried to bring my mind back to our previous conversation.

Eventually, I said, "So, what happened to the baby?"

"There never was one. It was what the doctors called a phantom pregnancy. Faith had all the symptoms, but there was no baby growing inside her. She was devastated, convinced they were wrong and that she had lost it, but all I could think was how that meant I now had a chance to be with you again. I went looking for you. I would have done anything to fix things. But Georgie told me you had moved on, you had a new man in your life, and you were very happy. So I gave up."

This was the second time tonight I'd heard that Georgie had made a decision like that for me. She had no right. Only I had that choice to make.

"I never stopped loving you," Jake continued quietly.

His words shocked me out of my thoughts about Georgie. I sat up straight and looked at him.

"I was worried about coming here tonight. I didn't know what I would feel when I saw you. Part of me thought that maybe I would realize that what I remembered we had was just a fantasy in my head."

"Was it?"

"No."

I didn't know what to say. All I knew was that my feelings for Jake were not what they once were. I knew I didn't hate him anymore, but I was definitely not in love with him.

"Don't worry," he continued. "I know what you're thinking. And I know what I had with Faith is real. It took me nearly five years to figure I was never getting back what I had with you and that I needed to move on. Tonight though, when she went missing, I thought it was my fault. I just had my life on track, and then I went and messed everything back up." Tears filled his eyes.

"In what way?"

"Faith and I had an argument earlier," he said, sniffing.

"I know. She wanted to know if you ever slept with Rachel. Did you?"

"No," replied Jake, his dark eyes looking at me. I felt my

stomach flip as memories of those eyes looking down into mine filled my mind. "She saw the way I looked at you. She was so upset. But what could I say? This time I had the chance to do what was right." Jake jumped to his feet and started to pace the small room, pulling at his hair. "I could tell her the truth, and we could work through it. Like a proper married couple would."

"But she didn't like that idea?" I asked sarcastically.

"No," sighed Jake, his shoulders slumping in defeat. "She stormed off to the toilets. To be honest, she's been accusing me of being in love with you for years. I didn't think she'd be so shocked at the truth."

"Yeah, funny that. Women don't usually like being told that their man is in love with someone else." All of a sudden, I had sympathy for Faith. Even though I still thought she was a little bit unbalanced.

"Then you told me that she was dead." Fatigue filled his voice as his head hung low. "I realized then how much she really meant to me. She couldn't be dead. I just had to find her, and everything would be okay." Jake looked up at me as he dropped to his knees on the floor. "I do love her, Alex," he said as the sobbing started. "And I wanted to make a life with her."

Tears silently fell down his cheeks, and I realized he didn't know. He didn't know that we'd found Faith, and she was okay. I jumped off my chair and quickly moved to him. Falling to my knees, I took hold of his shoulders and forced him to look at me.

"Jake. We found her. She's okay."

"What?" he asked, his eyes huge. "What? You found her?"

"Yes! Well, I didn't find her as such, but she turned up. Someone had hit her and locked her in the dub room, but she's okay." Well, she was. I wasn't sure what had happened to her when she was pulled down the stairs.

Relief swept Jake's face as he sat on his backside and buried his head in his hands. I listened as he cried and then laughed, finally moving to me and pulling me in tight for a hug.

"That's amazing news. I knew it had to be okay. I knew it."

"We still have to get out of here," I added, bursting his happiness bubble.

"We don't even know where *here* is."

"I think I do."

I'd figured out when I'd seen the photo of my twenty-first birthday. It was almost the same one I had found inside the old book of Westport. The one that was stuck in the pages telling me about the old house and the safe room the crazy mayor had installed.

"We're in a safe room." I quickly brought Jake up to speed with everything that had happened that night. "I'm sure Sam and Matt are looking for me by now." I left out the part about Faith and the stairs. I decided this wasn't a good time to bring it up with Jake. He'd only just stopped crying.

"Do you know where, exactly, the safe room is located?"

"No, but I'm guessing it's under the house and the entrance is somewhere in that room that was locked." It all made sense now. The pieces fell into place.

Jake nodded.

"You said you've tried to get out. What's stopping us?" Renewed energy surged through me.

"Two locked doors. At first, I thought there was only one, but when you were thrown in here, I heard a second door being unlocked. This door here," said Jake, moving to the metal door he'd been leaning against earlier. "And this one." He opened the door and showed me a second door. It was made of wood and looked solid. It was also locked. "There are no outside windows either."

"But we must be getting air from somewhere?"

"We are. We have some air vents. I think they're connected directly to outside as the air is cool coming in through them."

"You can't see out of them?"

"No. They're too small, and it's dark. Maybe if it was daylight we could."

"Where are they? Maybe we can make a lot of noise and get someone's attention. I'm positive Sam will be looking for me." I'm just not positive if he'd be out here looking for me.

"I tried that. Look, earlier this inside metal door was also locked. It was unlocked when you arrived."

"What do you mean?"

Jake moved to the doors to show me.

"This inside door is solid metal with a lock on both sides of the door. The outside door is timber, locked from the other side."

"Why? Wouldn't it make more sense to have the metal one on the outside?"

"I guess it gave the occupant time to quickly close the outside door as the inside one is bloody heavy, lock it and get some protection while you close and lock the inside door, making the whole room secure."

"What about ventilation? Didn't they think someone could gas them in here by putting something in the ventilation?"

"Well, if this room really was built in the 1920s, like you say it is, they probably weren't thinking of things like that," said Jake, shrugging.

I shrugged. It made sense, but it didn't help us get out.

"So this inside door was locked until I got here?"

"Yeah, I heard the outside door being opened, so I prepared to defend myself in here once this door was open. I heard the latch being thrown and waited."

"What did you prepare yourself with?" I asked, curious.

Jake blushed. "That doesn't matter."

"Yes, it does. I may need to use it. Who says whoever did this isn't coming back any second now?"

Jake looked at me and sighed. "I found a can of spray."

"What kind of spray?"

"Bug spray. I'd say whoever this all belongs to had a roach problem at one point."

I shivered, stood, and moved to look at the door Jake had his shoulder leaning against. "So, do you think we can get out of here?"

"I didn't until this metal door was unlocked, but now I'm wondering if we can ram this other door."

"It looks pretty solid," I commented.

"Yeah, it does, but the frame surrounding it doesn't."

Jake was right. The frame surrounding the door looked like it had dry rot.

"Probably the only time in my life I'm happy to see dry rot," I said, smiling.

We looked around the room for anything that might help us break a door down. Or at least away from its frame. The room contained a desk, a desk chair, and the armchair Stuart was lying in. Looking at him, I knew we had to get out of here as quickly as we could.

"Your shoulder looks nice and strong," I commented, giving Jake a look that hopefully conveyed I thought he looked like Mr. Universe. I'm not sure what he thought, but he took a step away from me.

"Ummm..." he said, eyeing the door suspiciously. To be honest, I probably had a better chance of knocking the door down, but I didn't think saying that would be a good morale booster.

"Well, do you have a better suggestion?" I asked.

The answer was obviously *no*, as he sighed and moved back into the room. "Stand back," he said, waving his arm at me.

I did as he asked and stood next to Stuart, my heart rate picking up slightly. I wasn't sure what I was more nervous about —getting caught before we got out or Jake failing and me having to have a go. "Hit the door near the frame with your shoulder," I said, encouragingly.

Jake took a deep breath and then ran at the door, his body slamming into it. I gulped as I heard the crack of the wood splitting as his body was ricocheted backward. He landed on the floor with a thud. Jake groaned as he sat himself up, rubbing his shoulder. "I think I've dislocated it," he moaned.

"Really?" My first thought was—*You don't see Gibbs from NCIS rolling around on the floor in agony after breaking down the bad guy's door*—but then I remembered he always kicks the door. *Oops.* Probably not a good time to mention that.

Instead, I moved to the door and tried to pull it open. It took a bit of force, but with the help of a whining Jake, we managed to pull it inwards, the rotten timber frame crumbling around it. We both gave a whoop of joy, overcome with emotion and gave each other a hug. Then we felt awkward as Jake hurriedly let go of me and stood back to look at the door and the dark passage beyond.

"Well," said Jake, gulping, "I say we leave Stuart here. I'm not completely sure he's okay to be moved without medical assistance, so I think we need to get help as quickly as possible and bring it back to him."

I nodded in agreement. "Yeah, okay." I promised Georgie we would find her dad and that all would be okay. I was damned well going to make sure that happened.

"I'll just check he's as comfortable as he can be, and then we'll go," continued Jake. "Stand guard on the door, and let me know if you hear anything."

I certainly wasn't going to enter the dark passage on my own, but memories of being locked in the dub room with Sam came rushing back, so I made sure I stood on the outside of the door. Not that any lock was going to keep that secure anymore. It needed a carpenter.

Jake carefully checked Stuart. The noise of the door frame splintering had woken him, and he murmured to us as Jake told him we were going for help and would be back as quickly as possible. I hated leaving him, but I knew this was the best option.

Switching my phone to flashlight, I checked my signal—still on zero, probably because we were underground—and the time, now three-thirty am. I shone the light into the passage. It was narrow, cold, and dark. It also had cockroaches. I couldn't see how long it was as my light didn't shine that far and there seemed to be no overhead bulb. Jake stepped up to me.

"Ready?" he asked.

The cockroaches were seriously creeping me out, but it was walk past them or stay here. "You bet."

I stood back and let Jake lead the way. Even though three people had been moved down that passage tonight, there still could be spiders hanging over my head. Cockroaches were bad. Spiders were worse. So, best to let Jake go first. Just in case.

With that, he moved ahead of me. I grabbed on to his belt and handed him my phone, allowing the light to lead the way.

The passage was narrow with cement walls, and I wondered how all three of us had been carried down here unconscious. Whoever was responsible was obviously very strong.

Thankfully, it wasn't very long before we reached some steps. Jake shone the light up to the top, and we saw another door. This one was much smaller, only looking like it was a meter or so high, but the hinges, the handle, and the lock all told us it was definitely a door.

My stomach clenched, and I hoped it wasn't locked from the other side.

"We don't know what's on the other side of that door," whispered Jake, turning his head toward me. "So be prepared for the worst."

I didn't like the sound of that, but I nodded and squeezed his arm reassuringly.

I heard his deep breath as he turned the light back to the steps and took the first step up.

CHAPTER 17

I held my breath as Jake touched the handle on the door at the top, and I waited to see what would happen. I heard the creak as he pushed on it and gave a silent whoop of joy. Jake flicked off the flashlight and gently pushed the door open. Not all the way—just far enough for him to have a look out. Impatience made me irritable.

"What do you see?" I whispered, standing on tiptoe, putting my head over his shoulder and trying to get a look. To do that, I'd had to virtually lay over the top of him as he squatted on the top step.

"Nothing," he hissed back, obviously not impressed with the position of my head. He then leaned his weight forward, stealthily pushing the door a little bit further open as he did so. My weight had other ideas, though. I was unprepared as he moved and fell onto him. That caused him to overbalance on his feet, and we both fell forward, the little door swinging all the way open, with us being propelled into the room. I squealed as Jake broke my fall, stopping when my full body weight squashed him like a bug, his face smashed into the timber flooring.

I heard his curse as I prayed no one was sitting in the room waiting for us.

"Get off me," he hissed. I was pretty sure he'd be pulling splinters from his nose for months.

"Sorry," I mumbled, rolling off him and looking around me. Not that I could see anything. The room was dark, too dark. "Jake, do you have my phone? We need a light."

I heard Jake roll over, the rustle of clothing, and then the relief of light. As he shone it around us, I quickly realized we were in the previously locked room in the old house. Just like I had thought we were. The only thing I hadn't figured was that the secret entrance to the safe room was hidden behind the fireplace. Humph. Smart.

"Let's hope *that* door's not locked this time," said Jake, pulling himself to standing and nodding toward the door to freedom.

I silently agreed, pushing the fireplace back into place in the hope that if anyone came back here, they wouldn't know right away we'd escaped.

As we made our way into the lounge room, my heart pounded with excitement that we'd made it out of the room and were heading back toward the station. Hopefully straight into the arms of Sam. Even if he didn't want me there, I figured I'd been through enough tonight to deserve one little treat.

Jake moved through the lounge and into the kitchen. As he turned the corner, retracing our steps from earlier this evening, he stopped, cursing loudly as he did so.

Because there, looking eerie in the glow of my flashlight, staring back at us, was a face. Sally.

I screamed. Jake screamed, and Sally screamed. I'm not sure which one of us was the most surprised.

"Arghhhh," I screamed. "Sally, you scared the shit out of me," I yelled, putting my hand on my chest in the hope it would stop the heart attack starting.

"Well, you scared the shit out of me," she yelled back. "What are you doing here? Everyone is looking for you!"

"Everyone?" I asked.

"Well, Sam and Matt are. Mostly everybody else is asleep."

Humph.

"Oh my goodness. I can't believe I found you! I've been so worried," she said, emotion causing her voice to crack.

"What are you doing here?" I asked, as Jake stepped around her and headed for the door.

"I was helping Sam and Matt look for you. Where are you going?" she asked Jake.

"Out."

"But this way is out," she said, pointing to the back door.

"Oh. I was just going the way we went earlier."

Personally, I didn't care which door we took. I just wanted to get out of here as quickly as possible.

"So, what happened to you?" she asked, following Jake.

I followed them both, giving her the short version of events as we all made our way out of the house and into the cool early morning air. The clouds from the earlier storm had moved out, and the partial moon was now bathing the wet grass in limited light. I couldn't tell you how cold I was. Adrenaline seemed to be helping me forget about that.

I was just telling Sally how we escaped from the locked room when she stepped closer to Jake, swung her handbag, and hit him hard across the back of the head. I had no idea what was in her bag, but Jake dropped to the dirt, the light from my phone dying as it landed next to him.

What the...?

"Sally! What did you do that for?" I asked, running next to him.

"He had to be stopped before he got too far," she explained. She moved to stand next to him.

"What?" I asked, completely confused, as she grabbed Jake's feet and started to pull him backward toward the house.

"I'm sorry," she whispered to him as she moved. "I'm sorry, Jake. But this is for your own good. Don't worry," she said to me. "He'll be fine. I didn't hit him that hard. Alex, there's a gate. Open it, will you?" she commanded. The meek and mild Sally from earlier was now gone, replaced with a woman who seemed strong and in control.

"No!" I yelled. "I won't open it."

My mind flicked to Wes and how he'd died from a blow to the head. Was Jake okay? *And what the hell was Sally doing?*

She dropped Jake's feet and looked at me. "Really?" she asked.

I shook my head as I moved to Jake, checking to see if he was still breathing, my own breath coming out in short, sharp spurts. I was fighting the desire to hyperventilate.

I gave a sigh of relief as I realized he was still breathing, but I knew that when he regained consciousness he was going to be severely pissed off as he now had mud up his nose from being dragged backward through it.

My mind raced through scenarios of what I should do next. It was having trouble comprehending Sally. My intuition definitely let me down on this one. I hurriedly looked around me, checking to see how far I could run before she caught me and hit me like she did Jake. And why did she hit him anyway? Was she the one who'd been hurting everyone tonight?

I spun to look at her. The only light we had was coming from the moon, and that wasn't great. But in it, I could see that Sally looked slightly deranged. Her earlier neatness had been replaced with messy hair and dirty clothes. I hadn't noticed that earlier tonight. Probably because I'd been so preoccupied with finding Jake and Stuart, I hadn't looked at anybody properly.

But why hadn't I? I was one of the few who knew a murderer was among us. Why hadn't I been looking closer at people? I smashed my forehead with my fists, frustrated with myself. But then, nobody else had looked at her either. Sally was a sweetheart. She always had been. She looked after her sick mother. She used to bring us all cake on our birthdays. She always organized secret Santa. She didn't hit people!

"Look, Alex, we can't leave him here," she said to me calmly. "Grab his arms, and then he won't have to be dragged through the mud. I don't like doing that to him." She placed her hands on her hips and looked at me, almost pleading. Panic bubbled up inside me as a few of the pieces fell into place.

I looked back toward the main building, assessing the distance. I had to first get around the building, and then I reckoned it to be a good few hundred meters to the station. Could I make that? And did I want to leave Jake alone with her? Probably not, but that wouldn't bring help to us. Jake and Stuart needed help, and I could bet my last dollar that Sally wouldn't be offering any. And unless someone was out here looking for us, no one would hear my screams for help, but what the hell? It couldn't hurt, right?

I took a deep breath and opened my mouth, allowing all the emotion from tonight to propel my voice as far as it would go.

"Help!" I screamed over and over again.

The mountain and the valley below it gave my voice an echo, and as I heard my own voice come back to me, I screamed again. I took off at a run for the main building. I didn't know if I could make it, but I guessed the fight-or-flight reaction thing had kicked in.

I didn't get too far, only to the other side of the house. It seemed that all the weight Sally had lost had definitely paid off. She caught up with me quickly, grabbing my arm and pulling me to a stop.

"Alex! *Stop!*" she yelled. "You're giving me a headache!"

I wriggled in an attempt to free myself from her and swatted her with my free hand. She pulled me backward toward her and put both arms around me, holding me tight.

When I was a kid, my dad and I had wrestled a lot. I was known as the wiggle worm, because I could wiggle my body so much that eventually he would lose his grip. And that's what happened with Sally. She lost her hold on me.

I didn't need another opportunity. I took off at a run across the car park, heading toward the main building, dodging and weaving every attempt she made to catch me. What I forgot about, though, was the pothole in the concrete.

My high-heeled pump caught the edge of it, causing me to go over on my ankle. I screamed at the pain shooting up my leg as I fell to the ground.

Sally caught up with me, lifting me under the arms and dragging me up. When she had me far enough, she fireman-lifted me over her shoulder and marched me back to the house. I was shocked at her strength.

I tried to get her to drop me, but she was a quick learner. Her grip was very tight. So tight, I could hardly breathe.

My heart pounded loudly in my ears as she walked around the back of the building, past Jake, who lay motionless on the grass, and into the house.

I cried as she stomped through the kitchen and lounge and back to the room with the secret entrance to the safe room without breaking a sweat. I didn't want to go back in there. If I did, I didn't think I would get back out.

She moved to the fireplace and used her free hand to open the secret door. She then attempted to get both of us into the small opening. Only I wasn't having that. I spread my legs wide and strong. She cursed and tried to ram me into the doorway. I felt the pain shoot up my leg. I wasn't sure if my ankle was broken from my fall or just sprained. Either way, the pain was excruciating.

But it didn't matter. I wasn't going back into that room. No way. Nuh-unh. It was like trying to get a square peg into a small round hole. It wasn't happening.

Sally screamed with frustration and threw me on the floor. "My God, you're an annoying cow!" she yelled as my head bounced off the boards.

I cried against the pain, but I sat up quickly, wanting to face my opponent at all times, even though I'd never have picked it to be Sally. My eyes had adjusted to the dark, and I could make her out quite clearly. "Why did I *ever* want to be like you?" she screamed.

I scurried on my backside to the wall farthest away from her.

"Do you have any idea what I've had to do over the years to be like you?" she continued.

I eyed the exit, shuffling that little bit closer to it. I remembered Stuart had left the key in the outside of the door. If I could get out there while she was distracted, I could lock her in. Even though I knew Stuart was in there too, there didn't seem to be too much I could do about that. I hoped she would be so mad at me for locking her in, she would forget about him. All I needed was to keep her distracted long enough to get to the door without her noticing.

"W…what…ha…have you had to…to do?" I asked.

Damn. I'd hoped my voice would sound a lot stronger than that. I guessed an office job was all I was ever cut out for.

Sally spun around, facing me. "The correct question, Alex, is *why* do I want to be like you?"

That was actually a very good question. "W…why do you want to be like me?" I asked. Wow, I was sounding stronger already. I only stuttered once that time.

"Do you know what I had to do to make people notice me? How many bloody birthdays I've had to remember or how many cakes I've bought? Hundreds, that's how many. How many have you bought, Alex? But it didn't matter, did it? Jake noticed you anyway. He never noticed me."

I was stunned by her statement. "Yes, he did! I remember him helping you with your mum. He used to go to your house and mow the grass whenever you needed it."

"Oh yes, Jake was my best friend. And if it wasn't for you, things would have been very different. Mum always told me so."

I shuffled a little bit closer to the door.

"As far as Jake was concerned, it was always you. It still is. Poor Faith. Even though I did do my best to try to get rid of her tonight. Personally, I can't stand the woman."

My heart stuttered at her words.

She laughed. "I didn't actually mean to get rid of her though. I never set out tonight to do that. That was kind of an accident." Sally sighed. "I nearly bloody died when she turned up later in the studio. I was sure she was dead after I hit her."

"You hit Faith?" I asked, moving another millimeter closer to the door.

"Yes. I walked into the toilets, and she was in there. I was going to quickly leave again, but I heard her talking on the phone complaining about you, so I stopped and listened. Man, did she go on!" Sally scoffed at the memory. "She was convinced Jake was still in love with you. Got to admit, I think she was right. Which was actually good for me. Anyway, I got a bit caught up in what she was saying and didn't hear her open the door. She stepped out of the cubicle and saw me. If I hadn't been dressed as you at the time, it wouldn't have mattered, but I did the only thing I could do. I grabbed the vase on the counter and hit her with it. She's a lightweight. Didn't take much."

"You...you were the one running around dressed as me?"

"Yeah, that was me."

"Why?" I asked, stunned yet curious.

"Another good question," she commented, moving toward me.

She squatted in front of me and grabbed a handful of my hair. Well, I was glad I was being a good student.

"But what do you want to know the most? Why I dressed as you tonight or why I dress as you at all?"

She leaned close and smelled my hair. Goose bumps broke out on every millimeter of my skin as it crawled under her touch.

I took a deep, calming breath and replied, "I don't mind. You choose. Whatever story you want to tell the most is fine by me." Sally laughed, dropping my hair and moving away from me.

"That's one of the things I've always liked about you, Alex. You have a weird sense of humor."

Good to know I was amusing her.

"Okay, I'll tell you, but it's a long story."

Good, the longer she talked about herself, the more time I had to scoot closer to the door and the more time Sam and Matt had to find me. I also had my fingers crossed that Jake would regain consciousness and go for help. Sally seemed to have forgotten all about him.

"Before I tell you, though, I just need to go and check on Jake." Damn. She stood and moved to the door. "Now, don't go anywhere, will you? I won't be long." With that, she closed and locked the door behind her.

———

WHILST SHE WAS GONE, I jumped to my feet and checked the window to see if it would open. It wouldn't. The timber frame was painted shut. At some point in time, the glass had been replaced with the opaque glass you find in a bathroom window. That prevented anybody from seeing in, but it wouldn't stop me from smashing it.

I looked around the room for anything that would help me smash the glass. I considered throwing myself through it, but I'd check for anything more suitable first. That glass was extra tough, and with my luck, I'd cut a main artery on the way out and bleed to death before I even made it for help.

Unfortunately, the room was empty. I remembered there was probably something in the safe room that would help, but did I have enough time to get down there and back before Sally returned? I didn't know, but I had to try.

I quickly moved to the fireplace. When I'd pushed it shut earlier, I hadn't noticed how to reopen it. The room was dark, and as my phone had died outside when Jake dropped it, I had nothing to help me.

I used my fingers to feel around the fire surround, hoping to find something that would open the secret door. It felt like I was moving slowly, even though I knew I was moving the fastest I had ever moved in my life.

Thankfully, I found a small divot in the timber which I pushed my fingers into and pulled. The fireplace moved. I pulled it all the way open and almost fell down the stairs in my hurry to get back to the safe room. I ran down the short passageway and into the room. Stuart was still lying in the armchair, so I gave him a very quick check over as I looked around wildly for anything I could use to break a window. His pulse was weak, but it was still there. Thank God.

I spotted a small timber stool pushed under the desk, grabbed at it, and turned to go back the way I came. Only instead of moving back down the passageway, I stopped as I came face to face with Sally. Damn. I hadn't been quick enough.

CHAPTER 18

"*I* had a feeling you'd try something," she said, her tone suggesting she wasn't impressed with my antics.

She snatched the chair from me and moved farther into the room, closing the metal door behind her. Oh God! Now what would I do?

Sally took some calming breaths and forced me backward, closer to the desk. She pulled up the desk chair. "Sit!" she demanded.

I did as requested.

Turning, she looked at the walls. "I found this room years ago," she said, losing herself in her memories. "When life got too hard, I used to like to come here and be alone. No one ever knew I was even in here. I was safe. I could do whatever I wanted, and nobody would ever know. A couple of times over the years, I thought I might be caught, so I had the locks fitted to the outside of these doors so nobody could get in. I always managed to steer Stuart away from it. Because nobody knew the room existed, nobody ever went looking for it. It became my secret. As you can see," she said, spreading her arms wide and sweeping them around the room, "I made good use of it."

I followed her eyes as she scanned the room. She picked the blanket up, off of Stuart and rubbed it between her fingers.

"I knew where we were," I said.

Sally's face paled as she spun to look at me. "What?" she spat.

"When I woke up in here with Jake and Stuart, I knew where we were."

"How did you know?"

"I remembered the book."

"What book are you talking about?" she asked quietly, sitting deadly still.

"The old book about Westport. Sam found it in the studio, and I read it while I was waiting for him. It told of the rumor of this room and how the crazy mayor had it built."

Sally stared at me, her eyes huge with a hint of insanity. I guessed this room was only useful to crazy people.

She turned to the desk and immediately started lifting papers. Haphazardly, she threw them aside as she hunted for something. Only once everything was scattered across the floor did she turn back to me, fear in her eyes.

"That book was mine!" she yelled. "It was mine! I found it. *It belongs to me!*" Okay, so she didn't like sharing her books. "You shouldn't have been reading it."

"But...but it was in the studio for everyone to read," I explained. I was starting to wish I'd kept my mouth shut about the damned book. She was obviously very attached.

"Who put it there?"

I shook my head. I had no idea. She pulled at her blonde ponytail, releasing her hair from its band. It fell rattily around her shoulders, making her appear even more like a crazy person.

She started to pace backward and forward, muttering to herself. I couldn't make out the sentences, but a few words caught my attention. Like *I made a mistake... they'll come...can't be found... worked too hard*, things like that. When she stopped pacing, she looked at me.

"Why can't the book be in the studio?" I asked, quietly hoping to calm her down. Really, though, I should have thought before opening my mouth. If I had, I probably would have changed the subject.

"Because, Alex, if certain people read it, they will find my secret, and all my hard work will be for nothing." She picked up the teddy bear that Jake had given me and started to once again pace the small area. "I needed to be you. That's what Mum said. Be like Alex then Jake will notice you," she said, looking around at all the possessions that had once been mine, completely lost in her own thoughts.

I eyed the door. The desk chair had wheels, so I rolled it a few millimeters toward it. "If you try to run for it again, Alex, I'll have to kill Stuart. You don't want that, do you?"

I stopped. No, I didn't. Tears stung my eyes as fatigue and guilt swept through me. Guilt that Stuart wouldn't be here if it weren't for me.

"I was going to tell you a story, wasn't I?" she asked, pulling herself from her memories, much calmer than a few minutes ago. "Before I got Jake, I was going to tell you why I had to become you."

She sighed and sat on the edge of the desk, pushing the bear under her arm and picking up a photo as she moved.

"See this picture?" she asked, turning it to me.

It was of a young Jake and me sitting on the beach. We'd spent a lot of time there when we were together. This time, Jake had his arm around my shoulders and was kissing my temple, his body language oozing the love he had for me. I wore my red bikini, smiling happily, snuggling into him as the glow from the sunset lit up our faces.

Even though the photo hadn't been taken front-on, it was actually a really good photo. One I would have proudly displayed at the time. However, until now, I didn't even know that it existed.

I remembered the afternoon it was taken. Jake had just told me for the first time that he loved me. After the sun had set and darkness had enveloped us, we'd made love on the beach, and the world had been perfect. We'd both thought we were alone.

"This," said Sally, pulling me from my memory, "is where it all started."

Nausea rolled in my stomach as I once again looked at every photo on her walls. She'd been watching me for years.

"Jake was meant to be mine. Mum loved him. She used to say to me, 'Sally, you need to marry that boy. He will look after you.' But once you came along, he didn't even want to know me anymore. At first, I planned to get rid of you, but when I saw this photo, I knew I had to change my tactic. He loved you, and even if you died, he would still love you. So instead of killing you, I decided I should *become* you. I had it all worked out. I figured becoming your friend would get me in closer, so I started the whole birthday thing. Mum always told me you could catch more flies with honey than with vinegar. So I became sweet Sally, the girl who did everything for everyone but who nobody really appreciated."

She stood and paced again.

"I started following you and Jake, taking a few photos when I thought I needed them, stealing a few of your things when you weren't looking. You never once noticed me though. All you were interested in was Jake. Not that I blamed you for that. He was all I ever saw when I looked at the two of you. But then Faith turned up and nearly ruined everything. When she seduced Jake, I thought all my hard work had gone to waste. But I could see that no, it hadn't. He may be with her, but it was you he still loved. So I *still* had to become you."

I wanted to say that none of this made sense, but I saw the crazy in her eyes and figured it didn't matter what I thought. It wouldn't change anything.

"What about Stacey and Dean?" I asked quietly. "Did you do anything to them?"

I might have been out of my depth here, but I knew the longer I could keep her talking, the more chance I had of getting both Stuart and myself out of here alive. I just hadn't figured out how yet.

"Yeah, I didn't mean to hurt Dean. Stacey was different though. I wanted to make my teeth crooked like yours, so I discussed it with her. She got a bit nosy and even accused me of having a mental problem." Sally scoffed. "All she had to do was write a referral to an orthodontist so that I could get some braces made to change my teeth. That was all. But no. She said she remembered me from school. How I would get obsessed with someone, and did I remember the girl in the eighth grade? Of course I bloody remembered her. She was gorgeous. Your hair reminds me of hers, Alex. It was all shiny and blonde. Only her eyes were greener than yours. Other than that, the likeness is uncanny. Look, I'll show you a picture."

With that, she turned to the desk and pulled out an old school photo from an album, showing me a photo of a young teenage girl. And I could definitely see the similarities.

"What happened to her?" I asked.

I knew the answer before I even asked the question. I recognized the girl's photo from the news, but I wanted to know if Sally was involved.

"Well, I got a bit carried away one day. She agreed to meet me after school, and I may have accidentally killed her. You know, I didn't mean to or anything. Anyway, I panicked and got rid of her."

"But didn't the old butcher get found guilty of her murder?"

"Yes, but he didn't murder her. He just went to jail for it. I got lucky with that because he was a bit of a perv and always watching her. It was *so* creepy."

Did she not see the irony in that?

"Anyway, back to Stacey. She got me so mad that day going over old times like that. She said I had mental issues. *I do not have mental issues!* Anyway, after I hit her, I still wanted your dental records and my referral, so I quickly copied it all and got out of there. I think I may have hit the wrong button, though, cuz it appears I wiped everything from her servers. Oops."

My stomach flipped, and I wondered if I were going to throw up as the crazy in Sally's eyes shone bright.

I put my hand over my mouth, willing the nausea to stop.

"Oh my God, Alex. You're not going to throw up, are you?"

Tears stung as I took some deep breaths, but Stacey filled my mind. Only when I got some control back did I pluck up the courage to ask, "Did you break into my apartment?"

"Yes, of course I did. When everything here was being organized for tonight, I saw an old photo of you wearing that WTN T-shirt. I never had one of those. I needed it. I remember you wore it all the time. However, your nosy neighbour, Dean, caught me climbing over the railing, so I hit him as well. A bit too hard. I really don't know my own strength sometimes." Sally laughed. "I used to be so weak and fat but not anymore. I'm strong now. It was part of my plan. I needed to be strong. It helped me get rid of the bodies."

"I still don't get it," I said.

"What don't you get, Alex?" she asked patiently.

"All of it!" I yelled, hysteria bubbling fiercely. "Is this about Jake? Because if so, why didn't you just tell him how you felt? Maybe he would have loved you."

"I did tell him," she replied, her patience quickly disappearing. "One night, I was in the production booth, and I overheard him talking to Brent about how he was going to tell you he loved you. When Brent left, I plucked up the courage to tell Jake how I felt. He said he could only love you."

Bloody Jake.

"When I followed him that night and took this picture, I knew what I had to do. It was simple. I had to become you."

"But what about Faith? He married her. *She's* the one sleeping with him every night, not *me!*"

"Calm down. Geez," said Sally. "Don't overreact."

I dropped my head between my knees, trying desperately to suck in air, willing the hysteria to settle itself down.

"Listen, when Rachel arrived at the station a few months ago and suggested tonight's reunion, I kind of had a plan." She sighed. "But I had lost sight of the prize, Alex. Jake. He was the reason I did all of this. I didn't *really* want to be like you. I just *needed* to be like you. Now I know he married Faith, and I know the two of you were so long ago, but I also figured that after tonight, that marriage wouldn't last. He would see you again and remember how he felt. Then all I had to do was get rid of you somehow and step into your shoes. Easy. And if it didn't happen that way, it was okay. There would be another opportunity. I'm a patient woman. I would wait an eternity for him if I have to."

She threw the photo she'd been holding onto the desk.

"I dressed as you tonight to see how Jake would feel when he saw me. To test the waters so to speak. Would he notice any differences? Other than the teeth, of course." She laughed.

I shook my head, my blood pressure causing a monster headache. I also gave in to my desire to throw up. Thankfully, the wastepaper bin was close by and caught the contents of my stomach. I saw Sally's eyes widen, and her skin turn green.

"Oh God! Don't do that! I can handle anything except vomit. It makes me want to throw up too."

Sally groaned and moved behind Stuart, who had started to stir. At least I knew he was still alive. She waved her hand in front of her face, attempting to get some air. But the smell was strong, and she quickly moved to the metal door, opening it and moving into the passageway.

210

When she'd calmed herself, she moved back into the room, leaving the door open. *I should have thrown up earlier.*

"That's the second time tonight that you've done that to me," she said, anger simmering in her voice. "When I hit Faith in the toilets earlier—which, by the way, felt *so* good—I was going to take her outside and throw her off the mountain so it would look like she slipped and fell, hitting her head on the way down. But you had to come in, didn't you? I'd forgotten how clumsy you were, which was good for me because when I heard you drop goodness knows what and heard you cursing, I had time to push Faith onto the toilet and jump up into the ceiling cavity with the vase. I've watched you from up there before, so I knew how to do it. When you fainted, I couldn't help but roll my eyes. When you came to and threw up, it took everything I had not to do the same. I was stuck in the ceiling, hiding from you, and I very nearly vomited all over you."

Seriously, I was never entering a public toilet ever again.

I sat up and death-stared Sally, waving my bin full of vomit closer to her. She took a step backward.

"Did you really lock Faith in the dub room?" I asked, stalling her as a plan came together in my mind—a plan that involved this bin.

"Yes," she sighed. "Like I said, I wanted to get rid of her properly, but do you have any idea how many people were wandering around the bloody station?"

Yeah, I did. About fifty.

"The dub room was as far as I could get. I figured she was safe in there for a while as I'm one of the few who have keys for that room. And I thought she was dead. I guess that should be a lesson to me. Check twice to make sure your dead body isn't breathing. Don't worry though, Alex. I'll make sure you're dead before I get rid of you. Of course, when I set out tonight, I never planned to kill anyone. All I wanted was for Jake to realize he still loved you, which is why I got Rachel to put him and Faith in your group.

When he saw the two of you together, he would realize she wasn't the one for him."

"You got Rachel to do that?"

"Yeppidee. It was easy. She loves drama, and as soon as I suggested it, she jumped on it. She's such a cow," said Sally, hatred in her eyes. "I'm getting her back though. You see, like I said, I never meant to kill anybody. All I needed people to do was mind their own bloody business and not stick their noses into mine. But anyway, shit happens. 'Always clean up after yourself, Sally,' Mum would say. So," continued Sally, the joy apparent on her face, "I'm setting Rachel to take the blame." With this, she burst into peals of laughter.

"It looks like you were trying to frame me!" I said, horrified.

"No, I wouldn't do that. Why did you think I was doing that? I need you to be a good girl for Jake to fall back in love with you."

"Well, you marked everyone with a butterfly, and I had the damned butterfly headband. Plus, Faith told everyone I'd hit her."

"Oh yeah, the butterflies. I forgot about those. But they were to set Rachel up, not you." Sally looked at me like I was an idiot. "I remembered you have one tattooed on your shoulder. See, you're marked with a butterfly just like the others! Rachel also marked you when she agreed to include my sketch design for the head-band in your invite."

"I don't have a butterfly tattoo," I said.

"Yes, you do. It's on your shoulder."

"No, I don't. That's a dragonfly."

Sally stopped dead and looked at me, her eyes wide. "Really?"

"Yep."

"Shit. Oh well, it doesn't really matter. Rachel made the head-band marking you, and I've built a really good case for her killing those people as well. She's insane, and I have a room full of people who will back me up on that one."

She had a good point there. Everyone did think Rachel was

insane. I suddenly had sympathy for Rachel for the very first time in my life. I looked down into the bin still in my hands.

I stretched my arms and wiggled my butt on the chair, hopefully making Sally think I was just adjusting my position. Which was partially true. I *was* adjusting my position. Just a little bit so that I could get much better coverage when I threw the bin's contents all over her. I was hoping that her reflex instinct to vomit would give me enough time to escape. The only downside to my plan so far was that Stuart was between me and Sally. I just hoped he would forgive me. Sally noticed me looking at Stuart.

"I didn't mean to hurt Stuart," she said, remorse affecting her voice for the first time. "I actually like him. He was always nice to me."

Stuart was nice to everyone and didn't deserve any of this. Actually, I didn't think anyone deserved any of this.

"He found my hiding place. He caught me leaving it when he came to unlock that door for you. He confronted me and was going to tell everyone. I couldn't have that happen. But anyway, I didn't kill him. I didn't hit him hard enough."

"What are you going to do with him after you kill me?"

"Hmmm, not sure yet. But I'll figure it out. I always do."

"What's your mum going to think about all of this when you get caught?"

"First of all, I'm not going to get caught. Second of all, Mum died years ago."

"What? But...but you said earlier she was well."

"She is well. She's sitting in a Royal Doulton bowl next to my bedside. I talk to her every night and make sure she's okay. It's me she's worried about, but soon she won't need to worry anymore. I'll have Jake, and he'll take care of me just like she wanted."

Okay, a few things were starting to make more sense. I could see how Sally had flipped a switch and lost the plot.

"But why not tell everyone your mum died?"

"No one cared, Alex. I'm not you. I don't have a bestie or a boyfriend. And I don't have any family. Mum was it for me."

I saw the sadness in her eyes. It didn't stay there long, the crazy slipping straight back into its place.

"Wes knew, didn't he?" I asked, adjusting my feet. "That's why you killed him."

"No, Wes was an idiot. I only killed him because he was going to get the police before I could get rid of Faith. I didn't have time to set it up to look like Rachel had killed her, and anyway, no one would have believed that because she and Rachel were besties. Well, at least Faith thought they were. Truth was, Rachel was just feeding her a heap of lies about you and Jake."

My stomach clenched, and I wondered if I was going to add to my bin.

"Of course, killing Wes meant I had to quickly stop all communications to the police. Luckily, cell signal sucks up here at the best of times—the storm just helped. But I still had to make sure the landline was down. And then I remembered the radios. God, killing someone is hard work. You have to think of *everything*!"

Sally moved to the desk and picked up a photo of Jake, her back turned to me. "I love this photo," she said, her voice softening. I stood slowly, my bin at the ready. "I love his eyes. I could get lost in them forever." She sighed as I took a deep breath. "I know this is all going to work out. It has to because I can't live without him. Alex…" she said, turning as she spoke.

But I didn't wait to hear what she was going to say. I saw my opportunity and took it, launching the contents of my bin—and I'll add that was quite a bit—at her. I hit my target dead on. As it ran down her face and into her open mouth, I dropped the bin and ran for the open door. I heard her retching over my own blood pounding in my ears as I said a silent prayer for Stuart and ran into the darkness.

I didn't stop running. The passage was short, and I made it to the steps quickly, but I could hear Sally coughing and moving behind me. I didn't stop to see how close she was. Instead, I pushed the secret door open and launched myself into the room, slamming the fireplace closed behind me.

My ankle throbbed as I sprinted across the room, pulling the door open. My intention was to close and lock it behind me and then run to the station building to get some help. I needed it before she took her revenge on me out on Stuart. Guilt coursed through my veins as I stepped through the door.

Only I didn't get as far as closing it. Instead, I felt the punch as I heard the crack of my nose breaking, blood gushing, and pain shooting across my face. I dropped to my knees, shocked and winded, as Faith stood over me, laughing.

CHAPTER 19

I screamed against the pain, angry that Faith had stopped my escape.

"I knew you were up to something," she yelled. "I knew you'd be with Jake. Is this your secret hideaway? Your love nest?" she screamed. Her switch had flipped also.

She was hysterical. Well, that was okay. I was pretty close to it myself. I could hear Sally's footsteps coming up the timber steps leading out of the secret passage. I had to get up and lock that door before she made it out.

I stood, ignoring the pain. The blood was a bit different though. Nausea rolled and my limited vision blurred as I tried to stand. I put my hand on the doorframe and moved my feet under me. The world spun as my blood ran over my lips. I had to ignore all of it. I had to close that door.

Sally screamed as she pushed the fireplace out. I screamed and stood, grabbing at the door handle, ready to pull it closed. Faith screamed and punched me again, this time in the temple.

"Don't touch that door, Alex!" Faith screamed. "Jake's in there. I know it!"

I batted her arm away as Sally emerged into the room. But

Faith was stronger than I gave her credit for. She launched herself at me, pushing me off my feet and into the room, my head hitting the floor with a thud. The world spun as the nausea once again rolled. I gave in to the desire and emptied my stomach, this time all over the timber floor.

Sally rushed at me but slipped, landing on her back. I wanted to run for the door, but Faith was blocking it. Instead, I launched myself at Sally, jumping on top of her and grabbing her hair. I then slammed her backward into the floor, banging her head as hard as I could, all emotion from tonight building to a hatred for this woman. Someone had to stop her, and it may as well be me.

Faith screamed at me, running and knocking me off Sally. She really had to stop doing that.

Sally was dazed but managed to get herself up, laughing manically as she did so.

"Oh Alex, you surprise me," she yelled as she ran at me.

Faith rolled off me but not before I managed to say, "She killed Jake."

As Sally grabbed at me, pulling me to my feet, I heard Faith's voice, "What the…?"

I needed to say the words again, but Sally had her hands around my throat. She was strong. As she tightened her grip, it became difficult to breathe.

She lifted me off my feet, her laughter ringing in my ears. I panicked, kicking out with my feet, trying my best to contact her somewhere it would hurt, my fingers digging into hers as I did so. But it was no use. She slammed me against the wall and held me up high, her grip tightening with every last breath I took.

As the world turned black, I heard Faith's scream, her footsteps on the floor, and Sally's hold on me stopped.

I fell to the floor, pain shooting up my leg from my ankle, twisting as it hit the ground. As I desperately sucked in air, I gave in to the desire to cry.

Honestly, I didn't know why it had taken so long.

I could hear Faith's uncontrollable screams and Sally's cries for her to stop. I didn't know what to do. Faith wasn't as strong as Sally, but she did have rage on her side. If I could get to my feet, I could help Faith hold Sally.

I wiped the blood from my nose with my jacket sleeve and attempted to stand. Only my foot wouldn't hold my weight. As soon as I tried to take a step, I fell back to the floor. But I needed to stand. Faith couldn't hold Sally forever. I dragged myself back up as I heard Faith punching her. Judging by Sally's screams, I'd have said Faith's aim was perfect. My plan was to go to the next room and find something to hit Sally with. It seemed to be working well for her, so why not use her own tactic against her?

I hopped across the room, panic screaming through me, and slammed into a large, hard body. I screamed as arms wrapped around me and held me tight. It was only as I saw the flashlight scan the room, its beams lighting the person holding me, that I realized I was in the arms of Sam. All was going to be okay.

MATT RUSHED INTO THE ROOM, pulling Faith off Sally. He was followed by Brent, Marty, and Jake. It took all of them to hold the women. Faith was still screaming and crying that Jake was dead. Sally was screaming and crying that Faith was a maniac. I was just crying. But I did manage to tell Sam that Stuart needed help and where he'd been hidden. Thankfully, Sam and Matt had come equipped with some serious flashlights, so Sam sat me gently on the floor and, with the help of Matt, moved into the secret passageway.

When Faith saw Jake she crumbled, falling to the floor hysterically crying. "I...I...thought you...you were dead!" she cried as he cradled her like a baby.

"Sssh," he said, soothingly. "I'm okay. It's all okay now."

He looked over to me, and in the glow of the flashlight, I

could see his concern. "Alex, are you okay?" he asked, not letting go of Faith.

I nodded. "Yes." Even though I didn't feel okay.

My ankle throbbed. I was positive my nose was broken. I was scared and alone. Tears filled behind my lashes. As they spilled over, mixing with everything pouring from my nose, the sobbing started. Faith matched my sobs, her own drowning out any noise coming from either Sally or myself. I prayed that Jake would get her the mental help she needed.

Brent and Marty were both sitting on Sally, holding her down so that she couldn't move. I had a moment of thinking I hoped she could breathe, but then I thought I really couldn't care less. I *then* thought what a bad person I was, making my sobbing kick up a notch. Before long, I was having trouble breathing. It was only as Sam stood over me that I attempted to get a grip.

"Geez," I heard him say, unsure what to do with me. "That's a lot of liquid coming from someone so small."

I had to laugh. He squatted in front of me.

"How...how's Stuart?" I managed to ask, wiping my nose on my jacket sleeve again. I was going to throw this jacket away as soon as I could.

"He's alive. He's lost a lot of blood, and his pulse is slow, but the police helicopter is on its way. Matt is going to stay with him until they get here."

The crying started again, relief that help was finally here. Sam pulled me into him. As the sound of his heart beat strong in my ear, I finally let go of the anxiety that I'd been feeling all night.

WITH THE HELP OF SAM, I made it outside. Daylight was peeking over the horizon, giving it a warm glow. It wouldn't be too much longer before the sun would be joining it. The wind picked up as the sound of the helicopter whooped through the air, and lights flicked across the grass. The helipad hadn't been kept in great condition, but it was good enough for the helicopter to land, and before we knew it, Sergeant Ed Helms was running across the grass. Sam stood and moved toward him. I saw him point to the house, and they both disappeared inside.

Jake came and sat next to me. "How are you feeling?" he asked.

"I've been better. You?"

"Got one hell of headache." He smiled down at me.

"How did you guys come to find us?" I asked him.

"Well, I woke up with Sam slapping my face and yelling at me. Turns out both he and Matt had been quite worried about you when you weren't in the studio like you were supposed to be. So they went looking."

"Where's Faith?"

"I took her inside to sit with Georgie until the police want to talk to her. She was freezing but unhurt."

"She's got one hell of a punch," I commented, feeling my nose, which seemed to be a few sizes bigger than an hour or so earlier.

"Yeah, I heard about that. Sorry. She thought you pushed her down the stairs and left to shack up with me. She had a bit of rage pent up against you."

No kidding.

"Jake, you will get her some help won't you? I'm sorry because I know you love her, but she has some serious issues."

He looked back at me, his expression one of concern. "I know. She has been getting help for her jealousy issue, but I think it's time to get her more serious help. Are you pressing charges against her?"

I thought about the implication of that for a moment, about what that would do to Jake.

"If I don't, will you promise to get her psychologically evaluated?"

He nodded. "I'm going to do that anyway."

"Okay then. I'll do my best to smooth over it when I speak to the police."

We sat in silence for a few minutes, Jake wanting to say something but not being able to find the words. Eventually, he spoke up.

"I'm sorry, Alex. For everything. For leaving you all those years ago without an explanation, for what I did with Faith, for hurting you. But most of all, I'm sorry about Sally."

I'd filled Sam, Matt, and Jake in about what happened after Sally had knocked Jake unconscious. No one had suspected her. Which actually made me feel a little bit better, as I wasn't the only one.

"Sally wasn't your fault, Jake. Well, I suppose technically she was as it was you she was in love with. It was because of you she became obsessed with being me, and because of you she killed people to do it. But what *happened* isn't your fault. She's insane."

He reached out and put his hand on my leg, squeezing gently. He then leaned over and gently kissed my forehead. Familiarity swept over me. But that was all I felt. As he pulled away, I looked up at him in the early morning light and smiled. Jake was finally out of my system, and I was out of his. "Go and find your wife. Have a good life with her. She may be psycho, but she loves you."

"I love her too."

"Good. Be happy, Jake."

"You too," he said, pushing himself to standing.

"I'll do my best."

As he walked away toward the main building and his wife, the sun broke the horizon, orange beams shooting across the sky. I felt the warmth touch my skin as Sam moved to sit next to me.

"What happened?" I asked, referring to the police.

"Well, Sally has been arrested and is now in handcuffs, and they've called for a medivac chopper to come and get Stuart. He's okay, but he needs a hospital. When it gets here, they'll stretcher him out and then probably come looking for you. Dawn's down there with them at the moment, ordering everyone around and telling them what they should be doing." Sam smiled.

"I guess it's her way of doing something."

"Yeah."

Silence filled the air between us.

"That's some wall down there," said Sam finally, referring to Sally's artwork.

"Yep. Creepy, hey?"

"That's quite a history of you and Jake."

"Sure is."

Sam shifted uncomfortably, pushing his back to the wall of the old house. "So. You and Jake."

I waited for the rest of the sentence. When it didn't come, I said, "What about us?"

"Are you...you know?"

I took a deep breath. "No." I wanted to *you know* with Sam, but I wasn't sure if he wanted the same thing. "Jake and Faith love each other. She's a bit messed up, but he promised me he would get her help. Hopefully then, they'll sort their crap out."

Sam nodded as the sun rose an inch higher, bathing his face in soft light. I sucked in my breath at the beauty. I'm not sure whether that was the sunrise or Sam. Both were stunning in my eyes.

The cool, crisp morning air soaked through my thin jacket as the morning dew glittered in the light, and not for the first time, I wished I'd brought a warmer one with me.

Sam saw me shiver and reached out, putting his arm around my shoulders, pulling me in close. His warmth seeped into me, and I knew there and then I'd found my happy place.

"I've been thinking," he said. "Would you like to go out for a meal?"

I pulled back and looked up into his eyes. They twinkled back at me.

"What did you have in mind?" I asked, my heart beating an erratic tune.

"I was thinking of breakfast." He smiled a super-wicked smile, his dimple flashing.

I thought about that for a second

"Sorry. But no." I shook my head.

I saw the disappointment flicker in his eyes. As the super-cute creases around the edges disappeared, so did his dimple.

"Oh. Okay. No worries," he said, his hold on me loosening. He removed his arm from its place on my shoulder.

"I have blood all over my clothes. I think my nose is broken. My ankle is twisted. I smell of beer, and I have bad morning breath. I need a shower and a doctor. How does lunch tomorrow sound?"

He grinned, making my heart miss a beat as he leaned down and kissed me. Light flashed through my brain the second he touched me. I wasn't sure if that was from the pain shooting through my nose or the shock as his feather-light kiss grazed my lips. Whichever it was, it took my breath away.

"You're right," he said, ending the kiss with a smile. "You definitely need to clean your teeth."

EPILOGUE

I watched the medivac chopper lift off, taking Stuart to the city hospital. After a lot of fussing, Dawn agreed to accompany him, even though she didn't like flying. I guessed her love of him outweighed any fears. The paramedics had already looked me over and agreed that the chopper could come back for me and Jake once Stuart had been dropped at the ER. As much as my nose and my ankle were both throbbing, I was more than happy that Stuart was getting the attention that he needed.

Georgie walked over to me and pulled me in for a careful hug.

"What a night!" she said, her large eyes puffy from all the crying she'd done.

"Yeah, that's one way to describe it." I grimaced in pain as I attempted a smile. Georgie and I needed to talk about what happened all those years ago and why she made those decisions for me. But right now wasn't the time. And I figured she only had my best interests at heart anyway. Jake wasn't the man for me.

"The police are with Wes," she said quietly. "I'm not sure what happens next."

"They'll take good care of him... Well, you know what I mean."

Georgie nodded. "Poor Wes. He was a good guy. He didn't deserve it."

"No, he didn't. None of Sally's victims did."

"But the police will sort it now, won't they? They'll see that justice is served."

I nodded and linked my arm through hers.

"How's the nose?" she asked.

"Painful," I replied.

Georgie's eyes filled with tears again. "I love you, bestie," she said to me, pulling my arm tight against hers.

"I love you too, bestie," I replied, smiling. To be honest, smiling hurt, but it was the thing I felt like doing the most. I looked over at Sam. He seemed to be the reason for that.

"There's some food left over from last night if you're hungry. Katie is setting up inside."

Katie may have been a bit strange, but it seemed she was a good person.

"Thanks," I said as my stomach gave a timely growl.

I wasn't sure how I would manage eating with my nose two sizes bigger than normal, but I'd be giving it a try. I linked my arm through Georgie's and turned toward the main building as Baxter ran up and joined us. I reached down and rubbed his ear, thinking how I would find him something special to eat before asking Sam to find his home.

We stopped at the ladies' on our way in, to give me some time to clean myself up. I gently washed the dried blood off my face and looked at the large purple rings growing around my eyes. My ankle still hurt, and I wanted to cry at the sight of my face, but I'd done enough of that in the last twelve hours, so I took a deep breath and walked out of the room before I changed my mind. Georgie searched her bag and found me some pain relief.

Entering the studio, I noticed the tired faces of the fifty people who had been stuck here last night. Every single one of them wanted to go home.

"Hey, who was the fake murderer?" I asked Georgie.

"Brent's girlfriend, Deanne. The story goes that his character had an affair with Rachel, and his girlfriend killed her."

Apparently, fiction was pretty close to fact.

"Humph. Did anyone solve it?"

"Yeah, Arthur's team."

"Ah, the wise ones."

"Rachel wasn't too happy. Deanne slapped her because she thought Rachel really did have an affair with Brent."

"Did he?"

"No, apparently he has standards, and Rachel didn't meet them."

Good to know Brent had a cut-off point.

"Did we ever find out what happened with Rachel?"

"What do you mean?"

"The bruise and the fact that she changed her clothes. I also found her acting very mysterious in the boardroom."

"Ah, well, it seems Kelly and Rachel had a catfight. That was before you found Wes. And she was arguing with Bernie in the boardroom."

I was impressed at how quickly Georgie found out gossip. "So Bernie definitely was here?"

"Yep, he didn't plan on being here for long. He had to pack for a plane trip."

"Yeah, I found the itinerary."

"Uh-huh, well," said Georgie, her eyes lighting up, "it turns out that Bernie had been embezzling company money to fund his gambling problem. Rachel found out and wanted a cut of the money. When he said no, she threatened to tell the police."

"How did she find out about it?"

"Wes told her. He'd been a bit suspicious of Bernie for a while and decided to look into what he was up to."

So that's what Wes had been doing.

"Wes wanted to go to the police immediately, but Rachel had

other plans. When Wes turned up dead, Rachel panicked and hid. That was until the police turned up, and then she squealed like a little pig."

"I bet she didn't squeal about wanting a cut though."

"No, I only found that out because Kelly told me. Wes had confided in her earlier this evening."

Wow, what a night. "So where's Bernie now?"

Georgie shrugged. "Probably on his way to the airport?"

I suddenly realized why the family photo on Bernie's desk was missing. I bet he'd come back for it, not wanting to leave it behind.

"But that's not all," continued Georgie. "Rachel has been a very busy girl." She winked at me, suggesting Rachel was up to her old tricks. "Blake seems to be very chummy with her at the moment. Nudge, nudge, wink, wink." Georgie laughed.

"So it wasn't a computer Blake was sleeping on. It was Rachel."

"Ha!" said Georgie, laughing again. "Apparently Rachel said the next reunion mystery wouldn't be so easy to solve."

"There's another reunion?"

"In another five years."

"Sorry, I don't care what the prize is," I said, frowning. "I am never, ever going to reunion again."

Would you like more Westport Mysteries? Then check out
Dangerous Deeds.
https://bethprenticenovels.com

When one door closes, another opens... or falls off its hinges.

They say that love is blind. Sure, they weren't necessarily talking about old houses at the time, but that's the story that Lizzie is sticking with. And she likes that theory a whole lot better than the one about her losing her mind.

She knew that buying a fixer upper meant stumbling into an unknown abyss of demolition, dust and unfathomable costs, but she never expected to find an engagement ring and letters of forbidden love hidden under the attic floorboards. Nor did she expect the lazy cat, or the drop-dead gorgeous handyman. And she definitely didn't predict the stalker.

As the renovation begins and the house starts to slowly return to its former glory, the letters dog her dreams. Who is the mysterious penman? Why was their love forbidden? And who is trying so hard to keep her from learning the truth about it all?

Working alongside her hunky handyman is proving to be quite the distraction, but Lizzie is determined to solve the puzzle of the long-lost love affair. But can she restore the house to its former glory, and solve the mystery before her stalker catches up with her? Or will she lose everything...including her life?

Find out in this spell binding romantic cozy mystery where hearts, along with homes, receive the renovation of a lifetime.

Dangerous Deeds is the first cozy tale in The Westport Mysteries series. If you like handy heartthrobs, suspenseful puzzles, and quirky characters, then you'll adore this series.

I'm offering a free e-book to everyone who signs up to my mailing list. I promise not to spam you and only send out a handful of newsletters a year!

www.bethprentice.com

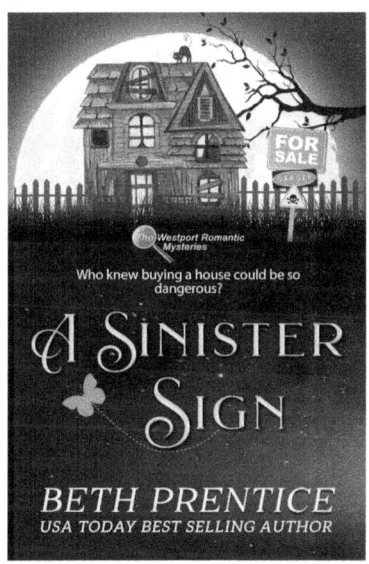

WHO KNEW BUYING A HOUSE COULD BE SO DANGEROUS?

Fed up with city life, Lizzie Fuller decides that moving home to the suburbs is just what she needs. But despite loving her family, the idea of living with them isn't all that appealing.

And it doesn't take long to find the house of her dreams...or nightmares—it's really just a question of perspective.

The lonely run-down old Victorian in need of major renovations tugs on her heartstrings, and before she can stop herself, she's fallen head over heels in love with it. Unfortunately, she's not the only one who wants it, and the other bidders aren't playing nice.

Deadly accidents, missing real estate agents and a chilling stranger, are all sinister signs that this is not the house for her. Still, Lizzie is determined to rescue this fixer upper or die trying.

Now all she needs to do is to win the auction and stay alive.

If only it was that easy...

A Sinister Sign is the prequel to Beth Prentice's light-hearted, romantic mystery trilogy. If you like crazy families, cozy reads, and a sweet romance, all tied together with a ribbon of danger, then you'll love The Westport Mysteries.

ABOUT THE AUTHOR

Beth Prentice is the USA Today Bestselling Author of the Westport Mysteries. Killer Unleashed, her GHP debut novel, received a bronze medal in the 2016 Readers Favorite International Book Awards. Her main wish is to write books you can sit back, relax with, and escape from your everyday life...and ones that you walk away from with a smile! When she's not writing you will usually find her at the beach with a coffee in hand, pursuing her favorite pastime—people watching!